piece

of my

heart

piece
of my
heart

Lynn Maddalena Menna

F+W Media, Inc.

Published by Merit Press
an imprint of F+W Media, Inc.
10151 Carver Road, Suite 200
Blue Ash, OH 45242. U.S.A.
www.meritpressbooks.com

ISBN 10: 1-4405-6105-2
ISBN 13: 978-1-4405-6105-4
eISBN 10: 1-4405-6106-0
eISBN 13: 978-1-4405-6106-1

Printed in the United States of America.

10 9 8 7 6 5 4 3 2 1

This book is available at quantity discounts for bulk purchases.
For information, please call 1-800-289-0963.

For Prospero,
with all of my love.

Acknowledgments

Writers may have an idea for a story, but it takes a village to turn it into a book. I've been blessed with many godmothers who helped my dream become reality. First and foremost is world-renowned author and editor-in-chief extraordinaire, Jacquelyn Mitchard. Thank you, Jackie, for believing in me and personally taking me under your wing. In my wildest dreams I could not have imagined such a talented mentor. Everyone at Merit Press has been wonderful. Thank you to my sharp-eyed copyeditor, Skye Alexander, for making me look good. I could not have submitted my manuscript to Jackie without the expert editing of the late Deborah Brodie. Deborah, your words of wisdom still echo through my brain while I work. You are now the angel who sits on my shoulder whispering helpful hints throughout the process. I was lucky to have you in my life even for such a short time.

So many friends helped me in so many ways. My thanks to Eileen Budd and Julia Hough, who read an earlier version of this story and gave valuable suggestions that appear in this book. I'd also like to thank my fellow students and all of my teachers at Gotham Writers' Workshop who helped shape my story. Laura Luhrs, thanks for keeping an eye on my stars.

Marisol's vocal ability was inspired by the beautiful singing voices of the students of School No. 18 in Paterson, New Jersey. In my years there I was constantly amazed at the raw talent so many of those young people possessed.

To my mother, Terry, thank you for instilling in me a love of reading, and thank you Grandma Rosie for buying my first chapter book for me to read while you played Bingo. Grandpa Tony, you were the first person to pay me for writing—a quarter was big money back then. I wish you were all still here to see this. I hope I made you proud.

Toonsie Menna, my fuzzy little black cat and the inspiration for so many of my short stories, was the best company a writer could ask for. Toonsie, you always stepped on the right keys when Mommy got stuck. Daddy and I miss you so much. We were blessed the day you wandered into our yard and our hearts. Thank you to The Boyz. I love you too.

Most of all, I want to thank my husband. Prospero, you always believed in me more than I believed in myself. You gave me the encouragement and opportunity to follow my dreams and make them come true. This book would never have been written without your support. I will love you forever and ever.

Contents

CHAPTER 1

Give Me a Break

I'm dancing to the beat, lost in my own world, when a slap on my butt brings me back to reality.

"Hey, Singer Girl, ready to start earning your keep?" Cisco grins at me, his white teeth shadowed by a short black beard. All he needs is an eye patch and a parrot; he'd look like a pirate. "What are you doing for your first number?"

"Doesn't matter." I resume my bopping while Cisco starts spinning a new tune, and I automatically adjust to the new beat. "Got any suggestions?"

This party's a little more high-class than the ones we usually work. It's a high school graduation party for some rich chick at Chelsea House, one of the hottest clubs in Manhattan. At least that's what Cisco told me when he called to say we had a gig. Cisco spins, and I get the karaoke going. Randy, who looks like a juiced-up mastiff, helps set it all up and break it all down again at the end of the night. He's also been known to do a mean beatbox into the mic.

Man, we're not in El Barrio anymore. These kids got megabucks. The birthday girl is wearing a simple white silk sheath encrusted with crystals. With her flowing blond hair and ocean-blue eyes, she looks like a little angel on top of a Christmas tree.

"Man, I'd like to get me some of that," says Randy, following my gaze.

"Yeah, like you got a chance." Cisco shakes his head while checking his laptop. He's probably thinking what I'm thinking—we're the help, and we've been treated like that since we got here.

At clubs, bartenders usually supply us with drinks and whatever else we want. At private parties, hosts or event planners will tell us to make sure we get a bite to eat or ask us if there's anything we need. But at this party, *nada*. There's an iceberg in the corner serving as a raw-bar for shellfish. Sushi chefs are slicing and rolling everyone's desires. Trays of bite-sized munchies that look like works of art have sailed past me. Carving stations are groaning with succulent roasts oozing juice. The waitstaff is passing bubbly cocktails created especially for the guest of honor, but I'm drinking the same bottle of water I brought in with me.

Who cares? We're getting paid super-bucks to entertain them. Unfortunately, my mouth is watering now.

The guys are out on the floor fist-pumping to the beat, but the girls are barely shuffling their red-soled shoes to Cisco's pulsing rhythms. Bejeweled zombies. This is so different from East Harlem. Everybody would be out on the dance floor showing off their best moves. And they'd be loud! Man, would they be loud. These chicks won't even have to take their dresses to the cleaners tomorrow. They'll never work up a sweat.

"Maybe we should slow it down," I suggest to Cisco. "Do something like 'Soul Spinning.' "

Suddenly Randy tunes in. "Uh-huh, a Diego Salazar song." He's grinning and nodding like he knows some big secret. "Won't Julian be jealous?"

Will these people ever forget that I was a crazy Diego Salazar fan when I was a kid? I mean, that's so over. I'll be eighteen in a couple weeks. Give me a break.

Cisco is shaking his head. "Nah, they're off again." He's talking about Julian and me.

It's amazing how these two keep track of my love life. Julian and I break up and get back together so much that it's almost impossible to remember where we're at. The cause of our break ups? Nights like tonight. It's tough to be in a relationship when you're out at parties and clubs several nights a week. It's not that I'm cheating on him— I'd never do that—but it's hard to hang out and be a girlfriend when your work makes you unavailable most of the time. I can't really blame Julian, any boy would be jealous of that.

"Mari's right though, slowing it down is a good idea," says Cisco, overriding Randy's comment. "It'll give Mari a chance to show off her pipes. You never know who's out there."

Besides the money-making factor, I'm doing this karaoke event—and any singing offer that comes my way—to get people to hear my voice. I'm good. Real good. I only need a break.

Cisco scratches the record to get everyone's attention. "Yo, yo, ladies and gentlemen, I need all of you to take your seats." Some groans come from the drones who don't want to relinquish the dance floor. "We're going to begin the karaoke portion of our evening." Now the drones are clapping and cheering. Go figure. "To get this party started, I'm going to bring a voice from heaven out here to show you how it's done. The one, the only, Marisol Reyes!"

I strut out onto the dance floor, arms raised like a prize fighter to acknowledge the cheers and whistles from the guys. When Cisco first asked me to work with him, he told me that I had to change my image, and I knew he was right. My basic everyday uniform consisted of jeans, a T-shirt and hoodie, and sneakers. Let's face it, with that outfit and my hair pulled back in a ponytail, I was a mouse. But the entertainment industry is a glitzy world, so here I am: black leather shorts, slinky sequined tank top dipping down to there, and the most adorable black leather ankle boots with thick gold zippers over the insteps. To die for!

The lights dim and a spotlight frames me like a halo.

Love, ooh, ooh, love . . .
A love like ours
Is a rare and wild thing.
It all began
When God created spring.

I start to circle the edge of the floor, singing to individuals, trying to gauge who might like to come up and give it a try. The guys look eager, but the girls seem icy. Little do they know that this isn't the real

Marisol. It's Singer Girl, the alter ego I create for myself in order to work up the courage to get out here.

I head back to center stage for the chorus and to give everyone the full impact of my range.

> *And when we meet between lives*
> *Our souls will spin among the stars*
> *Sharing our love*
> *That blossoms anywhere we are.*

Murmurs of approval echo through the dark. I'm winding up for the finale with a high note only dogs can hear.

> *Spinning . . .*
> *Spinning . . .*
> *Spinning . . .*
> *Soul spinning!*

"Thank you!" I pause graciously, accepting their applause. "Now who's going to come up and give this a try?"

There's always one. The karaoke star of the group. There's a low rumble—*Tyler, Tyler, Tyler*—and Tyler rises to accept his challenge. I get him situated and call his selection out to Cisco: "Proud Mary."

Surprise. Someone always does "Proud Mary." And badly enough to make Mary ashamed.

My job is done, for now, so I'm hanging with Cisco and sipping my water when a sharp-looking man walks up to the booth. I treat him to my best smile and ask, "Do you have a song picked out?"

Good-looking, for an old guy. He must be around forty. He's wearing a sleek black suit with a gold-and-black tie. On his wrist, he's sporting a gold Rolex that doesn't look as if it came from a case of watches on the corner of 116th Street.

"Actually, I want to tell you how much I enjoyed your performance." His intense eye-lock puts me on edge. "You have a very unique voice."

This always happens. Men see the flashiness and hit on me. I always turn them down. It's my rule, even when the guys are closer to my own age, which, this man is not.

"Thank you very much. I certainly appreciate it." Feeling trapped, I start to walk around him. Better to bow out gracefully before he starts laying on the lines. That's when things get tricky.

He cuts me off. "And I'd like to hear it recorded professionally." He hands me his card. "I'm Pablo Cruz."

Omigod, omigod, omigod! *Pablo Cruz!* I know that name. He's Diego Salazar's manager.

CHAPTER 2

Totally Buzzed

Diego Salazar. Omigod! I can't believe it. I have been in love with him since I was little—before he left El Barrio to become a big star. It was yet another silly source of Julian's—my on-again, currently off-again, boyfriend—jealousy. Even my friends make fun of me for being such a geeky fan, but I don't care. That man is *fine* and his music plays nonstop on my iPod. Singing with him has always been my crazy dream but, deep down, I always knew it would come true.

I hear a pounding on the ladies' room door. "Hurry up. Diego's here."

"Yeah, I'll be out in a minute."

I wait until the footsteps fade before I exit the stall and head to the sink. The cold water feels so good running over my hands and wrists. I pat some on my face carefully, trying to avoid messing my eye makeup. I dry my hands and take a deep breath. I still can't believe that Pablo Cruz is auditioning me to sing on Diego's new *Duets* CD.

Pablo looks relieved. "Ah, Mari, there you are. Come say hello to Teddy Bear Barnes, your producer."

Remembering my professional manners, I extend my hand. "How do you do?"

"Hey, girl, what's up?" Instead of a shake, he gives my fist a pound. Teddy Bear, literally a big bear of a man, is the number one record producer in the world.

Steering me over to the booth where the microphones are set up, Pablo says, "And this man needs no introduction."

Omigod, omigod, omigod. Knowing who he is and meeting him in person are two different things. I'm feeling as spazzy as the little twelve-year-old girl I used to be. Now I'm just praying that the bottle of water I drank earlier doesn't come up and baptize him.

He turns around and smiles at me. Diego Salazar is even more gorgeous up close and personal. His eyes are two chocolate kisses and I can almost see myself in his shiny black hair.

"Of course, Mari," he says, like we're old friends "*¿Cómo está usted?*" He takes both my hands in his and kisses me on both cheeks. I can smell his peppermint breath.

Now I may be Puerto Rican, but my Spanish sucks. I grew up speaking English and know only a little street Spanglish. I know enough to understand that he's asking me how I am, but all knowledge of responding in Spanish disappears from my brain. I stand there nodding like a bobble-head doll.

Sensing my nervousness, Pablo intervenes, "What do you say we get this session started?"

He looks me in the eye to see if I'm okay—and I am. Pablo Cruz is good at managing people. That's what he does. I'm hoping that if everything goes okay today, he'll soon be managing my singing career.

Teddy Bear fires up the opening bars to Diego's big hit, "Soul Spinning." I automatically begin swaying to the tune. "Diego, why don't you begin and, Marisol, you respond with the second verse. Kind of like a conversation. Then you'll both sing the chorus." He cuts the music and begins again.

Diego sings the intro in an ethereal voice:

Love, ooh ooh, love . . .
A love like ours
Is a rare and wild thing.
It all began
When God created spring.
The kind of joy
That only love can bring
And for a lifetime we will share
The kind of love that others dare

Until the end of time.

And when we meet between lives
Our souls will spin among the stars
Sharing our love
That blossoms anywhere we are.

I'm so entranced with listening to him sing that I almost forget my cue.

Spinning, spinning, soul spinning

Diego continues the stanzas with me singing the running line in a high soprano.

There is no greater thing
In the heavens high above
That can possibly compare
To the greatness of our love.

Spinning, spinning, soul spinning

Teddy Bear whips his hand in the air like a lasso. I'm thinking this is where I join him. Just guessing—I'm new at this.

And when we meet between lives
Our souls will spin among the stars
Sharing our love
That blossoms anywhere we are.

Spinning, spinning, soul spinning

Diego sings the final stanza with me echoing his lines in a higher key. I'm lost in the song and suddenly realize that I'm doing runs with the harmony.

How can a love be this wonderful to feel?
This kind of love can't possibly be real.
How can this love continue for all time?

Now we alternate lines and harmonize on the final *soul spinning.*

Because
Because
You're mine.
Spinning, spinning, spinning
Soul spinning

And so the day went. We did the song over and over, switching parts and harmonizing on others. Even Diego gives his input on the arrangement. "Hey, TB, can we try it with Marisol singing the third stanza?"

He says my name! My water bottle slips from my hand and I catch it before it hits the floor. Instant reality check! Suddenly the sound of my name on Diego's lips makes me realize exactly where I am and what I'm doing. I've been so crazy about him since Papi picked me up and put me on the stage with him at the Feast of Our Lady of Pompeii Church when I was a toddler. Diego was barely a teen, but he picked me up and we sang together and the crowd roared. I will never forget the look of love and pride in Papi's eyes. It's one of my best memories of him, and I can't shake the excitement I feel performing with Diego. This is not only my dream coming true, but Papi's dream for me as well.

So I have a major crush on Diego, but I know those feelings are not returned. This studio has more hot-looking girls working in it than they probably have jobs for. About every half-hour or so, one waltzes over with a fresh cup of tea for Diego. He stops what he's doing and thanks each of them as if he'd been given a cup of diamonds.

"*Muchas gracias,* _____!" Fill in the blank. He knows each of their names and kisses each one on the cheek. They walk away as if they'd been blessed by the pope. I'm getting a little sick of it by the end of the afternoon. I'm also a little jealous. Diego is getting cups of hot tea while I'm still nursing the bottle of lukewarm Poland Spring they gave me when I started singing.

"Okay, everybody, that's a wrap!" shouts Teddy Bear.

Diego throws his arms around my shoulders in a pretend faint. Funny, I'm not nervous anymore, even with his arms around me. We've been through so much today that we're more like teammates.

"I'm beat," he moans. "How about you?"

"Yeah, I love to sing, but I never sang this long," I say. "My throat is killing me."

He lifts the cup in his hand. "You have to keep drinking tea with honey through the session. Warm, not hot."

Pablo comes running over. "You nailed it, Mari!" He turns to Diego and gives him a hug. "My man, always a pro." Then he calls out to Teddy Bear, "Barnes, what did you think?"

"Girl, you've got it going on!" he booms in his deep bass voice. "You've got grittiness in your low range and you're clear as a bell at the peak. Smoking hot!"

My voice *is* unique. I have a four-octave range. That means if you sit at a piano and play *do, re, mi, fa, so, la, ti, do* up the keyboard four times, I can sing along. Not many kids can do that. Not many professional singers are able to sing that, either. But hearing someone like Teddy Bear Barnes tell me I'm good is slamming.

I want to ask if this will be on the new *Duets* CD, but I don't want to sound like a total dweeb. Besides, if the answer is no, I don't want to hear it in front of Diego.

"Diego, if you have a minute, I'll walk out with you," Pablo says. "I want to go over . . ."

That's it, I guess. Teddy Bear is talking to some of the technicians, so I call out, "Thanks, you guys!" I'm dismissed. No car service for me—just a long, hot subway ride uptown.

I am totally exhausted but I'm also totally buzzed.

CHAPTER 3

Second Chance

Casa de Felix is jam-packed, but I spy Vanessa sitting at our usual table with her sister, Tatianna. This place is kind of our hangout. All our friends meet here after school, but now that we've graduated, I'm not sure what's going to happen. Right now I'm starving and there's no point in going home because Lola has dinner plans.

Shortly after Pablo discovered me he also discovered my stepmother, Lola. As my guardian, she needed to sign an agreement for me to audition for the CD. Actually, he rediscovered Lola—they used to date when they were both my age. Now they are so into each other. When they're not working, they're always together.

That's a good thing. Ever since Papi was killed by that drunk driver last year, we've been existing in a dark place. He and Lola had only been married for two years, so we were still working out the kinks of being a new family, when our world turned upside down. Now it's just Lola and me. Papi was the ribbon that tied us together, and we're trying to figure it out as we go along.

At least I have my singing to concentrate on. Papi loved my voice and going professional would have made him so proud. Lola threw herself into her work as a paralegal in one of the big law firms downtown, but when the firm downsized, they let her go, and Lola's funk deepened.

See, that's another thing. With Lola doing freelance work, she's not bringing in her usual salary. I've been helping Cisco with some karaoke gigs, but that's not steady work. And now I have a chance to be on Diego's new CD, but it's not a done deal. I've got to keep working to make this happen and bring some money in, even though Lola keeps telling me not to worry about it.

Vanessa jumps out of her seat, her springy brown curls bouncing up and down, and hugs me. "So, how did your big day go?"

Vanessa's happiness for me is what spurred me on through my really bad times. We've always been good friends, but she stuck by me like a sister when Papi died.

"It was better than great!" I bend down to give her sister a kiss. "Hey, Tati."

Tatianna, two years older than we are, doesn't usually concern herself with what Vanessa and I are up to, but recording with Diego Salazar tweaks her interest.

"You sound hoarse," says Tati, flipping her silky black hair over her shoulder as she continues to thumb in a message on her phone.

"You would too if you'd been singing all day." Vanessa is always quick to defend me.

"Yeah, I'm not used to singing for that period of time, but Diego told me to keep sipping tea and honey to soothe my throat. Next time."

"Diego!" chorus Vanessa and Tati, which triggers the usual Latina catcalls and comments. Even their mother, Sylvia, who's working the dinner shift, comes over and chimes in.

Tati is especially interested. "Come on, tell us everything. Did he fall in love with you? Are you soul mates?" she asks sarcastically.

They will never let me forget that. I wouldn't mind if he wanted me, but it doesn't seem like it's happening. Still, there's a little piece of me that's going to go for it, especially since Julian seems to have moved on, but I'll never let my friends know that.

"No, come on, guys," I protest. "He's super nice, but we're just working together."

"Yeah, yeah," Vanessa sings. Then her head pops up. "Hey, are you going to Julian's party tomorrow night?"

This brings my little fantasy to a halt.

"Julian's party? This is the first I'm hearing about it. What's it for?"

Man, I'm pissed. Julian Pagan and I have a relationship, which is currently off. And every time we're off, I feel like I lost a piece of my heart. I can't believe he didn't even invite me to his party. We've been dating since we were fourteen. I know he's seeing Solange now, but I thought we were still friends.

Plus, it's more than just the two of us; we have the same group of friends, so it's impossible for us not to see each other. Julian is *the* most popular boy in school and possibly in all of El Barrio. Everybody likes him. I mean everybody. Including me. But I keep screwing up our relationship because I always put my music before him. If I have a gig, I go. Julian would rather I be with him every night, either hanging with friends or just watching TV together. I love that, but I love my music too.

Dating Julian was so cool. First of all, he's totally hot, with his caramel spiked hair and root-beer eyes that always give me that *I want you* look. Kissing was heaven, but what I loved most about him was that he was my best friend. We always had fun together. Then he had to spoil it by pushing me further than I wanted to go because *he* decided it was time for us to hook up. Well, the timing wasn't right for me and we had a huge fight. It was too much pressure. I was still upset about my father being killed in that hit-and-run accident. Didn't Julian realize I wouldn't be feeling romantic?

So we broke up. But I miss him and would give anything to have him back. He may be with Solange now, but they can't possibly love each other the way we do.

Still, not inviting me to his party is cold.

"It's a graduation party, tomorrow night on his roof." As if to soothe my feelings, she explains, "He didn't even tell me. Raven told me and told me to tell you. Tati's coming too, right?"

"Yeah, and Cisco is spinning. Come, it'll be fun."

"I don't know." I swirl the straw in my Coke, hoping to conjure an answer. "Let me think about it."

———— ♦ ————

The first item on my to-do list is to find something to wear to the party. I want Julian to notice me. That's why I'm heading into Vantage. Erika hooked me up with the really unique outfits for my karaoke gigs with Cisco, so she'll fix me up for tonight. Vanessa is right; I should go to the party.

As my eyes adjust to the dimness of the lighting and the flash of the strobe, one voice booms over the pounding beat of the music.

"Mari!" she screams.

Raven! *Frenemies* would be the best way to describe our relationship. Raven has morphed into a hater and is always making sarcastic remarks about my wanting a singing career.

Once upon a time, Raven, Vanessa, and I were really tight; we met in preschool and were inseparable ever since. Kids used to call us the Three Musketeers. We managed to always be in the same classes and even coordinated our outfits each day. On weekends we rotated sleeping over each others' apartments, and Sunday found us crammed into the same pew at Our Lady of Pompeii. Monday came and the routine continued like the movie *Groundhog Day*.

All that began to change when we started our sophomore year, and I'll admit it's probably my fault. Vanessa's cousin Cisco started hiring me for karaoke gigs and I became too busy to hang out with my old friends. Maybe it wouldn't have been so bad if I'd invited them along, but it's not as if they were my events—these were jobs. Still their feelings were hurt. I miss those times too, but sometimes things have to change. Anyway, I became the bad guy. Raven was the angriest, so I'm surprised she was the one who told Vanessa to invite me to Julian's party.

I'm also surprised that she's shopping here. It's not her style. Raven has the height and shoulders of her Jamaican father and has the hardest time shopping for cool clothes.

She runs over and gives me this huge hug and kiss and I have to brush her wild mane of kinky black hair out of my face. I mean, what's up with that? Part of me wishes she really means it, but in reality, I'm pretty sure she doesn't.

"It's so great to see you. You're coming to the party tonight, right?"

"Wouldn't miss it."

And I wouldn't. Maybe Julian wants me there because he wants a second chance too. There's something good between us. It was just bad timing.

"Well, I've got to run," she says, grabbing her bags. "See you later." The door slams shut and I turn to Erika. "I have to look fantastic."

"Gotcha." She heads to a rack of tops.

"I want to be able to wear the open-toe booties I bought last time," I tell her. They're cool-looking shoes and, although I have some money on me, new shoes would take a big chunk of it. I still need to mix and match.

An hour later I find it: a white cotton micro miniskirt and a black knit halter top with a really low neck. I'm okay with this now that I know the body-tape trick. I run one strip like a U under my boobs and, wham, instant cleavage. It's a killer to rip off, but it looks great on.

"Black and white pops," explains Erika, "and really shows off your hair." She fluffs it around my shoulders. "I love this dark reddish-brown. Are you sure you don't dye it?"

This is a standing joke between us, but it is my real color. Papi used to tell me that my mother had the same hair and that's what made him fall in love with her. Not that I would know. She split for Puerto Rico right after I was born. But she blessed me with a great head of hair.

Now that I think about it, Julian loved to play with my hair too, wrapping thick chunks around his finger and letting it spiral down, so if this outfit shows it off, good.

I turn around and stand on my toes to see how it will look with heels.

"Yep, this is it. Wrap it up."

I get dressed and meet her at the register. The damage isn't too bad.

"You know, you look good in minis. You should pick up a denim one and you can switch off tops or even a little T-shirt," offers Erika. "Show off those legs, girl."

She's right. On the way home I stop off at Regine's, my usual bargain store where everything is *two for*. Two for $7.99! Two for $15.99! Today it was denim miniskirts, two for $19.99! So I buy a distressed denim skirt and a black one. A girl needs her options. I pick through the rack of tops and find a couple cute ones marked down to almost free and add them to my pile.

If Julian isn't sorry we broke up, he will be tonight.

CHAPTER 4

Hot Stuff

Vanessa and I climb the stairs to the roof. Roof parties can't start until the sun begins to set because of the intense rays, but tonight there's a cool breeze to blow away the June heat.

The party has already started to rock. The roof is packed because Julian is really popular in the 'hood and of course he invites everybody. Except me, that is. Cisco and Randy are set up on one end, spinning tunes, and they wave hello. Somebody is pouring a bottle of Bacardi into the punch and a keg is set up next to it. Tables groan with trays of *empanadas*, rice and beans, plantains, *bistec salteado*, *chuleta frita*, and my favorite, *chicharron de pollo*—golden nuggets of Caribbean sunshine. No one ever goes hungry at a Puerto Rican party.

"Ooh, that food smells so good," says Vanessa. "Let's go and fix a plate."

But I spy Julian by the makeshift bar and I really want to talk to him.

"You go," I say to Vanessa. "I'm going to get a glass of punch."

When I look up again, Julian is surrounded by some boys from school who are laughing at a story he's telling. I don't want to talk in front of them. After all, Julian never really invited me. I'm kind of crashing here. So I head over to the DJ area to chat with Cisco.

"Hey, Singer Girl, you going to do your thing for us tonight?" His prickly black beard scratches my cheek when he gives me a kiss.

The kids from school have heard me sing, but they never saw me perform like I do when I'm on a karaoke gig with Cisco. I'm not sure I'm ready to share that side of me. "Nah, I don't think so. I'm going to let you do all the work tonight."

The group of boys that surrounds Julian starts to break up, so I go over to the bar and pour a cup of punch for myself. Before I know it, Julian is standing next to me.

"Mari, I was hoping you'd come," he says softly. There's a hint of sadness in those amber eyes as if he's missing the good times we used to have.

"Then you should have invited me," I say and take a sip of the punch. Strong.

He lowers his head and scratches an imaginary itch on his cheek.

"Hmm." I survey the roof. "Looks like a nice party. I'm glad I came."

I'm looking for signs that he wants to get back together, but Julian looks kind of, I don't know, nervous. This isn't the place to talk, but I did expect a little enthusiasm. Where's that smile that I love?

"Uh, Mari, we have to talk."

Well, here it comes. He does want to get back with me. I knew it!

"Mari," he continues, "I want to let you know that—"

I hear a screech, and a little black-clad banshee throws herself at him. "Julian! I'm sorry I'm late. I got here as soon as I could."

Her English is heavily accented, as she came over from the Dominican Republic this year. Even though it's almost dark out, she's wearing her ever-present knock-off designer sunglasses on top of her head, like a tiara crowning her sleek black hair.

Solange Solis is hugging Julian but, after giving her a quick hug, he spreads his arms wide in an *I'm not encouraging her* kind of way. I can tell he'd rather be anyplace but in the middle of this. Then it hits me—Julian doesn't want to talk about getting back together. He wants to tell me that he's still with Solange. That's why he didn't invite me to the party.

My throat is parched and I take a long gulp of punch, but I refuse to break eye contact with Julian. Let him sweat.

Another screech and a familiar voice interrupt my thoughts. "Solange!"

Raven!

Here she is jumping up and down and screaming with Solange. "You did it, *chica!* You did it!" Then she turns to me with those crazy eyes of hers that always look surprised. Raven had lead poisoning as a baby. Seriously. I'm not kidding. That's why she's a little slow and crazy. "Did you hear? Solange is dancing in the new Blend video! They filmed it today."

Solange's Chiclets teeth are glowing in the dark. "That's why I was late."

She's beaming like a neon sign and Julian is beaming at her like she's Shakira. That's it. I can't stand around here and take this crap. I head toward the stairs, my eyes filling with tears that I don't want to spill in front of this crowd.

As I head through the doorway, I have to step back because Tati-anna is coming up.

"Where are you going? The party's just getting started." Too late. I have tear-rivers flowing down my face. "Hey, what's the matter? Talk to me." Tati grips her arm around my shoulders to keep me from running off.

A whoosh of breath comes out of me. "It's Solange and Julian. They're still together," I admit.

"Oh, yeah, the hot tamale."

This makes me laugh.

"Did she film her video today?"

"You know about it too? How'd you find out?"

"Cisco, who else?" I keep forgetting how tight Cisco and Tati are. More like twins than cousins. "Raven was over the other day blabbing about it to my sister," Tati says. "That Solange really thinks she's the greatest thing going around here."

"So does Julian," I say. I can't believe everyone knows about this and no one told me. So this is the reason Raven told Vanessa to bring me. She wanted to watch my face when I found out in front of Julian. "Anyway, I'm out of here."

"Wait, you can't go."

"Watch me." I start to head down the stairs, but she grabs my arm.

"No, listen, if you go, that little poser wins," explains Tati. "Cisco keeps telling me how you kill onstage with him. Get up there and sing. Show them who the top dog is."

piece *of my* heart

This advice sounds like what Erika told me when I was shopping for clothes for my first karaoke gig. *Make the men want to be with you. Make the women want to be you.* Maybe it's time for my friends to meet my alter ego. Just like Beyoncé is Sasha Fierce, I am Singer Girl. I'm going to make Julian want to be with me.

I throw my arms around Tati. "Thank you," I whisper in her ear. "You are so right."

I turn around and look to the side of the roof where Cisco is set up. The lights of the skyscrapers glitter against the black velvet sky. The Milky Way doesn't have anything on the Manhattan skyline. Venus winks at me. I'm going to do it. I walk over to Cisco.

"Hey," he says, "you're just in time. Let's do 'New York Nights.' It's perfect for tonight."

"I don't rap," I snap. I want to do a song that blows them off the roof, like Whitney or Mariah.

"No, you don't," Cisco sing-songs like he's talking to a small child, "but Randy does. You can do the Alicia Chiavi part."

I raise my brow. Randy raps? First I'm hearing about this. It might be cool. I can work off him; do a little dancing and everything. Randy just better hold up his end.

"Let's do it!"

Cisco scratches the record he's been playing. "Yo, yo, everybody listen up!" he yells into the mic. "Come on, y'all, listen up!" It takes a few minutes to get everyone's attention. Then he continues, "Tonight we're lucky to have a new star on the horizon with us."

I can't help but sneak a peek over to where Solange is holding court. They're getting all excited. They think it's her. Dumb ass.

"Yesterday she was recording with our homeboy, Diego Salazar. Tonight she's singing for us. Give it up for our own Marisol Reyes!"

The opening bars waft through the night air and I begin singing the intro in a low sultry voice.

Nowhere on the planet
Takes my breath away
Nothing more to say
Than New York.

Randy jumps in with the beatbox, right on cue, and runs with the rap, his big body pumping in time to the music.

New York City, New York City
Center of the universe
New York City

I'm singing the melody in a voice as smooth as honey.

Whoa, whoa, whoa,
New York nights
Looking at the blackness of the midnight skies
Keeping all the wonders and sweet mysteries alive
With magic, whoa with magic.

I'm swaying to the tune and Randy is coming at me with a pulsing beat.

New York City, New York City
Center of the universe
New York City

This is good. We should do this in the clubs. It will really get the crowd going.

You can be who you want to be.
Shed your skin and now you are free.
Whoa, whoa, New York

New York City, New York City
Center of the universe
New York City

When I'm singing, I always make eye contact with the crowd. They are loving it.

Where else in this world can you see such sights
Feeling the excitement of the neon lights?
Where else in the world can you feel the beat
Dancing to the rhythms playing in the streets?

Vanessa and Tatianna are dancing and singing along with me. Their encouragement spurs me on.

Whoa, whoa, whoa,
New York nights
Looking at the blackness of the midnight skies
Keeping all the wonders and sweet mysteries alive
With magic, whoa with magic.

I scan over to a sulky Solange, a pissed-off Raven, and awestruck Julian. Oh, yeah!

New York City, New York City
Center of the universe
New York City

You can be who you want to be.
Shed your skin and now you are free.
Whoa, whoa, New York

Randy and I finish the tune and fall into each other's arms. Whew, he must have been as nervous as I was. I tell him he's great. That's no lie. Randy really brought it. Then I head over to the bar for another glass of punch.

The guys standing around the table start to argue with each other about who is going to get me a drink.

"Come on guys, I'm thirsty," I shout above the fracas.

This is great. They're all trying to hit on me. I hope Julian is watching, but I don't want to give him the satisfaction of looking. *Make the men want to be with you.* There's only one man I want to be with and I'm going to get him.

CHAPTER 5

Going Viral

I meet Vanessa at the restaurant for breakfast and to debrief about last night.

"Have you heard?" Vanessa looks like she's going to pop out of her seat.

"No, Pablo hasn't called or said anything to Lola." I think she means have I heard about the Diego CD.

"Not that, silly. You're all over the Internet!" She takes out her phone, hits a few buttons, and turns it so the screen faces me. There I am singing "New York Nights" with Randy. *Omigod!*

"Wait, how did this happen?"

"Someone obviously filmed it last night and posted it on You-Tube," she explains. "You went viral, girl!"

"*Omigod*, this is so great!"

Vanessa looks straight at me. "You rocked last night. I've heard you sing lots of times, but last night . . . I don't know, it was something else."

"I'm not comfortable with it yet, either." I take a sip of my OJ. Lola would kill me if she knew I'm skipping breakfast, but I'm not hungry. "Cisco likes me to be flashy onstage, so in order to stop the butterflies, I channel all the great singers in my head. It's the only way I can deal with it." Thinking about last night reminds me about something that's bugging me. "Why didn't you tell me Solange is dancing in Blend's new video? I know you knew."

Vanessa sighs and looks at her half-gnawed Taylor ham, egg-and-cheese sandwich. For a skinny little chick, she eats like a walrus. "Because I didn't want to hurt you. You're finally getting everything you ever dreamed about. I didn't want to spoil it for you."

How can I be mad about that? Vanessa would never hurt me, but I'm not sure about her other friend. "What about Raven? I'm thinking Julian didn't ask me to the party because he was going to be with Solange." See, this is why I'm not hungry; my stomach is still in knots from last night. "My guess is Raven invited me herself just to watch my expression when I saw them together and found out about the video."

"I think you're right," she admits sheepishly. "I didn't see it that way before, but watching her last night made me think that Raven set this up deliberately to hurt you."

Never in a million years would I think Raven would set me up like this. First of all, until we started high school Raven, Vanessa, and I were really tight—and had been since we were little. Secondly, Raven is—well, there's no nice way of saying it—dumb. She barely made it through her remedial classes and isn't cunning enough to pull this off.

"I don't get it. Is she that jealous of me? 'Cause I'll tell you, she started to turn when I began getting singing gigs. It's time for her to get over it."

Vanessa shakes her head. "I don't know. I honestly don't know anymore. Ever since she started going with Freddie last year, she's so full of herself. I hardly ever see her anymore. Kind of like . . . never mind." She looks away, but I can tell by the set of her lips that something's bugging her.

"Like what? Tell me. What's wrong?" I grab her hand and give it an encouraging shake.

"It's kind of like us. We don't see each other like we used to." Vanessa shakes her head. "I guess I miss hanging out at Felix's together after school, eating fries and drinking soda. That whole big group of us, laughing and having fun—that was the best." She looks at me with almost pleading eyes. "Do you think we'll ever do that again?"

I sigh. "I loved those times too, Nessa, but now we're all going our separate ways." The light goes out in her eyes. "I mean, of course we'll hang out again, it probably won't be as often, but we'll do it. That's the way life is."

"Yeah, but you're always out with Cisco, at clubs and all, and I'm stuck at home. Even Tati's out all the time. It's like she's living a secret life." She starts to choke up. "I miss everybody."

I swing my chair around next to hers and give her a hug. "First of all, it's not as glamorous as it sounds. Cisco and I are working, the same as if we had any other kind of job in the evening." I give her a kiss on top of her head. "Secondly, you won't have time to be bored once you start college in September. How lucky are you? You got a full scholarship to City College. Between classes and studying, you won't have time to feel lonely." I see a glimmer of a smile. "And best of all, Angel will be going with you. Think about it, both of you cooking up concoctions in the chemistry lab," I say in a sing-song voice.

Angel is Julian's cousin. He and Vanessa have been having a silent love affair since tenth grade, but both of them are too shy to make anything happen.

She blows her nose. "I guess you're right, but I still haven't seen much of Raven."

"Me neither," I admit, but that's a good thing. "And what's up with Solange? She just came here a few months ago. Now suddenly she's a video star? How did she even ask for an audition? No one can understand her."

"I know, right? But Cisco told me that she's been calling him and going over to his place all the time to see if he can get her music jobs. She wants to be a singer." Vanessa hesitates. "He said she'll do anything, he stressed *anything*, to get a job."

Huh, interesting. I wonder if Julian knows about this. Cisco loves his little cousin too much to get more specific about what Solange is offering, but we get the drift.

"Well, that's one thing Solange and Raven have in common," I say snidely. Raven once confessed that she'd do *anything* to get Freddie, and I guess she did, because they're a couple.

"Yeah, but it's one thing to hook up with a boyfriend and another thing to use it to get a job," Vanessa says. "You know what that makes her."

Yep, a skank.

CHAPTER 6

Think of Me

The door to the vestibule is never locked, so I walk in and pound on the door to the first-floor apartment. No one answers, so I pound even harder and kick it a couple of times, just in case.

The door opens. "Mari, what's up? What time is it?" Cisco is yawning and scratching his bare stomach. He's wearing only plaid boxers and a pissed-off expression on his face. "You know I never get out of bed before noon."

"We have business to discuss." I push my way past him.

"Well, come right in," he says sarcastically, but I don't care.

The only furniture in the room crammed with DJ equipment is an old worn-out sofa that probably never looked good. Smells of old Chinese take-out assault my nose, but I'm too angry to get fussy.

I spin around to face him. "You got Solange Solis a job in Blend's new video. What's up with that?"

"What's up with you? What difference does it make?" He's on the defensive. "So I got her a gig, so what. I can do a favor for a friend. I hired you."

I can't believe he's putting that skanky Solange in the same category as me. Cisco and I have known each other since forever. Now suddenly Solange is a *friend*.

"Yeah, you hired me and I've been doing a good job for you. You know how badly I want a music career. If something comes up, you should think of me first."

I mean, I know he doesn't have to, but we've been friends for a long time.

He throws his hands in the air in a gesture of innocence. "Whoa, whoa, whoa! First of all, you want a singing career. That's not what I got her."

"Duh, I know that, but she's still getting exposure and that's what I need."

I am so pissed that her face will be the first one out there. I've been working at singing all my life. She just sailed over and is trying to take my place.

He shakes his head. "No, you don't need that kind of exposure."

I start to protest, "Yes I—"

"No, no, trust me on this, Mari. Those jobs aren't for girls like you. You don't get it."

"So explain it to me," I insist.

His shoulders slump. "Listen, there's no musical talent involved. They give these dance jobs to anyone who will . . ." He looks embarrassed. "Do I have to spell it out? Come on, Mari, you're not that naïve. You know what these girls have to do to get those parts. Everybody gets a piece of that action, from the security guards who let her in to the director and producer of the video." Cisco lets that truth sink in. "Those chicks aren't dancers, they're *putas*."

I just stand there feeling foolish. Cisco laughs, then continues, "Heck, you should see what she did for me just for the introduction. That's not you. You're a class act."

I may be a class act, but those same talents that get Solange jobs got her Julian. Does he know she's doing all these guys, including his friend Cisco? I guess not. But he knows she was with Freddie and that didn't seem to bother him.

I'm still confused. "I don't get it. Why is she trying so hard to get into music?"

"Truth?"

"That would be a nice change, considering everybody knew about this but didn't tell me."

"Solange told me she wants to be like you," he says gently. "You should be flattered."

"Well, I'm not. I don't like that girl. First she steals Julian. Now she's jacking my style."

Cisco flops down on the couch. "Come on, Mari, she's not jacking your style. You're a singer. I heard you killed on that demo with Diego. Man, you're going to be soaring soon."

"She really said that she wanted to be like me?" That cheers me in a way, but it's also kind of weird—like a stalker. But Cisco's not getting off that quick. "Well, until then, I want to work with you every chance there is." I plop down next to him.

"Hey, fine with me. You're good for business. Trouble is, this is a slow season. Everybody's away. Big money, anyway. The only gigs are local clubs. That's why I had time to do Julian's party."

Cisco spins in a lot of clubs. Doing karaoke in college or tourist bars is a steady income, but he's performed in high-profile clubs downtown, too, and gotten rave reviews. He's made a lot of important connections and pretty soon he's going to be the number one DJ in the city.

"I saw the video on YouTube," I tell him. My anger is melting away. I can't stay mad at Cisco. We've become really tight since we've been working together.

"Yeah, me too." A smile spreads across his stubbly face. "You rocked, kid." He throws a tattooed arm around my neck and pulls me into a mini wrestling hold.

"All three of us did. We're a good team and it's all because of you, Cisco." Before I leave, I remind him, "So if you get a gig, you'll call me?"

"Sure. I was up for one this weekend in the Hamptons. Big-money party."

"What happened?" I ask, making my way to the door.

"They went with Crazy Joe."

Cisco may be on his way to being king of the DJs, but Crazy Joe is sitting on the throne. He hangs out with all the rappers—Kanye, Jay-Z, and Diddy. Crazy Joe is one of the boys. He gets first shot at the big gigs.

"Too bad," I say. "Hey, Cisco, thanks for hearing me out." I give him a hug. "I'm sorry I was so snarky. You were the first person to help me get my singing career off the ground. You saw me for what I could become. I'll always love you for that."

"No problem," he says.

"Seriously, I could always sing, but it was you who brought out the performer in me. You know, the clothes, the attitude, the whole show. Even I didn't know I had it in me."

"Nah, it was all there," he says modestly, but his smile tells me that he's secretly pleased. "I never knew you were such a hard-ass when you want something."

Neither did I. Neither did I.

CHAPTER 7

Sexy Chick

Hot summer weather turns the streets of East Harlem into a smelly frying pan. Kids and a whole bunch of adults, too, treat every square inch of space like their own personal trash cans. The mayor can put up all the signs he wants, but people still refuse to pick up their dogs' poop. So imagine this disgusting stew simmering on the sidewalk. Gross.

Vanessa called this morning to tell me she only has today to buy the perfect swimsuit for Fourth of July. That means field trip.

We've been spending the holiday at Coney Island since we were little kids. Vanessa's parents used to treat Tatianna, Vanessa, Raven, and me to a day on the beach with hot dogs from Nathan's. When the beach closed and the ocean breeze cooled the air, we'd walk on the boardwalk and hit all the rides.

Happy memories. Vanessa and I continue to celebrate the same way even now that we're grown. It's also the only thing on my agenda this weekend because Pablo is taking Lola and our Yorkie, Cha-Cha, to his house in East Hampton. I wonder if Raven will join us at Coney Island this year or if she'll be busy with her new friends, like Freddie, Solange, and *sob, sob,* Julian.

"So what kind of suit are you thinking about?" asks Vanessa. "Maybe we should get bikinis this year."

I can't imagine strutting my stuff in next to nothing on the crowded beach at Coney Island. We already get enough comments from the guys as it is. Wearing a bikini seems like an open invitation. Not that I mind when they're good-looking, but a lot of those guys are skuzzy.

"Nah, I don't think so," I say. "I'll probably stick with a two-piece. I want to be comfortable if I'll have to wear it all day."

We always throw on T-shirts and shorts over our suits because there's really no place to change clothes. It isn't too bad on the way down to the beach, but the train ride home with a salty, sandy suit grinding into your sunburned skin is pure torture.

We head into the department store on Third Avenue.

Vanessa holds up a white bikini with a filmy chiffon sarong cover-up. "This is so Tati."

"It's beautiful," I say. Her sister Tatianna is an exotic-looking girl with hair that resembles a flowing river of black water. With a hibiscus behind her ear she'd look like a Hawaiian princess in that suit. "Is she coming with us? You should buy it for her."

Vanessa hangs it back on the rack with a shrug. "Who knows? Everything she does is so secretive that I'm surprised she even went to Julian's party. And besides, none of the neighborhood stores are good enough for her. She only shops downtown."

Vanessa's been upset for a while about this. She and Tati used to be tight, but since Tati has been going to Fashion Institute of Technology and working in Soho, she's been going her own way.

I can't really blame her. Tatianna has been working in a designer's boutique for over a year now. Personally, I've never been down there, but I hear it's really nice. Tati's living her dream. Ever since we were little she's been designing T-shirts for us or altering her own outfits to give her a unique look. Plus, she sews like a pro. That's one of the things I love about Tati—she knows her talents and makes the most of them.

"Speaking of secretive, did you call Raven? Is she coming?"

It's going to be awkward, but Vanessa has her heart set on getting our triumvirate back to the way we were. Personally, I'm fine with letting the haters go their own way, but Vanessa is my closest friend, so for her sake I'll give it a try.

"I did, but she said she'd let me know, whatever that means." Vanessa holds a few suits she wants to try on. "Are you ready? Oh, look, here's the white bikini in your size. Try it on."

I protest, but she insists, "Just try it on. It won't kill you."

It feels so good to be shopping with Vanessa again like we used to do. I make a mental promise to myself that no matter how busy or tired I am, I will always make time for her. If you're lucky enough to have a friendship like we do, then you have to nurture it. I would feel awful if I lost Vanessa.

We get changing booths across from each other because we always discuss each item. I try on the suits I picked first, and they look like every other suit I've worn through the years, so much so that I wonder why I'm buying a new one in the first place. It's not like I wear them out, plus I've been the same size for the past two years, just taller.

Vanessa's face scrunches up at every suit I try on. She, on the other hand, always picks really cute bathing suits, like the red-and-white striped one she has on. She's so petite, she looks adorable.

"Everything you put on looks so good," I tell her. "You've got a rocking little bod."

"I think I'm going to take this one and the yellow-and-white print," she says. Both are bikinis, but don't show a lot of stuff. "You didn't try the white one on. I want to see it."

Reluctantly, I put it on. Vanessa is right. It does look amazing. I open the door to my booth to show her the suit.

"Oh, Mari, you have to get that," she insists. "You look beautiful in it."

I adjust the bandeau top. "One good wave and my headlights will be showing."

Vanessa fiddles with a little pouch on the side. "Here's the detachable halter strap." She helps me hook it in the middle and bring it around my neck.

I know it looks good, but I'm not sure it's my style. I'm not the glamorous type. On the other hand, I've been saying it's time for a change. Maybe this could be my new look.

I shake my head. "Nah, I feel too naked. This suit screams *exotic resort,* not Coney Island." I tie the sarong across my hips. "Besides, this will get all wrinkled under my shorts."

"So carry it in your beach bag and wear it when we go up on the boardwalk for lunch." She rolls her eyes and lets out an exasperated sigh.

Now this cracks me up. You have to know Coney Island. It's the last subway stop in New York City, picking up anybody and everybody who can't get to any other beach. Some people even swim in their street clothes. Believe me, it is not a high-class place at all. It's more like the Refugee Sea.

"Vanessa, think about it. Can you imagine me waltzing down the boardwalk in this suit?"

She starts laughing. "Okay, okay, I get it, but I think you should buy the suit anyway because it looks great. Don't waste your money on a suit that looks like everything you already own."

She manages to talk me into it, even though I have my doubts about wearing it this weekend. We stop at a rack of rubber flip-flops.

"Take the white ones to match your suit," she says, picking up a cute pair of yellow ones and a pair of red ones to match the candy-striped bikini.

I hate white shoes, except for kicks, so I take a pair of soft gold ones, thinking that I can also wear them with my new skirts.

On the way out, we run smack into Raven and her new BFF, Solange, who's erupting from the top of a flimsy black cami. She's got big boobs for a skinny little chick. She also cropped her cut-offs so the bottoms of her butt cheeks pop out. Tatianna's right; Solange does think she's hot stuff. A huge pair of black knock-off sunglasses with big gold D&Gs on the side covers almost all of Solange's face. Is she afraid her fans will pester her for autographs?

"Oh, wow," says Raven, not the least embarrassed to face me. "We came shopping for new bathing suits for this weekend."

I'm a little confused. Does this mean Raven decided to come with us to the beach? But I don't want her bringing Solange. There's no way we can be friends again if Solange is part of the package.

Solange is smiling her Chiclets smile. "Yeah, our boyfriends are taking us to the beach for the Fourth of July."

Well, I guess that answers Vanessa's question. Raven won't be joining us this weekend.

CHAPTER 8

El Barrio Poster Child

"Mari!" Cisco's voice booms into my ear. "Great news—Crazy Joe OD'd!"

Cha-Cha and I are out for our walk, and I can barely hear him on my cell phone with all the trucks groaning past. I could have sworn he said Crazy Joe OD'd. How could that be good news?

I stop, narrowly avoiding an ant-covered, half-gnawed slice of pizza. "Wait—Cisco, I can't hear you. There's a lot of traffic. Can you repeat that?"

"I said, Crazy Joe OD'd. Overdosed. You know, drugs?"

"Omigod, that's awful. Is he dead?"

"Nah, but just as good. He's in intensive care at Bellevue and can't do his Hamptons gig this weekend," he yells happily. "Mari, I got the job! We got the job!"

"Me too?"

"You, me, and Randy. Pack your bags. We're going to the Hamptons!" I can hear him whooping and hollering on the other end.

Every chance to sing is a good chance to promote myself. But this could be a big opportunity for me. There'll be a lot of people in the music industry out there for the holiday.

"This is phenomenal, Cisco, but I have to ask you—"

"Hold up, man, I'll be right there," he yells to someone in the background. "Listen, Mari, I can't talk now. I'll pick you up tomorrow afternoon. I'll let you know what time." And he's gone.

Great, just great. I want to know where I'm supposed to sleep. I'm not going to horn in on Pablo and Lola, especially considering I wasn't included in their plans in the first place. What am I supposed to do—sleep on the beach? I can't afford a hotel room, and I'm not sharing one with Cisco and Randy. *Eew.*

Whatever. I can't pass up the chance of a lifetime. This is so great! Wait until I tell Vanessa.

Vanessa! Omigod, I'm supposed to go to Coney Island with Vanessa this weekend. She's going to be so hurt, especially now that Raven isn't coming with us. Maybe I could ask her to come along. Forget that, her parents would never let her go. Besides, I don't even know where I'm staying, so how can I ask her to join us? Plus, the gig with Cisco is work. Not only will I get paid, I'll get exposure too. Vanessa is going to have to understand that. I'll make it up to her with another weekend. The summer is just beginning.

I feel terrible. I'm already breaking the promise I made to myself about spending more time with her. I should probably tell Cisco that I can't make it, and honor my date with Vanessa. But who knows when an opportunity to sing in front of all of those big shots in the music industry will come up again? Probably never. No, I've got to go with Cisco, but this is killing me. I hate hurting Vanessa.

Back in my apartment, I start practicing my vocals. Athletes exercise every day; I sing. You've got to keep the pipes tuned. Plus, I really love singing. It relaxes and excites me at the same time. I'm in a zone.

I run my scales over and over before flipping through the CDs in search of one that fits my mood. I love to sing along with really strong female singers who force me to stretch myself. When Lola came into our lives a few years ago, she introduced me to a lot of singers I'd never heard before. I pop one of her discs in and start to sing along.

The shrill sound of the phone interrupts my practice.

The caller ID surprises me. She *never* calls me. "Hey, Tati, what's up?"

"I'm coming with you this weekend." She must have found out about Cisco's gig in the Hamptons, because I can't see Tatianna slumming at Coney Island. "Get down here now. We have to plan clothes and everything."

"Tati, I'm not sure where you work, but I am sure I can't afford it."

"Never mind that, we'll work out something," she insists. I only wish I was as sure. "Write down the address and I'll tell you which train to take."

Thirty minutes later, I'm rattling downtown on a hot subway train filled with whackos. I keep my eyes focused on the gritty floor until I hear the announcement for my stop. When I emerge above ground, I realize once again that I really don't know New York at all. I feel like I'm getting off a spaceship after it lands on another planet.

Soho is like an old, little village with low buildings and old-fashioned storefronts featuring just a few expensive-looking things. It's the complete opposite of the crammed stores in East Harlem. No prices are advertised here. Most of the shops are art galleries and there are several sidewalk cafes. Attractive people bustle down the streets wearing clothes that are trendy to the point of strange. Not wanting to look like a tourist in my own city, I sneak a peek at the directions in my pocket and head left on Spring Street.

I open the glass door to Mystique. Nothing about this store invites me in. In fact, I feel like I have no business being here and there's a real possibility I might get thrown out. I'm regretting not taking time to change into something a little nicer. My cut-off shorts, T-shirt, and flip-flops are definitely not cutting it down here.

"Mari, thank God you're here," says Tatianna, coming from behind a counter. "And it's a good thing, too. You look like the poster child for El Barrio. You aren't wearing those rags to the Hamptons, are you?"

How am I supposed to respond to that? Truthfully, I hadn't thought about it. I'm more concerned with sleeping arrangements, but if Tati is coming, that makes it easier.

"Look, Tati, I warned you on the phone. I can't afford anything in here." I didn't need to see a price tag to know there was nothing in my budget here.

"Just be quiet," she whispers. "I've got a—"

I smell floral perfume before I notice a woman in the room with us.

"Ah, Tatianna, this must be your little friend that you were telling me about," purrs a voice with an accent so posh that I can't place it.

"Kell E, this is my friend Marisol Reyes." She gives me a *don't blow this* eye. "Marisol this is Kell E, the famous fashion designer."

Well, I've never heard of her, but that doesn't mean she's not famous. How many designers do I know? Unless their initials are plastered over knock-offs on East 116th Street, I don't know who they are. But Kell E doesn't need to know this.

I smile and extend my hand. "Hello, Kell E, this is a real honor for me. Your designs are beautiful."

Kell E is a wisp of a woman with a dark-brown bob and heavy black eyeliner.

She preens a little. "Oh, my. And I'm a fan of yours as well. Tatianna showed me your video earlier this morning. *Très charmant.* I hear you'll be performing at Blend's Fourth of July party this weekend. Is that correct?"

Everyone knows more about this gig than I do! I had no idea it was Blend's party we were working. And how in the world does a woman like Kell E—who looks like a high-society type—know about a rapper like Blend?

"Yes, we'll be performing," I reply with more confidence than I feel.

"Well, that's wonderful. I'm looking forward to your performance," she says sincerely.

Wait, Kell E is going to be at a rapper's party? Too weird, but *whatever.*

"I also told Kell E about your duet with Diego Salazar on his new CD," Tatianna says indicating that I should play along.

"Oh, what a delight he is!" says Kell E into the air. "Such a talented young man." Then she's all business. "Now we have to decide on your look." She gives me the once-over. "If you're going to be a Kell E girl, you have to maintain a certain image at all times. I have a reputation to uphold," she says, looking pointedly at my cut-offs and flip-flops.

Tatianna is beaming with pride. Okay, I get it. Beautiful new clothes will be mine, in exchange for Kell E getting to brag about designing for a new star. Works for me.

Kell E says to Tatianna, "She'll need a white dress for the party. You're wearing the Gatsby, correct?"

Tati's eyes widen. "Yes," she stammers.

"Bring it to Marisol. You can wear one of the others," orders Kell E. Her voice is no more than a whisper but has enough strength to command an army.

Tears glisten in Tati's eyes, but she does as she's told without a hint of protest.

She emerges from the back room carrying a simple white silk dress with spaghetti straps on a padded hanger. I notice a hint of clear beading on top, giving the dress a little sparkle. I slip it on. It reminds me of pictures of flappers from the twenties. For such a flimsy little dress, it's surprisingly heavy.

"You see," begins Kell E, "everyone must wear all white to the party. No color, not even shoes, or you will not be admitted."

Great, just great. Now what am I supposed to do about shoes? Maybe I should have bought those white flip-flops—not that they go with this dress.

Being poked and prodded and told what to wear is not my idea of a good time. After several tedious hours, I'm surrounded by piles of clothes. The ethereal Kell E has long since vanished, *poof*, into the atmosphere.

I look at Tatianna. "How am I supposed to get all this home on the train?"

She looks at me like I'm an idiot. "We'll messenger it up to you. Just worry about what you're going to pack it in for the ride out."

I hadn't thought of that. All I have are my ratty little-girl suitcases that I used for sleepovers with Vanessa and Raven.

"Maybe you can find something in the neighborhood. Just make sure it's black; that way it will blend in, even though it's cheap. No gold initials. You don't want to look ghetto."

"Yeah, I'll do that as soon as I get uptown, but I have another problem."

She lifts her hands as if to say, *Haven't I done enough?*

"No, I don't need anything else," I tell her. "And thank you for all of this." I survey the cache. "No way could I have done this without you. How'd you ever think of it?"

Tatianna looks pleased with herself. "We both win. I want a weekend out there so bad I could scream. Now I get to go with you as your stylist."

"Well, I'm happy you're coming. I hated the idea of being alone with two boys for the whole weekend, even if it is business," I admit.

"So what's your problem?"

"Vanessa," I tell her. "We have plans to go to Coney Island, just the two of us. Raven made plans with Solange, Julian, and Freddie. Now she'll be all alone this weekend."

"She'll just have to deal with it. This is business for you." She brushes the problem away with a flick of her wrist, which she must have picked up from Kell E.

I blow out a *whoosh* of air. "I feel so bad. She's going to be hurt."

"She'll get over it," Tati says dismissively.

But I don't think she will. I'm not sure I would.

CHAPTER 9

Meet Me Halfway

I owe Vanessa a personal apology—not a text or a phone call from the street. She's meeting me in front of her building. I can see her scrolling through her messages as she waits for me.

"Hey!" I say when I get close enough.

She looks up, smiling. Vanessa is always so happy to see me. It kills me that she'll be so disappointed.

"Hey, yourself!" she calls. We give each other a kiss.

"Vanessa, I have bad news." Better to get it out of the way. "I can't go to the beach with you on the Fourth."

Her brow furrows. "Why? What's up?"

"Well, the good news is I'll be working with Cisco that night." I force a weak smile in the hopes that she joins me in celebrating this turn of events. "The bad news is that the gig is in East Hampton. We'll be there all weekend."

She purses her lips and rolls her eyes.

"Vanessa, it's work. I've got to do it." I immediately regret the harshness of my tone. It's a double whammy. Not only am I ditching on our plans, but now I'm yelling at her in defense of myself. I'm a crummy friend.

She starts off down the street without me. I run to catch up, jumping over a dried puddle of pee in the process. I've never seen her get like this, so I don't know what to expect.

"Vanessa, at least talk to me. Meet me halfway on this," I plead.

She looks me right in the eye. "I understand. I really do. I know this is work, but my feelings are hurt." I can see her eyes getting watery, and I feel like crying too. "I feel like everyone is moving on with their lives except for me."

"Vanessa! That's not true. You have a great career ahead of you. You're going to college. This is all I have. These singing jobs are my college. If I don't make it doing this, I'll be flipping burgers with Raven at Mickey D's for the rest of my life." I move in to give her a hug, but she pushes me away. "There'll be other weekends at the beach. We can go next Saturday if you want."

"But this is special. It's a holiday," she snaps. "Everyone else has plans. Raven has Freddie and Solange has Julian." Ouch! "Tatianna is going off wherever. And now you're off to the Hamptons while I'm stuck in smelly old East Harlem." She kicks a crumpled Tico's Tacos bag into the gutter. "It's not fair."

Oh, boy! "Actually, Tatianna is going with me," I say sheepishly. She glares at me. "It's a long, long story. Come with me to 116th Street. I have to buy luggage and I'll tell you the whole story."

She starts walking again and I hurry to catch up. At least she's heading in the right direction.

A lot of the stores along the way have knock-off luggage out front.

"What about that?" Vanessa points to a brown duffel bag covered with gold LVs.

I shake my head. "Tatianna said that knock-offs are ghetto."

"Figures."

We head into one store that carries a little bit of everything. Surprisingly, they have a three-piece luggage set on sale. There's nothing special about it, just plain black nylon with wheels and retractable handles, but I like the way the duffel can be hooked onto the suitcase.

We walk toward the restaurant with me pulling my luggage behind me. Vanessa holds the door so I can wheel myself into Casa de Felix. Julian and his cousin Angel are seated at our usual table, and Sylvia is placing burgers and fries in front of them. Julian looks up and sees me. Neither one of us can look away—like we're invisibly connected.

"Hey, Mari," he says softly, pulling out the chair next to him.

I take that as an invitation and sit down. My stomach grumbles and I realize that I haven't eaten since breakfast. I snatch a fry off of Julian's plate. "Umm, good!"

"That does look good," says Vanessa, smiling for the first time since I told her my news. "Can I have the same, Mammi?"

"Me too," I add.

I'm not sure if it's the burger or Angel that's making her smile. Vanessa likes Angel, but so far, the only hooking up they've done was in chemistry lab, mixing weird concoctions.

"What are you guys up to?" she asks.

I really hope the name *Solange* doesn't come out of Julian's mouth.

"We're going to see *Alien Invasion IV*," Angel says.

"Ooh, that sounds like fun!" squeals Vanessa. "What do you think, Mari? Should we go too?"

I think it sounds boring, but there's nothing else on my agenda for tonight. Lola texted earlier today; she and Pablo left for his beach house this afternoon. I'd have to sit home all alone. They even took Cha-Cha with them.

I sneak a peek at Julian to see if I'm wanted. He's busy with his burger, but sensing the lull in the conversation, he looks up. "Yeah, why don't you come with us?"

He sort of sounds like he genuinely means that. I hope so because I miss him like crazy. Maybe this will give us a chance to get back together. We need some alone time without Solange barging in.

We finish the burgers and Julian finishes my fries. I can tell by the way he smiles at me that he's still interested. Now it's my job to reel him in.

"I've got to drop this off at home first," I say as we head to my building.

"Where are you going, anyway?" asks Julian.

"Cisco and I have a gig in the Hamptons this weekend," I say, so pleased with myself that my plans are better than his. He may be taking Solange to the beach, but I'm going to a really exciting spot and hanging out with the rich and famous.

"Cool," he offers, without any enthusiasm, as we get to my building. "I'll help you get this upstairs."

The boxes from Kell E are stacked in the living room.

"What is all this?" he asks.

"Tatianna got the designer she works for to dress me for this weekend."

Julian raises his eyebrows. "You're moving in pretty fancy circles these days."

I'm not sure how to take that comment, so I let it go.

We get to the movies and Julian and Angel pay for us. This is starting to feel like a date.

"Want to split a soda and popcorn?" he asks.

"Sure," I say, even though I'm stuffed. I wolfed down that burger and now it's sitting in my stomach like a lump of cement.

Vanessa and I sit in the middle and I see her squeeze Angel's hand. Go, Vanessa—make a move. I pick a few kernels from the top of Julian's bag and snuggle against his shoulder. Even if we're not dating, we're still friends, right? He switches the popcorn bag to his right hand and puts his left arm around my shoulders. Oh, yeah!

My mind is racing with a thousand things, so I'm actually surprised when the credits roll.

Nobody's hungry and I'm kind of pooped.

"I'm going to walk Mari home," Julian says. "I'll see you guys tomorrow."

We take the elevator up to my apartment.

"I'm glad you're walking me in," I confess. "I've never spent the night alone before. I didn't even leave a light on."

He pulls me in and hugs me. We walk arm in arm down the hall. When we get to my door, he takes the key, flips the switch, and walks in first.

"Everything looks fine," he says, flipping on the rest of the lights.

He looks up at me with those puppy-dog eyes. "I've missed you, Mari."

He pulls me into a hug and kisses me long and hard. I've wanted this for so long. His tongue pushes through and begins dueling with mine. Without breaking contact, he maneuvers us to the couch. His arms are strong. This is the way I always thought it would be. Natural, not forced.

"I've wanted you for so long." His voice is husky in my ear. Just the feel of his breath gives me chills.

His hand sneaks under my T-shirt and I feel tingly as he unhooks my bra. A soft moan escapes from my lips. After a while he takes my hand and lowers it into his unzipped jeans. This time I don't resist. Now I have Julian moaning.

"Let's go into your room," he says huskily.

This is it. It feels so right. I get up and take his hand.

Then an unexpected, unwanted face pops into my brain. Solange.

"What about Solange?" I pull away. "Am I filling in for her tonight or are you serious about me?"

"What kind of question is that?" he snarls. The mood is broken.

"I know you're taking her to the beach this weekend. She made a point of telling me that herself." He might as well know that I know. "I'm not sharing you with that skank."

"She's not a skank," he barks. I can't believe he's defending her! "And you don't have to share me with her. I'll talk to her this weekend."

"Before or after the beach?" I demand.

"What's it to you? You'll be in the Hamptons." His voice is tinged with sarcasm.

It's everything to me. If he takes her to the beach and tells her at the end of the weekend, they'll still be a couple. That makes me—nothing!

"If you want to be with me tonight I have to know it's over between you."

"It's over, I told you. But we already made plans to go to the beach with Raven and Freddie, plus Angel told me tonight that he's asking Vanessa. Why should I stay home by myself? It's not like you're going to be around."

Great, just great. It's going to be a big triple date. All of my friends will be partying together, except Solange is taking my place. This news cancels my excitement of being in the Hamptons and I'm pissed. Suddenly I wish I was going to Coney Island with my friends. Weird.

"I can't share you with her," I say, pouting. "Cisco told me she's been doing all the guys at the video production company. That's how she got the part in Blend's video. She even did Cisco. That's how she got the audition."

He's staring at me. Flames are shooting from his eyes. I know it's mean of me, but he's got to face reality. If he's going to decide between us, he should know all the facts.

"You know, Mari, you really are a bitch." He adjusts his clothes and walks to the door. Before he opens it, he says in a low voice, "You've been getting a lot of singing jobs lately. Did you ever stop to think that people might be saying the same things about you?"

CHAPTER 10

Two Mojitos, Dudley!

I keep replaying the scene with Julian over and over, only this time "Breakeven" is playing in the background. I am falling to pieces. Julian was and always will be the best part of me. At least that's what I'd always thought, but what if love isn't enough? We never used to fight like this—and never before have I intentionally tried to hurt him. He didn't deserve that. Julian is right. I am a bitch.

We were always so close that our friends used to call us Peanut Butter and Jelly. There *was* something sweet about our relationship. Julian looked out for me, always making sure I was okay and having fun. I was his princess. Everything was great until I started working with Cisco and our jobs got in the way of our good times. Julian, like Vanessa, felt left out and it's all my fault.

When this weekend is over, I've got to sit down with Julian and sort this whole mess out. If we can't figure out a way to be together without hurting each other, then maybe it's time to go our separate ways, no matter how painful it is. I love him too much to go on this way.

Sleep eludes me all night. I fling off the covers and head into the living room. I might as well pack my suitcases for tomorrow. Maybe the effort will make me drowsy enough to get a few hours of sleep in the morning.

The boxes of clothes are packed beautifully with layers of blue tissue paper in between. I'm so afraid to mess it up that I take the entire pile and place it in the large suitcase. I pack underwear, which reminds me of the body tape. I toss in the roll. Vanessa must have ESP because the white bikini will be perfect for the weekend. That goes on top, along with the gold flip-flops.

I've never splurged on fancy PJs, which would have come in handy. I grab a couple of camis and flannel boxers. My faded blue hoodie is on the back of the chair. I pack it, just in case it gets cold out there. Ziploc baggies will have to hold my toiletries and makeup because I don't have anything else to put them in.

That's it. I have a weird feeling something's missing, but I can't put my finger on it.

Shoes! White shoes! Kell E said that I have to wear white shoes to the party. I completely forgot. Where in the world am I supposed to buy those now?

I head into Lola's room and rummage on the floor of her closet. If she even has white shoes, she must have taken them with her to the beach. I plop my behind onto the rug. Shoot! Now what?

Then I remember. Lola showed me an old, favorite gown of hers last month and Lucite shoes to go with it. They'll be perfect. They're clear plastic so there's no color to worry about. Plus, I'd rather look barefoot than walk around with clunky white shoes on my feet. I grab them out of her closet.

There, now I'm done. But I'm still not sleepy. The sky is beginning to lighten.

I make myself a cup of tea to warm my throat so I can get my vocal practice in. Running scales is soothing for me. I guess that's why some people chant when they meditate. The repetition is otherworldly. I can't turn the music on this early without waking the building, so I practice singing a few tunes a cappella, remembering to breathe from the diaphragm.

When I learn a new song I listen carefully and try to internalize the words so I can make them my own. I never want to copy the original artist, even if I can sing the song better. Phrasing is everything, but you really have to own the lyrics to make them ring with truth. That, in addition to my range, is what makes my singing unique.

Still thinking about Julian, I work my way through the oldies: "Walk on By" with Dionne; I'm pleading "You Don't Have to Say You Love Me" with Dusty; singing "Memories" with Barbra. Enough! I'm going to make some new memories today.

I sip another cup of tea and find Lola's stash of Milanos. Breakfast of champions. The day dawns bright and clear. I'm getting excited. This is a whole new adventure for me.

Remembering Kell E's warning about appearances, I take a little extra time getting ready. Tatianna already told me that if she sees me with a ponytail held up with a ratty sweatband she's going to pull it right off of my head, so I let my hair dry naturally. I don't want to get my new clothes all crumpled and sweaty on the ride out there. I decide to wear my denim miniskirt and a cute little top. So what if it's cheap? It's so adorable no one will know.

I pull my suitcase to the elevator and wait on the sidewalk. After a few minutes, Cisco's Jeep comes rolling up with Randy and Tatianna already inside.

He lifts my suitcase into the rear. "God, Mari, what have you got in here, rocks?" It's obvious that it won't fit in with all the equipment, so he shoves it onto the backseat floor and tosses my duffel on top. "This suitcase is huge. How long do you think you're going for?"

"Ask Tati," I reply. "Hey, Cisco," I ask as we start to roll, "I know how you got this gig, but how do I fit into this? A big rapper like Blend isn't going to have a karaoke party. Not with all those singers there."

"I know, right?" He looks in the rearview mirror at me. "But you'd be surprised what these rich people do for a hoot. Besides, when we were talking at Apple last week, he asked me who you were."

"Aah!" yells Randy pounding the dash with his big ham fist. "Blend's got the hots for Mari! That's how we got the gig."

"Whatever," says Tati. "At least we're getting a weekend in East Hampton out of it."

The ride is long and boring. I must have dozed off because suddenly the scenery is way different from the City. We're rolling along a flat county highway dotted with low buildings and stores. A sign on top of a little shack of a restaurant reads LOBSTER ROLLS, and I wonder what in the world they could be. They're probably like egg rolls, but I never had lobster before.

"How long before we get there?" I ask.

Cisco answers, "An hour with this traffic, maybe a little less."

"Omigod, this is taking forever."

Tatianna responds without opening her eyes, "That's why they call it *Long* Island, Mari."

Amazing! She's even sarcastic in her sleep.

I'm so fascinated by the scenery that the time slips by. Before you know it we're pulling into a long horseshoe-shaped drive and up to a white marble porch, which is attached to a dazzling white-and-glass mansion. The place is jammed with trucks, vans, and workers buzzing around. As if on cue, a butler in a white jacket and black pants comes out to greet us.

We are actually staying in this place. How great is that? Clive, the butler, has a maid show Tatianna and me to a room on the second floor. I always thought Vanessa and Tatianna's room was fit for a princess, but this is a hundred times better. The wooden floors are stained a dark brown; everything else is sparkling white, including the gauzy bed linens and billowy curtains. I walk to the window and see the ocean outside! I can't believe that I can sit here and watch the ocean from my room.

Tati's eyes are wide and glistening. "I can't believe this!" We stare at each other and then turn back to the view.

"Let's get down there," I say. "Did you bring a suit?"

"Well, duh, Mari, where did I think I was going?" It doesn't take long before Tati is back to her jaded old self.

"Hey, look at this," she says, flipping the switch. We have our very own pink marble bathroom with gold-and-crystal fixtures. There's a sunken Jacuzzi tub big enough for a few people to sit comfortably. I want to turn it on right now, just to watch the water pour out of the swan's mouth.

We change into our suits and Tati eyes my new white bikini. "That's really nice. Where did you get that?"

"Vanessa picked it out for me at Epstein's."

"Hard to believe the two of you could pick out something like that."

She has on a midnight-blue bikini held together at the top center and bottom sides with round gold discs with K and E cut out of the metal. She looks magnificent, but then she always does.

I start sweeping my hair into a ponytail, but Tati snatches the sweatband out of my hand and tosses it into the wastebasket.

"What did I tell you about that?" she snarls.

"But we're going swimming."

"We will *not* be swimming. We're not walking around this place looking like drowned rats," she insists. "We just got here. First impressions are everything."

I'm not going to argue with that, but I still feel naked. I start to reach for my blue hoodie.

"Put that down!" She walks out the door, leaving me no choice but to follow her.

We make an impression all right. We impress every workman all the way down to the pool. How could we not? Two tall, lanky girls with hair flowing past our waists, walking through the mansion in bikinis, are hard to miss. Dead men would wake up and notice.

I gulp and try to mirror Tatianna's super-cool attitude as we walk out to the pool area. People are already starting to party. The bartender is serving brightly colored cocktails in fancy glasses. Most people are on chaise lounges or sitting on cushions dangling their feet in the pool. Two blond twins, splashing in the water, make some noise as they toss a beach ball to each other. They don't look like drowned rats to me. In fact, most of the guys around the pool can't stop looking at them.

Until they notice us, that is. Blend himself gets up from a round glass table and walks over to us. I'd know him anywhere. Not only is he the number one rapper in the world, but he also has his own record label and clothing company. In fact, he's wearing his totally hip golf ensemble right now—peach shirt and white shorts. Underneath is a rocking bod. I know that from his underwear ads; he models them himself.

Blend gets his name from his nationality. He claims to have the blood of every race on the planet running through his veins. I don't know if that's true, but it mixes together really well. This is one good-looking dude!

"And who might you be?" he asks, eyeing us appreciatively.

This gives my confidence a boost. "I might be Marisol Reyes," I answer cheekily. "I'm working with Cisco at your party tomorrow night." I flash him my best smile. He kisses my hand! "And this is my friend, Tatianna Fuentes."

She looks boldly into his eyes, almost challenging him when he kisses her hand.

"Welcome to my home. You add to its beauty." He walks us over to the bar. "You must be thirsty." He calls to the bartender, "Two mojitos, Dudley."

I would kill for a cold bottle of water, but I don't want to be rude. I take a sip from the icy glass. "Delicious," I compliment my host.

"If there is anything, and I do mean *anything*, you girls desire, you have only to tell one of my staff. They'll be happy to fill all your needs." He sweeps his arm, indicating the entire property from the pool to the rolling green lawn, all the way down to the golden sand. "Enjoy."

We take our drinks over to two lounge chairs at the far end of the swimming area and a pool boy brings us the most luxurious towels I've ever felt. As comfy as this is, I'm itching to run through the hot sand and feel the cold saltwater on my feet. But I'll have to wait until Tatianna is otherwise occupied or I'll never hear the end of it. I close my eyes and feel the warm rays of the sun kiss my face. I may have had a bad night, but right now I don't have a care in the world.

A deep voice interrupts my thoughts. "Hello, ladies." I look up to find one of the guys who had been sitting with Blend. He smiles at me, but then turns his attention to Tatianna. "I'm Reggie Wainright. Blend and I were wondering if the two of you would care to join us for dinner tonight."

Tati and I look at each other and nod. It's not like we had plans.

"Sure," Tati replies. "That sounds great."

Reggie is as fine as Blend. You can almost feel his rock-hard body under his preppy Blend outfit. A bright smile flashes across his chocolate-brown skin.

"Wonderful," he says. "Nothing fancy, mind you. Blend is in the mood to sit by the water and have some lobster."

"What a coincidence," replies Tati smoothly. "So are we."

CHAPTER 11

The Claws Are a Little Tougher

You can't really call this a date. Besides Blend and Reggie, there are three other guys who were hanging with them at the table by the pool. Also sitting with us are the blond twins and an assortment of really hot girls whom I don't know and am not introduced to.

Not that it matters. This place is amazing! The Shark Shack looks like an old fishermen's wharf that has been here for a century. We're sitting on a wooden deck overlooking the water. Sleek boats are pulling up to dock and people are coming in for dinner. So cool.

I'm trying to take everything in so I can learn about this life. People aren't dressed up and yet they are. I mean their clothes are casual but really put together, not sloppy. Women are in sundresses or light capris with pastel T-shirts and sherbet-colored sweaters draped like shawls across their shoulders. Men are dressed in golf shirts and tan pants, their sockless feet stuffed into brown moccasins tied with cord. They all look so clean and polished.

In El Barrio people walk around in shabby clothes. If a woman from home were eating here tonight, she'd be in a tiny little camisole and really tight jeans with a roll of fat sticking out in between. Either that or she'd be all dressed up in sequins or lace with her long talons polished to match. There's no going halfway.

These people look classy. Lola would fit right in here.

Blend and his posse are sporting the casual classy look, but a few of the girls at the table are definitely hootchie mamas. Even Tati looks a little too flashy in a red strapless dress. We argued about my outfit, but I'm glad I didn't back down. I mean, Reggie had said that it was nothing fancy. Tati wanted me to wear a midnight blue spandex dress that I thought would look better in a Manhattan club. My white mini and lightweight mango cashmere tunic by Kell E are a better fit in this place. At least my gold flip-flops aren't getting stuck in the boards of the deck like the other girls' heels.

Waiters bring over silver buckets with bottles of Cristal champagne, which they pour nonstop. Silver three-tiered trays are loaded with clams, oysters, crab claws, and shrimp nestled on crushed ice. Blend scoops up an oyster and puts it on my plate.

"Ever try one of these?" he asks.

He did insist that I sit next to him. Tatianna is down at the other end, but not next to Reggie, who's paying a lot of attention to one of the twins. She's pouting, which is not a good sign.

"Well, I've had clams. Do they taste the same?"

"Even better." He squeezes a few drops of lemon juice and drizzles some of the sauce on top. "Try it."

Normally I just pick up the shell and slurp it down, but I notice the little forks and use mine to pick out the meat and pop it into my mouth.

"Umm! Creamy." I can't resist picking up the shell to drink the juice. "These are delicious."

Blend chuckles and fills my plate with shellfish. "Enjoy."

And I do. I sip my champagne between bites of seafood—I never knew life could be this good. There's a whole new world outside of my neighborhood and I can't wait to discover every bit of it.

Blend leans over. "I saw your video on YouTube."

Omigod, this is news.

"I like to browse through to find new talent for my label," he continues. "You really rocked it, Marisol. Are you signed with anyone?"

I honestly don't know if I am or not. So far it's only been talk. I never signed anything. But it's probably best to be straight with Blend and let him know where I stand.

"I just recorded a demo with Diego Salazar for his new *Duets* CD. We recorded 'Soul Spinning.'"

"Nice. So did my man TB Barnes sign you?"

"No, I haven't signed anything," I admit. "Pablo Cruz said he'd get back to me when they make a decision."

"So you're Cruz's client?"

This is a little embarrassing. "Well, I'm not sure. He arranged for me to sing with Diego, but I'm not sure if he actually took me on as a client."

Blend is shaking his head. "No, no, no, don't let them jerk you around. They should be jumping through hoops to sign up a talent like you. If you didn't sign anything, you're free."

Well, I don't know about that. Pablo Cruz and Teddy Bear Barnes have been really nice to me. I may not have signed anything, but we do have an understanding. I don't want to jeopardize our relationship.

"Look, I can see you're unsure about all this, but you have to trust me. I know this business. You have to look out for yourself because no one else will do it for you." He looks me right in the eye. "But I'm going to let you think about that. When you're ready, you come see me." He nods in the direction of the inside of the restaurant. "Now here comes our dinner."

A squadron of waiters brings out platters of huge lobsters still in their shells. I stare at mine, wondering what I'm supposed to do with it.

"I'm guessing you never had lobster before."

"This is a first," I admit to him. The creature in my plate looks interesting, but I don't know where to begin.

"Here, let me show you." Blend is the best teacher. He breaks off the tail with his big hands. "Stab the small part of the tail with your fork and twist it out."

Like magic, the meat pops out of the shell. I start on that while he tackles his own. Everyone at the table is drenching their lobsters in the butter boats, but I'm not crazy about butter so I just give it a squeeze of lemon. Delicious. I take a sip of my champagne and wait for Blend to give me my next lobster lesson.

He notices me waiting. "The claws are a little tougher. Let me give you a hand." He rips them off and cracks them with a nutcracker. "You're going to have to work for the meat," he says, indicating my little fork.

I'm having fun. It's like a treasure hunt. I look at Tati, who's sitting back drinking champagne, her untouched lobster in front of her. She's pouting and eyeing Reggie. I'm surprised the sparks from her eyes haven't set him on fire by now. Tatianna doesn't place second to anyone.

I'm absolutely stuffed and a bit light-headed. The sun set long ago and tiny diamonds dot the indigo sky.

Blend signs the check and the waiter says, "Thank *you*, sir!"

Smacking his palms on the arms of his chair, Blend announces, "I'm feeling Shells!"

Even I know that Shells is the hottest club out here. Last summer it made the news when pop tart Chelsea Channing caught her boyfriend there with another girl. After he ran out of the club, she tried to run him down with her SUV and took out the line of people waiting out front. Every local news reporter was broadcasting from the front of the club.

We pile into the Navigators and head over there. Walking across the gravel parking lot is a challenge for the girls in their platform stiletto sandals. Either that or they have a thing for playing the damsel in distress. I'm happy to see Reggie giving Tati a hand as she steps gingerly across the pebbles.

A horrible retching sound brings us to a halt. One of the twins is losing her lobster while her sister holds her hair back. I'm glad I avoided the butter. After wiping her mouth with a tissue, she looks up and announces, "Okay, let's go!"

We sweep past the line and head into the club. Blend gives her a look of pure disgust. Something tells me this is the last time she'll be a guest at the mansion. Blend is a very classy guy. Everything in his gleaming white home is hospital clean. I can't imagine him digging girls who puke in parking lots.

A tall blond with pin-straight hair that falls down her back leads us to a guarded area a few steps above the crowded dance floor. It looks like a mini living room with three low couches set around a square coffee table. A giant conch shell surrounded by tea candles decorates the surface. Waiters appear with buckets of Cristal, and the twins are busy guzzling it down without a care in the world. They may not have learned a lesson, but I did and take little sips.

Blend pats the place next to him and I take a seat. Tati tosses her bag on the table and heads to the dance floor with Reggie. Her slinky body is already grinding in her red spandex dress as they push their way into the crowd. I'm itching to dance, too, but Blend seems to want me here and I don't want to offend my host. After all, I'm not here as a guest; I'm working his party. It was very nice of him to invite Tati and me to dinner—he didn't have to. Cisco and Randy weren't invited.

So I sit silently as Blend holds court. Most people aren't allowed past the guards, but lots of actors and singers in the VIP area stop by to chat with Blend. It's exciting to see them at first, but then it gets pretty boring. They're not here to see me; in fact, they only stop by to see and be seen by Blend, who doesn't even introduce me. That doesn't mean he's not paying attention to me. Every now and then I feel his long tapered fingers run up and down my thigh. Not too far up so that I'm freaked, but just enough to keep me on my toes. I'm not sure if I should relax and let him continue because it does feel good, or push his hand away because, well, I hardly know him. I mean, this is crazy, he hired me to sing, but does he think that I'll do *anything* for this gig?

I'm tired and wishing I could slip between those crisp white sheets back in the room I'm sharing with Tatianna, so I'm not unhappy when Blend gives the command to split. At the house I'm a little nervous about what comes next. I remember how snarky Julian got the two times he wanted to hook up and I turned him down, and I don't want that to happen with Blend. I'm afraid of being pressed into something I'm not ready for. This could be difficult considering I am staying in his house and have to be here all weekend.

Tatianna, Reggie, and the others head to the barroom that extends out to the patio to continue the party, but Blend and I remain in the foyer.

"I had a great time, Marisol. I hope you did too." He gives me a kiss on the cheek.

"Oh, I had the best time!" I mean it. "Thank you so much for everything—dinner and the advice."

"You know," he begins, "we could continue our little party up in my suite." He's kissing my neck and working his way down and I'm getting a little uncomfortable. "I'll have a bottle of champagne sent up, or whatever you like to party with. Come on, what do you say?"

Blend is really hot and it's hard not to get turned on by his actions. I mean, he is good at what he's doing and he's pushing all the right buttons. I'm not a zombie. Still, I always expected that when I decided to go to bed with someone it would be someone special whom I loved very much. Someone like Julian. Blend is hot, but he's not the guy I'm going to give it up for.

I place my hands on his shoulders and gently push him away. "Blend, I'm sorry, but . . ."

He sighs. "Okay, I get it. Is it another guy?" He holds up his palm. "Never mind, that's not important. But know . . ." He kisses my left cheek. "That I intend . . ." He kisses my right cheek. "To keep working on you." With that, he gives me a full-blown kiss on the lips, swirling his tongue around mine.

Wow! I'm almost sorry I said no.

I head up the stairs to my fairy-princess room. That was all easier than I thought it would be.

CHAPTER 12

Sea and Sun, Mar y Sol

Cawing seagulls bring me out of my sleep just as the sky begins to brighten. I open my eyes; slivers of mauve and salmon are layered between the inky ocean and sapphire sky. I turn to Tati's bed to see if she's awake, but her bed hasn't been slept in. No surprise there. After a rough start to the evening, she and Reggie seemed to be getting along *really* well. I'm glad they picked his room instead of ours.

With no one to disturb, I slip out of bed and kneel on the chair under the window to watch the sun rise. I always wanted to do this, but I never had the view. In Manhattan, only the people living in luxury high-rise apartments get to watch the sun come up over the horizon.

I open the window to take in the whole experience. The air is salty with a tang of fishiness. Seagulls caw against the rhythm of the waves. I can still catch Venus shining in the dark morning sky and make a wish. Now it's more than just a singing career. I want this life. Not the mansion and the hangers-on—I want a life full of new experiences. I want clean instead of gritty. I want quiet instead of noise. I love Manhattan, but it would be so nice to have a place to escape to when the city gets too hectic.

Maybe this is the way my mother felt before she moved back to Puerto Rico. I always believed that she ran away from Papi and me, but maybe she felt the city closing in and ran to where the sun always shines. I wonder if she would be proud of me now. I know Papi would be. He always had the biggest smile on his face when he listened to me sing. How I wish he could be here tonight to watch me perform for these people. *God, if it's in Your power, please let Papi look down on me tonight.*

A sliver of sun pops up on the horizon; daylight begins to break. I watch until the full ball is up, sending glistening ripples on the water. I can't wait another minute. I have to get down there and be at one with the beach.

The bedroom door slowly opens and Tatianna saunters in still wearing the red spandex dress from last night, but carrying her pumps.

"I thought you'd still be sleeping," she murmurs, so as not to disturb the quiet of the house.

"Just got up." I watch her slither out of her dress, sit at the vanity in her underwear, and begin to remove her makeup. The entire top of the table is covered with her potions and lotions. "What are you doing here? I figured you'd still be with Reggie."

"I came back for a nap because I can't stand going to bed with makeup on and lying in bed after, you know, without a shower. I can't rest."

She takes a delicate cream-colored silk cami and tap pants out of her drawer. Even Tati's lingerie is perfect. She's perfect, so worldly and sophisticated, it's hard to look at Tati and believe she's a poor girl from El Barrio. She always looks as if she's in control of the world.

"Can I ask you something?" I ask. She shoots a look at me. "Why did you decide to spend the rest of the night with Reggie?"

She sighs. "Mari, I'm a big girl, I can decide for myself whether or not I want to sleep with someone. I don't need anyone's permission." And she is a big girl, Tati's nineteen going on twenty.

"No, no, I'm not judging you, it's just that, well, I had a little situation, and I wasn't sure how to handle it."

She turns around in her chair, giving me her full attention. "Like what? Spill."

"It's just that Blend . . ."

"He didn't force you to do anything, did he?"

"No, but he was kissing me and touching my leg in the club."

"Is that all? That's what you call a situation? Honestly, Mari, I think you and my sister have a bet going to see who will be the last remaining virgin in El Barrio." She shakes her head and turns back to the mirror.

"That is so not true," I insist. We're not in a contest, we simply haven't, I don't know, found ourselves in the right situation. "And anyhow, what's wrong with being a virgin?"

"Nothing," she says, "there's nothing wrong with it. It's just that you're making such a big deal about a little kissing. That's what guys do, they give it a shot. Haven't you done that kind of stuff with Julian? I mean you two have been dating since like when, junior high?"

"Freshman year, on and off, but that's Julian and that felt right. I met Blend yesterday, I don't even know him."

"Then just say, no." With that, she picks up her cami and tap pants and heads into the bathroom.

She makes it all sound so easy. I need to think about it some more. Right now, the beach is calling me.

With Tati in the shower, there's no one to stop me. I throw on a pair of cut-off sweatpants and pull my faded blue sweatshirt over my cami top. Despite the morning chill the sun feels warm on my face. I run down to the ocean through the still-cool sand and only stop when the waves break up to my knees.

This is me, sea and sun. In Spanish it's *mar y sol*—Marisol!

I wish I had the nerve to start singing at the top of my lungs, but the early morning runners and fishermen might think I'm crazy.

I start walking down the beach on the hard sand. The water flows in, depositing pebbles and shells on the beach. I wonder what happens to the pearls from the shells. Maybe they're sitting on the ocean floor waiting to be found. A pretty little shell with accordion pleats stands out among the big old clam shells. I put it in my pocket for luck. Maybe someday I'll get a pearl to go with it.

People are out for an early morning run or walk. A few surfers are bobbing on their boards. It's so different from the noisy crowds of Coney Island.

I turn and head back down the beach in the direction of the house. The white mansion glistens in the early morning sunlight, just behind the dunes. I wash the sand from my feet at the outdoor shower and sit on a chaise lounge to let them dry. Blend walks out of the house with two smoothies and hands one to me.

"I saw you coming up the beach and thought you might like to join me."

"Ooh, this looks yummy, thank you." I take a sip. "Delicious. What's in it?"

"Some whey powder for protein, nonfat milk, Greek yogurt, berries, a banana and, oh yeah, a sprinkle of flaxseed. I made it myself," he says proudly.

"It's good. I'm not a big breakfast eater, but this slides down." I take another sip.

He studies me for a while. "I can tell you're a pure girl," he says, like it's a pronouncement. "I kind of thought that as soon as I saw you, but after last night I could tell you're not like the others." He indicates the lounges around the pool even though no one is there.

I'm not sure how to respond to that. Well, at least there are no hard feelings from last night. But what's pure? And how does he mean it? Purity isn't an *on* or *off* switch; it's more like a sliding scale. I'm not a saint, but I'm not one of the hootchie mamas running around this place. Maybe it's a good thing if he thinks I'm pure. Then I won't have to fight off any more of his advances this weekend. That would be awkward.

Blend leans on his elbow and continues softly, "You're someone I can mold." He's looking me over like I'm a pastry in a bakery window, but then he continues in a businesslike voice, "I want you to think about our conversation last night. I can take your career in the right direction."

That's flattering! I've been trying to get my career off the ground for so long—and now I have two record labels interested in me.

"I have been thinking about our talk and I am interested in working with you." I pause and smile up at him to soften my point. "But I do have an unofficial agreement with Teddy Bear Barnes and Pablo Cruz. I'd like to give them a little more time to consider signing me before I dump them for you. It just wouldn't feel right."

"Okay, I respect that. See, that's what I mean by *pure*. Another girl would have jumped at the chance and not cared about hurting others. I respect that," he repeats. "But remember what I said last night about looking out for yourself—no one's going to do it for you. I'll give you a week or so to decide, then get back to me."

I nod in agreement.

"Okay! Enjoy your drink. I have some phone calls to make." He heads back into the house.

"Blend," I call after him, "there is one favor I'd like to ask."

"Shoot."

"I like to practice my vocals every morning and Cisco won't be ready for a sound check until afternoon. Is there a quiet place I can sing without waking the house?"

"C'mon." He puts an arm around my shoulder and walks me into a cavernous all-white living room. In one corner is a white grand piano. Blend sits and plays a little arpeggio on the keys. "Let's hear what you can do."

He plays along while I run one scale, two scales, three scales. He tosses a questioning look at me. At my nod, he continues on to the fourth scale and I follow without breaking.

"Whoa, girl, four octaves! I'm impressed." He shakes his head to clear it. "Damn, let's make some music this morning."

"Won't we wake everyone?"

"That's their problem. This is my house," he snaps. "You know this one?" He starts playing the opening bars of "Tough Love," the hit song he wrote for his friends, the singing duo Nick and Nikki. Blend, who usually raps, has a surprisingly beautiful voice.

When I was just a little bitty baby
Love came so easy to me.
Just a smile and laugh got me going
Everybody gave their loving to me.

Things got tougher when I got older
But it still was pretty simple to me.
Smiles and laughter still worked their magic
All the girls came running to me.

Then I met you one sunny summer
On the beach you were cute as could be.
I knew then there'd never be another
Only you would be the one for me.

I come in and join him in full voice, harmonizing as if we rehearsed the tune.

Loving you is climbing a mountain.
Loving you is swimming the sea.
If I knew then what I know now
I wouldn't do it, 'cause loving you
Is tougher than I thought it would be.

I sing Nikki's part in that same high soprano she does so well.

You talk of love
Of wanting me only
Yet you treat me bad
You make me sad
Even with you I'm lonely.

Blend jumps in and we finish the song in perfect harmony.

Loving you is climbing a mountain.
Loving you is swimming the sea.
If I knew then what I know now
I wouldn't do it, 'cause loving you
Is tougher than I thought it would be.

For the last stanza, I echo the lines after him, really wailing them.

When I was just a little bitty baby
Love came so easy to me.
Just a smile and laugh got me going
Everybody gave their loving to me.

We come together in perfect synchronicity for the finale.

Loving you is climbing a mountain.
Loving you is swimming the sea.
If I knew then what I know now
I wouldn't do it, 'cause loving you
Is tougher than I thought it would be.

I didn't think it was possible to love singing more than I do, but singing with Blend is a new kind of high!

CHAPTER 13

Feeling It

We get the music going long before the guests are due to arrive, so that they feel like the party is in full swing when they get here. Blend wants the karaoke portion of the performance to start after the guests have had a chance to eat, drink, and mingle. It's true that people only get up and sing after they have a lot to drink. I still have my doubts about tonight. A lot of people coming to the party make their living singing or rapping. I can't imagine them getting up to sing along with taped music for free.

I'm hanging out with Cisco and Randy, but until I'm up, I'm free to walk around. Tatianna is going to film the karaoke portion with a camera Cisco brought with him. We got a lot of publicity from that YouTube clip of Randy and me singing, so we decided to generate our own. Now I know why Cisco agreed to take Tati with us this weekend—she's working the camera. And she said she was coming as my stylist. *Please.* I should know better than to believe her.

Guests are mingling and the waitstaff is passing trays of champagne and tiny little goodies that people are gobbling up faster than the servers can get them out. There are individual spoons filled with dollops of mac and cheese, mini pizza rounds, tiny bagels smeared with cream cheese and topped with smoked salmon, mushroom caps stuffed with a crusty gold filling. Oh, and sliders, every type of slider imaginable—pulled pork dripping with barbeque sauce, meatballs parm, crab cake sliders, and of course, hamburgers and cheeseburgers. The cutest mini treats are the tiny little hotdogs with mustard and sauerkraut. They're only about two inches long and being served from a real New York pushcart with a yellow-and-blue umbrella. After all, what's the Fourth of July without hotdogs?

Leave it to Blend to do things in a big way. Instead of a sit-down dinner or a buffet, New York food trucks have formed a semicircle on the edge of the property like covered wagons circling for the night. His fancy-pants guests that would probably never dream of eating food from a truck on the sidewalk are falling over each other to sample the fare.

"Try one?" A waitress is holding a tray loaded with shot glasses, each filled with a colorful liquid.

I wrinkled my nose. "Are they Jell-O shots?" This party seems too fancy for something like that.

"No, they're cold soups." I follow the direction of her nose. "Tomato basil, vichyssoise, potato and leek, cherry-berry, and gazpacho."

"They look good." The cherry-berry sounds interesting, but I sample tomato basil. "Delicious, thanks."

Bars are set up in various parts of the property so that no one has to trudge up to the pool area for a refill. Most guests are indulging in topical concoctions decorated with fresh fruits and flowers. Waiters circle with bottles of champagne wrapped in white linen napkins and can't seem to fill the glasses fast enough.

Everyone looks so summery in white. I'm wearing my Kell E flapper dress that's really more like a tunic. The deep V-neck cuts to mid-chest; clear sequins and bugle beads run patterns down the front. It's casual flashy, not wedding flashy, and the clear sandals make me look like I'm barefoot.

"Hey, Cisco, I'll be back in a minute," I say. At least I hope I'll be back. I may be in a whole lot of trouble.

An elegant tan woman in a white sueded-silk dress is sipping her glass of champagne. As if she feels me coming, she turns to me and says, "Marisol, what are you doing here?"

Lola is too cool to cause a scene, but I understand that look on her face. She thinks I'm back in the apartment or at Coney Island with Vanessa.

"Lola, I can explain."

She's still staring at me, too much of a lady to start giving me the third degree in front of all these people.

"I'm working the gig with Cisco," I explain. "He got the job at the last minute when Crazy Joe, the other DJ they first hired, OD'd."

Maybe that wasn't the best explanation.

She shakes her head gently. "Where did you get that dress? And more importantly, where are you staying?"

"Again, very last minute. Kell E, the designer Tatianna works for, dressed me for free as long as I tell everyone this is her design." I want to take deep breaths, but I have to appear cool. "And Tati and I are sharing a room right here."

"Here? You're staying in some rapper's mansion?" she asks incredulously. "Marisol, I know you're a little naïve, but you're still a smart girl. You have to know that's not the best idea."

"I was a little nervous at first, but I felt better when I found out that Tati would be with me," I say. Lola and I have been through some tough times, and it's still kind of weird taking orders from someone who's only been my stepmother for two years, but I never want to lose her respect. "And this gig will get me a lot of attention. There'll be a lot of music people here tonight."

She starts to say something, but is cut off by Pablo's arrival. "Hey, Mari, I didn't know you'd be here."

"She's working the *gig*."

"That's great." He's cut off by a pat on the back.

"Hey, man, glad you could make it," Blend says, shaking Pablo's hand.

"You trying to steal my client?" Pablo's smile is tight on his face.

"From what I hear, Marisol's not signed to anyone," Blend says kiddingly, but in a way that leaves no doubt that he's dead serious when it comes to business. He gives Pablo another pat. "Hey, enjoy the party. I'll catch up with you later."

After he walks away, Pablo says to me, "Watch out for that guy."

I feel my nose crinkle. Watch out for Blend? He's the nicest guy. Kell E is across the lawn waving me over. Good excuse to get out of here.

"Catch you guys later."

Kell E is talking to a young woman who is writing something down on a notepad. Kell E looks like a goddess in a one-shoulder chiffon tunic that I'm sure she designed herself. A photographer is standing by.

"Marisol, dear," begins Kell E, in that lilting accent of hers, "come show Harper your dress." I twirl around slowly, giving Harper a chance to take it all in. Kell E goes into a long description of the dress that I totally block out until I hear, "Where did you get those shoes?" Kell E, Harper, and the photographer are staring at my feet.

"Vintage," I reply. "From the '80s."

Kell E tilts her head. "They work." Thank God.

I see Tati standing in front of the DJ stage, trying out the camera. Her heels are sinking into the grass. The dress she's wearing is really cute and suits her. I saw another version of it in the store and liked it. It's called a cut-out dress and has a racer back and bare sides that ride low on her hips. Tati has the perfect body for it—tan skin and just enough curves.

I head in her direction. but a familiar voice calls to me. "Marisol, what's the matter? You're not going to say hello to me?"

Diego Salazar is standing with three amazing-looking guys who seem completely aloof, as if they were gracing the party with their presence. Their tropical drinks are the only splash of color against their white shirts and pants. I hurry over and give him a hug. The man closest to Diego stares at me with disdain. How dare I touch the big star?

I ignore him.

"Oh, Diego, I'm so glad to see you. I didn't know you were coming."

Omigod, if you told me last year, or even last month, that I would be greeting Diego Salazar like a long-lost friend, I'd think you were crazy.

"Yeah, I'm out here most weekends in the summer. What are you doing here?"

A waiter comes up, holding a tray with skewers of chicken stuck in a papaya half. "Satay?" he asks.

Diego's friends each grab a stick, but Diego and I shake our heads. The waiter doesn't leave.

"Diego, I just *adored* your latest CD," he says, rolling his eyes heavenward. " 'Soul Spinning,' well, what can I say?"

Yeah, tell me about it, I think, *it got to me too, now beat it.* But Diego is always gracious.

"Thanks, man," he says. "Be sure to watch for my new *Duets* CD coming out this fall. I think you'll love it." The waiter floats off. Diego turns back to me. "I'm sorry, you were saying?"

I point to Cisco. "I'm working the party. Cisco likes me to get the karaoke started, although with this crowd, I'm getting a little nervous."

Diego's friend is still studying me as if I were a lost species that might possibly be lethal.

He protests, "No, you'll be good. Hey, maybe we can do our duet together. We practiced it enough."

Nothing would be better for my career than to sing "Soul Spinning" in front of this crowd of music people. If that doesn't light a fire under Pablo and Teddy Bear Barnes, nothing will.

"I'd love that! Just come up when you're ready." I give him a kiss on the cheek. "I have to run. Cisco wants to start soon." I ignore his friends. Rude people shouldn't be acknowledged.

I head across the lawn, admiring all the party dresses. Everyone looks so beautiful. I notice that the smart girls are wearing wedgies so their heels don't sink into the grass. The supermodels are in flip-flops and smug smiles. *We don't need heels—our legs are long enough.*

I climb the steps up to the stage and check the playlist Cisco has set up. He's still fiddling with his laptop so I scan the tunes to make sure I'm familiar with them all. This isn't the place I want to fake it. As it is, the butterflies are shuffling in my stomach. I look up at the crowd. Mistake! The entire music world is out there, along with famous actors, directors, and models, and I'm sure the faces I don't recognize are important people too.

It's crazy. I always wished that I could sing in front of people in the music industry, and tonight I'll get that chance. The problem is—I'm terrified! Why didn't I visualize that part of it when I was making my wish? You've got to be careful what you wish for. I close my eyes and try to summon Singer Girl.

"Get out there, Mari. We're going to hit it," orders Cisco, bopping to the beat. He scratches the music real loud and then lowers the volume. "Okay, everybody, listen up! We're going to sing a little karaoke tonight. Give all you singers and want-to-be singers a chance to strut your stuff." A murmur of laughter rustles through the crowd. "Come on now, don't be shy. How 'bout we let Marisol get you started?"

Cisco begins spinning the number one dance record of the summer. The bass starts thumping and a cheer erupts from the crowd. I prance out there to the music, clapping my hands above my head, until I'm right under the lights. This feels so good.

> *Feeling it*
> *Feeling it*
> *We're all going to have a good time*
> *Have a slam-bang rocking good time . . .*
> *Because we're feeling it*
> *Feeling it.*

Randy jumps in, supplying background rap that thunders through the tune.

> *Dance, dance, da, dance, dance*
> *Da dance, dance, da, dance, dance*

We didn't have to wait long for a brave soul to join in. I can see the top of a woman's head as she carefully makes her way up the stage stairs. She walks across the stage and lifts her face to me.

Omigod! Omigod! Omigod!

Princess!

I start to back up to give her center stage—after all, it's her song—but she throws her arm around my shoulders, inviting me to join her.

> *Hanging with my homies*
> *Playing funky golden oldies*
> *Getting down to the beat now*
> *And we ain't leaving no how*
> *'Cause we're feeling it*
> *Feeling it.*

Randy had moved backstage, but now he's up here with us.

Dance, dance, da, dance, dance
Da dance, dance, da, dance, dance

He steps back, giving over the stage to Princess and me.

We're all going to have a good time
Have a slam-bang rocking good time . . .
Because we're feeling it
Feeling it.

Dance, dance, da, dance, dance
Da dance, dance, da, dance, dance

I'm having such a great time with Princess that she couldn't get me off this stage if she wanted to. Anyway, she seems to want me here.

Running with the A team
Drinking black rum and ice cream
Chilling out on the side streets
Stomping boots on the concrete
'Cause we're feeling it
Feeling it.

Dance, dance, da, dance, dance
Da dance, dance, da, dance, dance

The crowd is going crazy, clapping to the beat and singing along with us. Their energy is contagious.

Feeling it
Feeling it
We're all going to have a good time
Have a slam-bang rocking good time . . .
Because we're feeling it
Feeling it.

Dance, dance, da, dance, dance
Da dance, dance, da, dance, dance

Princess holds the microphone towards the audience and they all sing as one:

Hanging with my homies
Playing funky golden oldies
Getting down to the beat now
And we ain't leaving no how
'Cause we're feeling it
Feeling it.

Dance, dance, da, dance, dance
Da dance, dance, da, dance, dance

Up until this moment I thought singing with Diego Salazar and Blend was the best thing that ever happened to me. This tops it by a mile.

The crowd is insane! They're screaming and cheering. Fists are pumping the air. Princess is a goddess and everyone knows it. She gets more play time that any other singer and her face is on the cover of every magazine. The entire party is joining in on the finale.

Feeling it
Feeling it
We're all going to have a good time
Have a slam-bang funky good time
Because we're feeling it
Feeling it
Feeling it
Woo-hoo!

We finish the song and Princess gives me a kiss smack on the lips!

"You're beautiful!" she says to me. Her dazzling cobalt-blue eyes are even more sparkly up close and in person.

"So are you," I mumble or at least I think I did. How am I supposed to finish this set? I'm shaking.

That's a hard act to follow but surprisingly, a couple of the singers in the crowd do get up and perform a few of their tunes. Randy and

I do "New York Nights." Alicia Chiavi watches the stage while we perform, but she doesn't climb up and join us.

It's a relief when the fireworks guys hook up to our sound system to prepare for their display. My voice is getting tired and I haven't had anything but a bottle of water and a soup shot all night. Now I'm starving. I wander over to the bar area, hoping that a few of those little goodies are left, even though the buffet tables, carving stations, and food trucks have closed down.

Jay-Z and Beyoncé smile at me as I walk past. I wonder if that means he liked what I did with his song. Just a few months ago these people were names on my CD jewel cases. Never in a million years could I have pictured myself not just performing for them, but hanging with them as well.

A couple shrimp remain in the giant ice clam shell. I put a few on a plate and add a scoop of cocktail sauce.

"Did you get a chance to eat anything tonight?" asks Blend.

I shake my head; my mouth is full of shrimp.

"Go in the kitchen and have them fix you a plate," he insists. "Tell them I said so."

Never much of an eater, the shrimp actually do it for me. "That's okay. I'm good."

He's about to protest when the first firework explodes in the night sky. Watching the colorful display and listening to the music make my thoughts drift to Vanessa. I wonder what she's doing tonight. I hope Angel invited her to the beach with the others. I don't care if she's on a big triple date with Solange and Julian and Raven and Freddie. I want my BFF to be as happy as I am right now.

Blend and I walk toward the beach. He holds me in front of him as we watch the display, rubbing my arms and cuddling me to protect me from the nip in the night air. It feels kind of nice; after all, Blend is one of the hottest-looking guys on the planet. And, if I let myself be totally honest, I feel like somebody important standing with him. Here he is treating me like a girlfriend, even though I'm not, in front of all these superstars. I'm no longer just the singer girl with the DJ; I'm part of their group. I'm finally fitting in.

It's funny. Here I am in the arms of the hottest rapper in the world, who is treating me like a princess, but I just don't feel turned on. He doesn't do it for me. I take a step away from Blend. It feels wrong to encourage his feelings for my professional gain. If it were Diego, I'd be ecstatic. And if it were Julian—if I were wrapped in Julian's arms, I'd feel like I was home.

CHAPTER 14

Wishing on the Sea

The sun wakes me up again. We're leaving today, but as Cisco doesn't get up until noon, I have the morning to enjoy the beach.

Tatianna's bed hasn't been slept in again. No surprise there; she and Reggie have been tight since that night at Shells. He keeps calling her his beautiful Brazilian. Whatever. I guess she thinks that sounds more exotic than Puerto Rican, so she ran with it. As long as she shot the video of our performance last night, she can be whoever she wants to be.

I don't have time to waste thinking about her. I want to soak up every minute I have left of this place. Who knows if I'll ever get out here again? The mornings are a little chilly so I'll need my sweatshirt and shorts for now, but I have my bikini underneath for when it warms up.

The house is silent as I pad through to the back door and grab a couple towels from the pool house. I walk straight down to the ocean and toss my towels and tote on the sand. The sound of the surf and seagulls is so tranquil that I don't want to spoil my walk with music from my iPod.

I shove my hands into my pockets and feel the shell I took from the beach yesterday. It did bring me luck and maybe it will bring me more. If wishes can be made on stars, then why not the sea? I kiss the shell for luck and toss it back into its home.

Big mansions can be seen behind the dunes. I wonder if Diego Salazar is staying in one of them. As nice as he is to me, there's a part of him that remains, I don't know, secretive. I spent my entire life dreaming about him, so part of me thinks we should be great friends. But Diego always seems to hold a little piece of himself back. Even last night, he never mingled with the other guests and he never came up to sing our duet as *he* suggested. He just hung out with those three guys, who were unbelievably hot, but not very friendly.

Not a lot of people out here this morning. The die-hard surfers are bobbing out there as usual. A runner is approaching me.

He does a double-take. "Hey, nice singing last night," he tosses over his shoulder.

"Thanks!" I yell, even though I have no idea who he is.

It's so strange to be recognized—I've always been the kind of girl who blended into the scenery. It makes me wonder how famous people deal with this. Maybe that's why Diego keeps to himself.

The sun is up higher and glistening when I decide to turn back. Maybe if I soak enough rays into my skin and get enough saltwater up my nose, I'll always have a little bit of this place with me. I dive into the surf and splash around a while before returning to my towel to dry off.

Blend comes down the sand, fully dressed in shorts, a long-sleeved shirt, and a French Foreign Legion-type hat on his head protecting him from the sun's rays.

"Thought you might like one of these," he says, handing me a smoothie.

"Ooh, yum, yes, I'd love one." I take the plastic cup from him and savor a long sip. "I didn't realize how thirsty I am."

"I'm guessing you like the beach," he says. "You have to come out here more often. I'm here most weekends."

As much as I love this place, I'm not sure where this is going. Blend, talking about a professional relationship but inviting me to stay for weekends, might mean he's thinking of me as girlfriend material. That's taking it too far, too fast. I'm not sure I want that. In fact, after giving it some thought last night, I know I don't.

I decide to dodge around it. "Well, next time you have a party, call Cisco. We'll be out here in no time."

He studies me. Then he says, "Give me your phone."

I fish around in my tote bag, pull it out, and hand it to him. He punches some keys with his thumbs then gives it back to me.

"Now you've got all my numbers—my cell, office, the beach house, and my apartment in Manhattan. You call me anytime you're ready for me." He keeps looking at me like he's trying to read my mind. If he is, he's out of luck. Even I don't know what to think. "You want that music career, you just have to call me." He pauses. "If you're looking for something more, well, you call me for that, too."

I don't know what to say. "Thanks, Blend."

"I like you, Marisol. Like I said the other day, you're pure. I like that in a girl. You're the kind of girl I can see myself getting real close to." His thoughts seem to drift off as he runs the tips of his smooth fingers over my face and onto my shoulders. "Young, innocent . . ."

I'm getting a little weirded out. Before I have a chance to process this, he says, "Can I ask you a question?"

"Okay."

"Are you a virgin?"

I can feel my face getting hot. My brain is screaming, *None of your business!* But I don't want to piss him off, so I say absolutely nothing.

"Hey, I'm sorry. I can see that you are from your reaction." He's not pissed, in fact, he seems thrilled. "My bad for even asking that question of a beautiful young lady. But my offer still stands. Give me a call if you need me."

"Thanks, Blend, I really appreciate that." The relief rolls off me.

"All right, if I don't see you before you leave, have a safe trip back to the city." He takes the empty cup from my hand and heads up to the house.

Blend might be the music connection I've been looking for. But am I ready for all that comes with it?

CHAPTER 15

Replay

"We have to talk," orders Lola first thing Monday morning.

I'm still replaying the dream I was having right before I woke up. Diego and I lived in one of the old mansions on the beach in East Hampton. We had just finished a worldwide singing tour and came home to unwind. We were sitting on the beach watching the sunrise and he was kissing the side of my neck. I was just turning my head to kiss him when I woke up.

Lola's sharp tone zaps me out of the mood.

"What's up?" I ask, even though I have a pretty good idea what's on her mind.

She pours an extra cup of coffee, puts the mug in front of me, and gives me a look that says, *What are you—stupid?*

I play dumb, so she continues, "About this weekend? About staying in some rapper's house without even a phone call? That's what we have to talk about."

I stir sugar and half-and-half into my cup. "I told you, I found out about the gig after you left with Pablo. I didn't think it would be a big deal."

Damn, why is she on my case? I'm going to be eighteen in a few weeks.

"Well it is. Why do you think I pay for that cell phone, to chat with your friends? You only had to push one button and you would have gotten right through to me."

I shrug. "Like I said, I didn't think it would be a big deal. What difference did it make if I were sitting here in this apartment or not. If anything, I was actually closer to you."

Lola lets out a gust of breath. "Look, Marisol, you're a smart girl, but maybe I give you too much credit for having common sense. I think we need to set up some ground rules."

The English muffins pop up and Lola brings them to the table. I busy myself with the butter and raspberry preserves.

"First of all," begins Lola, "when two people live together, letting the other person know where you are is a courtesy. I assumed you were here and notified Sylvia Fuentes to be on call if there was anything you needed."

I nod. Fair enough.

"After all," she continues, "if your father were still alive would you take off without telling him? I think I deserve the same courtesy, don't you?"

Low blow, but what can I say? She's got me there.

"I'm sorry. Next time I will call," I say contritely and take a bite of my muffin.

"Secondly, staying in the home of a rapper—or any man for that matter—can be a dangerous thing for a girl your age."

I start to protest, "But I was with—"

"Yes, I know. You were with Tatianna. And Cisco. And whomever. But that doesn't make it any better." She pauses to take a sip of coffee, then begins more gently. "Your friends, no matter how well meaning they are, can't protect you from all the possible things that can happen. Someone could have forced drugs on you or you could have been raped. You had no idea what kind of people would be staying in that house."

Talk about overreacting!

"Well, where was I supposed to stay?"

"You could have stayed with Pablo and me," she says. "Tatianna too. The boys could fend for themselves."

"I actually *did* think about staying with you, but—"

"But what?"

"I didn't want to intrude on your romantic weekend."

"You wouldn't have been intruding," she says. "There's plenty of room—not like that rapper's mansion, but you and Tatianna would have had your own room." She folds her arms and leans against the table. "The important thing is not to get yourself into something you can't handle."

"I understand. Believe me, I was a little scared when Cisco told me we had the job. I wasn't sure where we'd be staying and I hated the idea of being the only girl."

Lola spreads her hands as if to say *there you go.* "At least you were thinking. Then what happened?"

"Tati called me and said that she was coming too, so I felt better. And I really needed to take this job."

"Why?"

Now I give her a look that says she's crazy. "Because Cisco paid me more than he usually does and we could use the money. But mostly because I knew that all the big names in the music business would be at that party and would get to hear me sing. One of those people could launch my career."

"Your career is launched. You recorded with Diego Salazar last week. And I told you that we're doing just fine financially, so save your money." Lola squeezes my hand. "I have to tell you, your performance Saturday night was phenomenal."

"Thanks, but that recording with Diego was only a demo. I don't know if I'll get it." Doesn't anyone realize that I'm trying to work at a real career here? There's a lot of luck involved, but sometimes you have to force it along—give luck a chance to work its magic. "I can't afford to pass up an opportunity to be heard by professionals if my singing career is going to happen. Besides, Blend says that if Pablo or Teddy Bear really wanted me, they would have signed me."

She holds up a finger while she swallows. "Speaking of Blend, Pablo said to be careful of him."

"Of Blend?" I ask incredulously. "He couldn't have been nicer to me. In fact, he respected the fact that I wasn't like the hootchie mamas out there." Still, something about Blend is nagging me, but I'll never admit it to Lola.

"Be that as it may, just be careful. How old is he anyway?"

"I'm not sure. I think I heard he was twenty-five or twenty-six, not old."

"And you'll be eighteen in a few weeks. Seven or eight years are dog years at this stage. He may be interested in the type of relationship that you're not ready for." She finishes her coffee and takes the cup to the sink. "Don't let any man ever rush you into something you don't want."

Lola's advice was kind of like Tatianna's. She told me to just say no, and Lola is telling me not to let a man talk me into anything. They're right. I'm the only one in charge of me and I have to be brave enough to make my own decisions. In the end, I'm the person who needs to be happy.

"Lola?"

"What sweetie?" See, that's Lola, a class act. When the argument is over, it's over.

"I was thinking so much about Papi yesterday and wishing that he could watch me perform. Do you think he'd be proud of me?"

She gives me a hug. "Proud of you? He'd be bursting at the seams. And believe me, if I know your father, he found a way to travel through the dimensions just to watch you perform." She ruffles my head. "Never doubt your father's love for you. He's your guardian angel."

That makes me smile.

Before practicing my vocals, I check my messages. Vanessa texted me—Come 2 pk aft lunch.

She's been sitting for the Colon twins. The twins like to go to the park for the day camp activities. The camp counselors do all the work. Vanessa just has to walk them over and sit on a bench.

That's exactly what she's doing when Cha-Cha and I get there.

"Hey, girl," I call to her.

As usual Vanessa is busy texting someone. "Hey," she says distractedly. She hits a button and looks up. "I have news," she sings tauntingly.

"Tell!"

"Guess who broke up?"

I feel my eyes widen. "No!"

She nods *yes*.

"Julian and Solange?"

"They were fighting like crazy at the beach."

"Tell me *everything*," I demand. I don't care how mean I am; this is great news. I am so happy they broke up.

"Well, we went to the beach on the Fourth of July, right?"

I nod. "Which beach did you go to?"

"Coney Island, where else?" she answers sarcastically. "It's not like we have a place in the Hamptons." She gives me a piercing glare. "So the whole day from when we got on the train, Solange keeps checking her messages and texting. At first Julian tells her to put it away and let's have a fun day together, but she ignores him and keeps it up." Vanessa scrunches up her nose. "It's like she wanted to be somewhere else, you know?"

"Uh-huh, uh-huh," I say nodding. I need to hear the whole story now.

"And I could tell that something was bothering Julian even before the day started. You know what I mean?"

Yeah, I know what she means. I think I also know what was on his mind. He was probably thinking about what I told him about Solange doing all those guys to get in Blend's music video. Blend. I wonder if she did him too?

"So we get to the beach and take off our shorts and stuff and Solange is wearing this black thong bikini that showed *everything!*"

"Omigod!" I knew she was a hootchie mama and I knew she'd be wearing black, but a suit like that? At Coney Island? Man, that's insane.

Vanessa continues, "So Freddie starts acting all crazy about how hot she looks and even Angel can't look away."

"Did she look hot?" Stupid question. Of course she did.

"Yeah, but still—"

"So what did Julian do? Was he all on top of her too?"

"No! That's the thing. Julian looked really pissed because she was attracting everybody's attention. All these guys on the beach were hooting and yelling stuff and you could tell she was loving every minute of it. She was twirling around and strutting her stuff."

"What about Raven? She couldn't have been happy about Freddie falling all over Solange."

"No, she wasn't. You know how Raven pouts when she gets angry? I could see it coming." Vanessa pauses just to torment me. "So Raven walks a few feet in front of us to where another group of boys are sitting and spreads her towel. She lies down on her stomach, unhooks the top of her bikini, and flings it away! It hit one of the boys in the head!"

"Oh, no, she didn't!" I yell. Just picturing Raven in a bikini makes me laugh. She's a big girl. Maybe she's not fat, but there's a lot of jelly in that belly.

Now we're howling with laughter, which gets the attention of the twins, Derek and Alex, who leave their playgroup to run toward us.

"Mari! Mari!" they scream.

"Hey, guys," I say, taking time to twirl each of them around. "Hey, you're missing all the fun. Your buddies are playing that game you like."

No, they aren't, but I need to hear the rest of this story. The twins run back to their playgroup.

"Omigod, this is too funny." I start laughing all over again. "But wasn't Freddie pissed at her?'

"Oh, yeah! He was so mad. He walked over to the guy, picked up her top, and said, 'Sorry, dude.' Then he tossed it back at Raven and told her to put it on. We sat there staring as if the whole scene was on some imaginary TV set. I can't even imagine how Raven found a bikini top to fit those boobs. What a sight! What a crazy day! The whole day played out like that with the four of them pissing each other off. On the train ride home, Angel and I were the only two still talking."

"Did you stop in Brooklyn to see the fireworks?" I ask with false innocence.

"Are you kidding me? We're lucky nobody killed anybody on the way home." We sit a while then Vanessa says, "Anyway, Julian told Angel that the next time he gets a girlfriend, he's going to make sure she doesn't need to attract a lot of attention."

I wonder if he was talking about Solange or Solange *and* me. Julian always gets upset when I choose my career over him. I could tell he was jealous that I was going to the Hamptons with Cisco. That's what always causes a rift with us.

"Anyway, maybe the two of you will get back together," suggests Vanessa. "How did things go after the movie?"

"Don't ask," I say. "I told him he'd have to break up with Solange before he could be with me."

I omit the rest of what I told him. I don't care if Vanessa knows about Solange's sex-for-jobs policy, but I'm not proud of myself for flinging it in Julian's face.

"So now they're not together. You got your wish."

"I'm not so sure," I say hesitantly.

She shoots me a look. "Why? Did you meet someone *in the Hamptons?*" she asks sarcastically. "How was it anyway? Tatianna hasn't said a word about the weekend, but then she's always secretive about everything."

"It was good, really good," I say, even though I'm no longer sure if Vanessa is truly happy for my success.

I've always heard that some friends only stick around when things are going good for you. Now I'm learning that some friends *like* to feel sorry for you. It makes them feel good about themselves, like they're doing a good deed or they're better than you are. When good things start happening to you, it pisses them off. They're down because you're up. Crazy.

But I tell her, "The performance went well. Everybody loved Cisco." Then I add, "Tatianna shot the whole thing. It's up on YouTube if you want to see it."

Knowing Vanessa, she will check it out. I'm curious to hear if she'll have anything to say.

"So, it sounds like you and Angel are finally a couple," I say in a sing-song voice. She blushes which only encourages me. "Did you hold hands? Did he kiss you goodnight?"

"Stop it!"

She's laughing now, too. Good. I love it when Vanessa laughs. When she's happy, I'm happy. And if Vanessa's happy, maybe, just maybe, we can get our friendship back on track.

CHAPTER 16

Hit Me with Your Best Shot

This week is dragging. Cisco warned me that summer is a slow time for him. Most New Yorkers—at least the rich ones who throw big parties—are out of town. He said we'll have to rely on the tourist trade, although who would come to walk the steamy sidewalks of Manhattan is beyond me.

I don't care, I just want to work. I miss the buzz I get from performing in front of a crowd. And I have to be honest with myself—I like getting out of East Harlem. Invisible walls are starting to close in on me. Now that I've had a chance to see that a better world exists, El Barrio seems stuck in a gritty time warp. I want to be out there with the people wearing cool clothes and hearing the latest music.

Now I know why Tatianna is never around. She got a taste of that life and she doesn't want to give it up. I don't blame her. I'd call her to hang out, but she works all day and I'm not sure what she does at night. I'll bet she's seeing Reggie. If that's the case, she won't want me hanging around.

Walking Cha-Cha is my only escape. Thank goodness, money isn't a problem. I'm not rolling in it, but I've been making enough with Cisco to store some nuts for lean times. I have a nice little roll of bills in my sock drawer and I even managed to sneak a little cash into Lola's mad-money jar. Hopefully, she won't notice. Lola doesn't want me paying for household things.

My phone rings. Ah, life still does exist.

"Hey, Mari, it's Pablo."

Omigod, he never calls me. This is it. I know he's going to tell me I got the spot on Diego's new CD. I can just feel it.

I try to calm down before replying. "Hey, Pablo, what's up?"

He hesitates for a beat, then begins, "Say, I know it's short notice, but can you meet me later for dinner?"

Maybe he wants to see the expression on my face when he tells me the good news.

"Sure," I reply. "Is there any news about the CD?"

Again, I can feel his hesitation through the phone.

"Uh, yeah, there's some news," he says. "We'll talk more at dinner."

"Okay."

He probably has a lot of details to go over with me and contracts to sign.

"Meet me at El Nuevo Caridad around six. You know where that is?"

"Yeah, 116th and, is it Second?"

"That's it, the place right on the corner. I'll see you then."

"I love the steak *empanizado* here," Pablo says, sliding into his seat. "I don't get to eat good Caribbean food as often as I'd like."

I got here exactly at six and I'm already waiting at the table, but I only ordered a Coke so far. It felt too weird to be sitting in a restaurant all by myself.

"What are you having?" he asks. "Do you want to try the steak?"

What I really want is to stop the chatter and get down to business, but I say, "That sounds good."

A waiter approaches and Pablo says, "Bring us two orders of *bistec empanizado*, a side of rice and beans, and an order of plantains." The waiter turns to walk away, but Pablo adds, "Oh, and bring us two salads with avocado. And more Coke." The waiter writes it down and heads to the kitchen. "I told you I don't get this food very often. The salad is a specialty."

I don't care about the salad, or the plantains, or the rice and beans. I want to know if I have a record deal or not. Because if the answer is no, none of that food is going to stay down.

The waiter returns with two more Cokes, even though I haven't touched the first one.

"So, how's it going?" asks Pablo. "I was surprised to see you at Blend's party. You killed, by the way, *killed.*" Then he adds, "That Randy has got it going on too. Is he with anybody?"

Forget Randy, I want to scream. *What about me? Am I with anybody?*

When the waiter returns with our food, Pablo busies himself with salt and pepper and lime juice—anything but my career.

"Did Teddy Bear make a decision about the *Duets* CD?" I ask.

I figure it's the only way I'm going to get some information around here, or else I'll have to wait while Pablo finishes his flan. He swallows and takes a long sip of his soda, then painstakingly wipes his mouth and returns his napkin to his lap.

"As a matter of fact, they did. Just this morning."

"And? Will I be recording 'Soul Spinning' with Diego?"

He looks at me with the saddest eyes I've ever seen. "Mari, I'm afraid they went with Taylor Fox."

"Taylor Fox?" I yell, causing everyone in the restaurant to look at me. I don't care. "I sing better than she does."

I'm not being bitchy. I do sing better than Taylor Fox.

"Calm down," he says softly. "Everyone in the meeting agreed that your demo was the best one. Diego loved it. Barnes loved it. And you know I'm your biggest fan."

"Yeah, so? If everybody loves me so much, why didn't I get the deal?" I think that's a fair question. I know I nailed that demo and I deserve to be on the CD.

"Mari, it's not that simple," he says gently. "The best person doesn't always win."

Well, that much I know. I've learned that lesson the hard way too many times. But nobody does "Soul Spinning" better than I do. Not even Diego!

"Look, I know Taylor's pretty and she is a great songwriter. I'll admit that. But her delivery is just okay. It's nothing special." I stop because I can feel my voice cracking. I will not cry. I take a sip of my Coke and continue. "I have a four-octave range. Taylor Fox's singing doesn't come close."

He leans in across the table. "Mari, I know that. You don't have to explain it to me. This is what I do. This is my business."

"Then why did they go with her?"

"For the crossover," he explains. "Taylor Fox has a huge fan base. She's got the pop audience and a country following too. That's what she brings to the table. It's a business move, pure and simple."

I understand, but I'm not happy with it. I sit there and drink my soda. My food remains untouched.

"Let me explain a little bit of the music business to you," says Pablo. "The whole reason for doing a duet CD is to make your collaborator's fans your fans too. Understand what I'm saying?"

I can only nod because I'm afraid that, if I start to talk, I'll cry.

"Diego has a nice Latino fan base and he has a dance following too. But dance music is volatile. It changes fast. And both of those demographics are mainly urban-based—mostly New York."

The waiter approaches and wants to know if anything is wrong with the food.

"Just give us a minute," Pablo says to him. "Diego wants to break out into the pop audience."

"But he has songs on the radio," I protest. " 'Soul Spinning' is a huge hit. And before that, there was 'I Want to Dance with You.' That song played constantly."

"No, it played in the New York market. It died everyplace else in the country," explains Pablo. "So I got him this duet deal. The whole idea is to get the other artist's fans to buy Diego's CD. Bottom line."

"So they don't really care who sings the best song, do they?"

"No, Mari, they don't. And I'm very sorry about that," he says. "But listen, you're young, you have time. Other things will come your way. Trust me."

Trouble is, I don't have time. I'm ready to record now. If Pablo isn't as anxious about getting me into a studio as I am, then he's not the manager for me. Maybe I should take Blend up on his offer.

"Pablo, I want a singing career now, and if you can't help me, I'll find someone who can." I get up from the table. "Thanks for dinner."

All I can think of is getting out of that restaurant before I completely break down.

CHAPTER 17

The Way You Make Me Feel

I feel like I've been crying forever. The room is completely dark, with only the neon lights from outside illuminating the crumpled white tissues surrounding me.

There's nothing left inside me. Lola tried to console me when I came in, but I had to send her away. Sometimes there's nothing anyone can say to make you feel better. Sometimes the hurt has to come out before you can heal.

I'm done. I refuse to cry anymore. There's nothing I can do about it.

Ping! Nothing like technology to snap you into the here and now. I scroll down and retrieve Vanessa's text.

u got 2 vu NOW!

I hit the link hoping it's not another one of the squirrel-chasing-a-cat videos that Vanessa is so fond of. The black screen comes up and the video loads. The image is small but the faces come into view.

Omigod! This is unbelievable!

They're all naked! Raven and Solange are on their knees kissing over the legs of some guy. They pull apart to reveal a smiling Freddie. Then they both begin kissing him. It's obvious how *happy* he is to be there. They all begin to touch and play with each other. They're having a great time.

Raven! Our innocent Raven who was always falling in love with boys who never noticed her is . . . well, they'll notice her now. She's not the least bit ashamed to be naked—in front of a camera! I mean, I figure Solange wouldn't have a problem with it. She probably thinks she's starring in a movie. And we all know Freddie is shameless. Being with two girls makes him even more of a legend in the 'hood. But Raven? She was always such a good girl.

I can't stop watching the video. Now I don't have to wonder if Raven ever did *that*. She just did. And so does Solange. Freddie must love being a human Popsicle.

Solange and Raven resume their original positions and kiss, a slow, deep, sensual kiss. The camera zooms in on Freddie with those short crazy dreads and a big white grin plastered on his brown face. *The End.*

I play it again. I'm still shocked, but the reality of what I'm watching begins to sink in. Poor Julian, he and Solange may no longer be a couple, but to have everybody see her like this has to be embarrassing. Plus, I always knew Freddie was a sleaze-bag, a funny, life-of-the-party sleaze-bag, but a sleaze-bag nonetheless. He and Julian have been best friends forever. They grew up in the same apartment building—on the same floor, even. For him to snake Julian's girlfriend not even a week after they broke up really stinks. Yeah, Freddie may have been with Solange first, but she wasn't exactly a girlfriend, if you know what I mean.

The thought of watching it a third time makes me queasy and kind of sad. At first it was shocking and funny, but now, I don't know, I feel bummed out. Raven, Vanessa, and I were like the Three Musketeers. We were always together and thought it would stay that way. Seeing Raven in this video makes that impossible. She's changed so much, I feel like I don't even know her anymore.

First I had to face the reality of the music business and now I realize that one of my best friends is moving in a direction I don't want to go in. Not like this, anyway.

Vanessa is probably home waiting for me to call her, but I don't feel like doing a play-by-play right now. Strangely enough, there's only one person I want to be with, but I'm afraid to call. I can't take any more rejection tonight. So I text:

want to talk?

My phone rings.

"Where are you?" asks Julian, like nothing had ever happened between us.

"In my room," I reply softly.

"I'll be out front in ten." And he clicks off.

I go into the bathroom and splash cold water on my face. There isn't enough makeup in the world to hide my swollen eyes so I don't even try. I never changed out of my shorts and T-shirt, so I just head downstairs.

I see him walking toward me. I didn't realize how much I miss him.

He takes me in his arms and gives me the most passionate kiss in the world. Wordlessly, we wrap our arms around each other and head to the park.

I pick the same swing that I always do. He gives me a push to start me going and takes the swing next to me.

After a pause, he asks, "Did you see it?"

I drag my foot on the rubberized matting to slow my swing. "Yeah. Vanessa just forwarded it to me."

"So what? You want to tell me that you were right?" he says, his voice husky with sadness. "Too late. I kind of knew it, even before you said it to me. I just didn't want to face it."

"No. That night I wanted you back, but there was no way I was taking second place to Solange."

Julian looks at me and brushes my cheek with the back of his fingers. "You could never take second place to her, not in anything."

We get off the swings and head to our bench. I snuggle against his shoulder.

"The video grossed me out," I admit. "I mean we weren't in it, but I feel dirty by association. It feels like we're not kids anymore. What was she thinking?"

Julian is shaking his head in disbelief and staring out over the East River. The lights of Queens twinkling in the distance make it look much prettier at night than in the daytime.

"Freddie probably talked her into it. For a while, I've been feeling like he and Solange were hooking up behind my back. Raven just wants to hang on to him."

"Why?"

"Who cares? I only care about us," he says, and begins to kiss me softly at first, and then with an urgency that makes me feel wanted. I really need this after the day I had.

I pull away from the kiss and tell him, "If it makes you feel any better, my day was awful too. I didn't get the duet with Diego Salazar."

He looks confused. "I don't get it. Everybody's been saying how great you were."

A bitter little laugh comes out of me. "Yeah, everybody in the studio thought I was the best too."

"So what happened?"

"They went with Taylor Fox."

"Taylor Fox! You sing way better than she does."

"That's *exactly* what I said to Pablo Cruz earlier this evening. It seems that doesn't matter. What does matter is that she brings her fan base with her and hopefully they'll buy the CD and be Diego's fans too."

"That sucks," he says with genuine feeling, "but maybe this will give us a chance to spend more time together."

"I guess." Although I don't see why I can't do both. What does singing have to do with a relationship anyway? "We could be together anyway now that Solange is out of the picture." I smile at him. "That's what our problem was, not my singing."

"Face it, Mari, every time we get together *your career* comes between us."

I can tell he's getting worked up over the past and I've already had more than my share of drama for the day. Right now I just want to feel loved.

"You don't have to worry about my career coming between us because as of six o'clock this evening, I don't seem to have one. Now kiss me," I demand.

We kiss in the shadows for the longest time. If Lola wasn't home right now, tonight might be the night. My feelings for Julian are deeper and stronger than my little-girl crush on Diego Salazar. And Blend just doesn't do it for me. I can tell he wants something more but, even though he's been super nice to me, I don't feel he has genuine feelings for me. There's no connection. I'm not sure what he wants from me.

Julian is the real deal. And this time I'm not going to mess it up.

CHAPTER 18

Pissing Off Everyone

Cha-Cha and I are headed over to the park to hang with Vanessa. We're about to enter when Cisco calls.

"Hey Mari, what's up?" he says. Before I can even answer, he asks, "Hey, you see the video?"

He doesn't have to explain which video. It's the most viewed scene in El Barrio.

"Yeah, *How to be Skanks,* starring Raven Sinclair and Solange Solis. It was hard to miss."

Cisco laughs his crazy laugh. "See, that's what I love about you, your sarcastic sense of humor. So anyway, I got a gig tonight."

Yes! I punch the air with my fist. I've been antsy to work.

"It's a guest DJ spot over at Apple. It's not karaoke, but I thought you might like to come over and hang with us."

I feel myself deflate. First Pablo tells me I didn't get the job. Now I don't even get to sing karaoke to tourists. But hanging in a hot club like Apple is better than sitting in an apartment in El Barrio watching bad TV.

"Yeah, that's great," I say.

"That's my girl," he says. "Pick you up at nine. I go on at ten."

Vanessa is sitting on a bench watching the Colon twins play on the swings—my swings—where Julian pushed me last night.

"Hey, I got your message last night," I call out to her. "That was something."

Instead of her usual smile, she glares at me. "I thought you would have called when you got it."

Whoosh. I plop down next to her. I can't handle any more drama.

"Sorry," I say as contritely as I can manage. "I was having a rough day myself. I didn't get the duet deal with Diego."

Vanessa turns to me. "I'm sorry. I know how much you wanted that. Did they give you a reason?"

"Yeah, they went with Taylor Fox because she's popular and her fans will become Diego's fans." Every time I have to explain this, I get pissed off all over again. Maybe I should send out a mass message and save myself some aggravation.

"Bummer. What are you going to do?"

"I told Pablo that if he couldn't help me, I'd find someone who would."

"Whoa, big words." Vanessa chuckles and I glare at her. "So, do you have a plan B?"

"Kind of," I say. "Blend offered to help, but I'm not sure about him."

Vanessa grabs my arm. "That's great! Give him a call." She notices the look on my face. "Wait, what's wrong?"

"Pablo told me to watch out for Blend."

"Maybe he's jealous about someone else representing you."

I nod. "I thought about that, but there's something that bothers me about Blend. I'm not sure what, just something not quite right." I turn to face her. "You know how you get that little niggling doubt in your brain, like there's something more that you're not getting? Well, I've got that."

Vanessa narrows her eyes like she always does when she's analyzing a problem. "Why? What set you off?"

"I'm not really sure. I mean we made out a little, but when I asked him to stop, he did."

"Wait, you made out with Blend?" she asks incredulously. "Oh man, he is so hot! You are one lucky girl."

I glare at her. "Vanessa, I was just telling you that something about him made me uneasy. How does that make me lucky?"

"I know, but he's so cool." She scrunches her nose. "Okay, back to the problem. If he stopped when you asked, he seems pretty decent."

"Yeah, but, I don't know. Sometimes he stared at me, and it was like wheels were turning in his head. It's like he was thinking thoughts that had nothing to do with our conversation. It was weird."

She smacks her hands on her knees. "Here's what I think. Keep on your guard, but let him help you with your singing career." She nods for emphasis. "And if that rapper tries anything funny, he'll have to deal with me."

For the first time in a long time, I feel like I'm with the Vanessa I used to know. We were always each other's go-to person when we had a problem. This is like old times.

She continues, "So wasn't that video something? I can't believe Raven made it. Do you think it was filmed without her knowing?"

"Oh, I don't think so," I say sarcastically. "That performance looked rehearsed to me. It was all set up." I shake my head. "I feel so bad about it. I feel like we lost a friend."

"Tell me about it," says Vanessa. "I feel like I lost everybody."

I snap my head around to look at her. "What do you mean *you lost everybody*? You still have me."

"Do I?" she asks. "You're never around anymore. You're always off with Cisco or recording with Diego. Sorry, but you did record with him, even though it didn't work out. Everybody's doing exciting stuff and I'm stuck babysitting." Tears well up in her eyes. "We don't even go to the restaurant anymore and when I do go, my mother tries to sit with me while I eat so I don't have to be alone."

She starts crying full out now, causing Cha-Cha to yelp and put his front paws on her knees. I dig in my pocket for a tissue and hand it to her. Scootching closer, I hug her while she lets it all out.

"I'm sorry, Nessa," I say, using her baby nickname. "I've been so into my own life that I keep leaving you out. I would never do that intentionally."

She blows her nose loudly. "It's not just you. First Tatianna started spending all her time downtown and not just when she's working. Who knows what she's doing?"

I do, but this isn't the time to go into details about Tatianna's social life. Besides it's not my news to tell.

"Then you started hanging out with Cisco."

"I was working!" I insist. This is killing me. Doesn't anyone realize that I'm fighting for my life here?

"I know, but you were still busy every night and then you sleep late," she explains. "Then you cancelled for the Fourth of July."

"Again, working!"

I feel really bad about hurting Vanessa, but I'm getting a little tired of defending myself for trying to make money and launch a music career. I'm not going to pass up job opportunities to hang out, gossip, and eat French fries. Vanessa is headed to college. She has a game plan. If I can't make this music thing happen, I'll be flipping burgers at Mickey D's.

"Well, it still hurt!" she yells. "And now this with Raven. It seems everybody's doing something glamorous except me."

"I wouldn't call that video glamorous. It's not like she made a movie. They filmed themselves doing Freddie. It's porn."

"You know what I mean," she insists.

Yeah, I do, but I don't see Vanessa hanging out at club gigs. Tatianna and Vanessa may be sisters, but they are worlds apart. Vanessa is a geek with a thing for her lab partner, Angel. When they both start City College in September, she'll be too busy to care about all this. Vanessa's a homebody. She loves hanging at Casa de Felix with her family and she's the perfect sitter for the Colon twins.

Tatianna left El Barrio in her mind before she was old enough to take the subway by herself. When she was ten, she had a subscription to *Vogue* and talked about traveling the globe. Now she's moving in new circles—fashion, clubs—and making her dreams come true. She hasn't shared any of this with her family or invited her sister to be part of it. If Tatianna and their cousin Cisco wanted Vanessa to be included in their lives, they would have asked her. It's not up to me to bring Vanessa in. She wouldn't like it anyway.

"Look, I know you're right, but this is the way it is now." I love Vanessa and hate to see her upset. "Why don't we have dinner tonight? I could go for some *chicharon*. What do you say?"

She smiles and nods her head. "I'd like that. Then maybe we could go to see that new movie."

I groan as I drop my head and run my fingers through my scalp. "I'm sorry, I can't. Cisco is picking me up at nine. I've got to go home right after dinner to get ready."

"See? That's what I'm talking about!" Then before I can say anything, she says, "Fine, we'll have dinner."

"Good, I can't wait," I say as cheerfully as I can manage. I'm afraid I'll set her off again if I say anything else. "Now I've got to finish walking Cha-Cha and run a few errands for Lola."

I'm almost back at my apartment when my phone rings.

"Hey, Mari," says Julian. "I miss you."

"I miss you too." Actually I haven't had time to miss him today, but that's not what girls say to boys. I know that. So I play the role even though my head is on getting ready for Apple tonight.

"I would have called sooner but we've been swamped today."

Julian's father owns a motorcycle shop in the neighborhood. They sell motorcycles and accessories and do repairs out back in the garage. This makes Julian a little better off financially than most of us in the 'hood. He always has money, but that's because he works for it. He works in the shop on weekends during school and full-time during the summer. He even does his father's books. He'll be starting NYU in September. Julian's smart.

"Listen," he continues, "tonight's our late night, but how about we do something later?"

"Oh, I'm sorry." I seem to be saying that a lot lately. "Cisco is picking me up at nine. He has a gig at Apple." Everybody knows it's the newest club in the city, so I'm sure he'll understand.

A loud silence fills the air.

"Julian? Are you there?" I ask, hoping we were cut off.

"Yeah, I'm here," he says with an attitude.

First Vanessa and now Julian. I'm pissing everyone off without trying.

"Hey, why don't you come hang out?" I suggest, hoping to make him feel included. "I'm not really working tonight. We can hang out together. It'll be fun."

"So this isn't even a job and you still can't blow it off and go out with me?"

"Come on, Julian, it's Apple. How often do we get to go to a club like that?" I'm hoping he'll see my side of it. "Come on, we'll dance and have a good time. We'll be together."

"No, I don't think so," he says coldly. "On second thought, I'm a little tired. I'm going to go straight home after work."

"Fine." I don't even try to hide my aggravation. "If you change your mind and decide to stop by tell the doorman that you're with Cisco." And I click off.

Once again I'm back with Julian and once again we're fighting. Why did I ever think this would work?

CHAPTER 19

Feeling Gritty

Dinner with Vanessa was strained and tense. Everything I said set her off. Maybe she should hook up with Julian; they'd have a lot to talk about.

Oddly enough, my anger at them makes me more determined to jazz up my appearance and have a great time tonight. I go heavy on the black kohl to bring out the greenish-gold glow in my eyes. Bending at the waist, I blow-dry my hair over my head to maximize fullness.

Flipping through the rack of my rapidly growing wardrobe, I take out the blue dress from Kell E and wrinkle my nose. Not that it's ugly—far from it—but it's cool and sophisticated and I'm feeling gritty. El Barrio girl goes downtown and gets her jam on. I flick through until I come to the bronze top I bought for my first karaoke gig with Cisco, but instead of wearing it with the leather-like capris; I team it with my black denim miniskirt. I slip into my open-toe shoe boots with the fat gold zippers across the instep and admire myself in the mirror.

Forget all of them if they don't like it. I'm not pulling back the reins on my new life just because of jealous old friends. Julian could have come. He chose not to, so let him deal with it. I am so sick of everyone complaining.

Riding down the elevator, I try to psych myself into a more positive zone. By the time I hit the fresh air, I'm feeling better.

Cisco comes rolling up. "You look like a hooker standing out there," he says. "I mean that in a good way."

"There's no way that can be good, so don't even try."

Honestly, is everyone in the universe trying to piss me off today? I've got to start reading my horoscope before I leave the apartment.

We ride downtown without further conversation. I'm not stewing on my day because I'm focusing on the sights. I will never get tired of looking at the different neighborhoods of Manhattan. For moles like me and millions of others who travel only by subway, getting a chance to explore New York by car is a real treat. I'm a tourist in my own city.

It's amazing how neighborhoods change every few blocks. Crossing Ninety-Sixth Street is like entering the world of the rich and fabulous. The apartment buildings are much nicer with uniformed doormen out front. Not only are the people dressed better, they're busy walking to their destinations. No loitering on these streets. And the cafes! Oh, how I wish that someday I could eat in one of those adorable outdoor cafes. What a perfect date that would be.

We bustle through midtown, but get caught in the snarl of traffic headed toward the west side of town. Cisco is swearing in Spanish and English, and Randy rolls down his window to yell at a truck driver who is unloading his double-parked vehicle. "Hey, leave a little room for the rest of us, will you?"

The driver flips him the bird.

Finally, Cisco pulls his Jeep up to the front door of a nondescript club in the meat-packing district. I smell a faint whiff of old meat mixed with river water in the air. It's hard to believe this is the infamous Apple. I would have walked right by it. A line to get in is already forming, even though the club won't open for another hour. We start unloading quickly so Cisco can get his Jeep into a lot before he gets a ticket.

Once inside we set up in no time. We have it down to a science. Cisco sets the loop going for background music and we head to the bar until it's time to spin and the crowds are allowed to enter. I order my usual.

"A bottle of water, please." I get so hot and thirsty in these places.

"Sparkling or still?" asks a very cute bartender with possibly the bluest eyes I've ever seen.

Now this throws me. Usually they just hand over a bottle of Dasani and are done with it, except for the time I drank the fancy French bottle of Evian. Either way I'm slugging down water straight out of the bottle.

Because tonight is a night for me to explore new things, I say, "Sparkling, please."

The bartender places a glass of ice with a slice of lemon in it in front of me with a wink. Then he twists off the cap of a green bottle of Pellegrino and fills the glass, leaving the bottle in front of me. I take a sip of the bubbly water—delicious. I think this is my new favorite drink.

"It's go-time!" shouts the manager, and we all head to our places. Even though I'm not performing, I follow Cisco and Randy to the DJ booth. I have nowhere else to go. I'd feel funny hanging out at the bar by myself, especially since Cisco told me I look like a hooker.

The music is pumping as the club fills up with hot-looking people in super-cool clothes. Something tells me the doorman is there to prevent anyone who does not fit the image of the club from entering. That's cool. Some of the people on the line outside must still be hanging out there because some of them didn't even make the effort to try to look the part. Some guys are wearing sports jerseys from their favorite teams, and the girls, let's just say they look dumpy and frumpy.

About an hour into the night, I catch sight of Tatianna and Reggie on the dance floor. They're a good-looking couple. Tati is rocking the dress she wore to the white party and Reggie is wearing a white linen suit and black shirt. I head down to the dance floor and join them.

Lady Gaga is belting out "Bad Romance" over the sound system and I dance up to Tati. The two of us make a sandwich out of Reggie. I'm belting out the song right along with Gaga, but no one can hear me over the sound system. I'm working up a sweat and having the time of my life when I see him.

Blend is sitting in an elevated area cordoned off by a red velvet rope. He's wearing a light-weight charcoal suit with a black shirt and no tie. Vanessa's right, he's definitely hot. There are several people at his table, but sitting silently at his side is a girl with long blond hair and huge turquoise eyes. They're so blue I can see them from here. They've got to be contacts. The strange thing is that she looks about twelve or thirteen. She can't be anyone's relative because all the other people at the table have some color to them and this girl is snow white.

I pass by to say hello to Blend, but I'm stopped at the rope. "Sorry, private party."

Not a problem, I'm not here to make a scene. I only felt that, after he was so nice to me at his house, it would be rude of me not to say hello.

I'm heading back to the DJ booth when someone grabs my arm. It's the velvet rope Gestapo. "Blend would like you to join him."

He allows me to lead the way back to the VIP area and the first thing I notice is the blond girl's missing. Blend invites me to take her seat. Whatever.

"Sorry to hear your deal with Salazar fell through," he begins. Boy does bad news travel fast. "Why didn't you give me a call?" Am I imagining it, or is there a slight edge to his voice?

"There's really nothing you could have done about it. They're going with Taylor Fox."

A clean champagne flute appears before me and Blend fills it himself from the bottle in the silver cooler.

"No, I mean why didn't you call me to say you're free to sign with me?" His tone *is* a little rough, almost angry.

I take a sip of champagne to give me time to gather my thoughts.

"Honestly?" I ask. "I thought you were just being nice to a girl with big dreams. I didn't think you really meant what you said."

Blend is shaking his head as if he's annoyed with the antics of an unruly child. "Of course I meant it," he says. "Why would I bother to say it if I didn't mean it?"

He tops off my glass and I take a big sip. All that dancing made me thirsty. Now I have to move Pellegrino down to second place on my list of favorite drinks; Cristal is number one.

"So where do we go from here?" I ask. "As long as you're serious, so am I."

Blend is right. I should have called him to ask what he had to offer. I do have a plan B and I should have played it immediately. If Pablo and Teddy Bear Barnes didn't care enough to fight for me to sing on the CD, then I don't owe them a thing. I salute my new attitude with a little more champagne.

"So what we're going to do . . ." Blend leans closer and begins to run through his plan, but we're interrupted by shouting over at the red velvet rope.

"Let go of me, man!"

"I told you to step away. That's a private party."

Julian! Julian is being dragged away by two burly security guards. I automatically get up and chase after them.

"Wait!" I yell over the music. "Stop that! He's with me."

It's breaking my heart to see him like this. They're treating him like a criminal.

"Julian!" I scream, hurrying toward him.

The guards let go of his arms but instead of walking over to me, Julian storms toward the entrance to the club. I run and catch up.

"Wait, Julian, where are you going? It's cool. Come back in."

He turns to me with that same face he was wearing when he called me a bitch. "What is it you want, Marisol? First you invite me down here to have a fun night and then I find you guzzling champagne with some rapper. Make up your mind."

He turns and starts walking. I catch up and grab his arm, ignoring all the faces of people stopping to watch the drama.

"Julian, stop, it's not what you think," I protest. "It was—"

"Business. I know. You don't have to tell me again. That's always what it is with you."

He heads outside into the night. I stand there a while, hoping he'll turn and reconsider, but he's long gone.

I go back into the club and over to the red velvet rope. I want to hear Blend's plan for my music. At least one good thing will come out of tonight.

The velvet rope Gestapo blocks my way. "Sorry, private party."

"But I'm with . . ." I point to Blend, but the girl with the long blond hair and vacant turquoise eyes is sitting in my place and he's pretending like he doesn't even know me.

Looks like I missed my chance. I missed it with Blend and now I missed it with Julian. Again.

CHAPTER 20

Love Bites

I've been calling and texting Julian all day, but he won't answer. The image of him being dragged out of the club by those gigantic security guards keeps playing through my mind on an endless loop. It was so unfair. Julian wasn't trying to get to Blend; he was trying to come to me. I had invited him.

And Blend—I never saw anyone do a 180 so fast. One minute he's trying to launch my career and the next minute he doesn't know who I am. I feel like I'm getting a crash course in the music industry and I don't like what I'm learning so far.

I've got to go over to the motorcycle shop where Julian works. He can't ignore me if I'm standing right in front of him.

When Cha-Cha sees me getting ready to leave, he runs over to the door and starts yipping.

"Sorry, Chach, but I'm not sure how this is going to go. I promise we'll go for a long walk when I get back." Now I can add guilt to my list of woes.

I walk the eight blocks north to the motorcycle shop, picking my way over the chunks of broken sidewalk and the other detours caused by new construction that's going on in the area. There aren't many people on the street and I'm starting to regret leaving Cha-Cha at home. My little dog is too tiny to protect me, but at least he's good company.

I take a deep breath before opening the door. What if Julian tells me off in front of all the bikers inside? That would be humiliating. *Man up*, I say to myself. If he goes off on me, I'll just turn around and walk out. At least I tried.

Buzz. The buzzer goes off when I walk through the door. All heads turn to see who enters and, when they realize it's a girl, they stare and smile. Embarrassing! I look straight ahead at Julian sitting behind a cash register. I can see his face soften. That's all the encouragement I need.

"Hey, Mari, let's get out of here." Then he calls through the doorway behind him, "Dad, come out front. I'm taking ten."

He grabs my hand and leads me out the front door.

"Hey, Julian, that your girlfriend?" some man calls.

Julian ignores the guy, and we walk down the deserted street past the construction.

I begin, "Julian, I'm so sorry about last night. If I could change everything, I would." My eyes are welling up with tears.

He's shaking his head. "Oh, Mari, I'm sorry too." He kisses away a tear that escapes down my cheek.

My hopes soar. If this is all a giant misunderstanding, we can pick up where we left off. I couldn't sleep last night so I had a lot of time to realize just how much I care about Julian. In fact, I think I love him. I know how strange that sounds considering so much of our time together has been spent apart. Every time we get our relationship going, it seems we fight and break up. But not this time. I'm really going to make the effort to be the kind of girlfriend Julian wants.

"Mari, this is hard for me to admit." He's kicking up chunks of broken concrete with the toe of his cool white kicks.

I interrupt him, "You don't have to explain. It's going to be all right from now on."

He walks a few steps away and then circles back to me. "You're right—I am jealous of the life you lead when you're involved with your music."

See, that's the first step. Once he admits that, we can work on it.

"I mean there's Diego Salazar," he says. I start to protest. "Don't say no. Everyone knows you were crazy about him. Those feelings don't go away. I could see it in your face when you had the chance to record with him."

There is one small ring of truth to that, so I let it go.

"Then there was the Fourth of July. You know I would have dropped Solange right then and there. I would have called her right in front of you and taken *you* to the beach. But why should I? You were going to spend the weekend in the Hamptons with a lot of cool celebrities. What was I supposed to do? Sit home?"

I never really thought about it from his point of view. But the idea of him taking Solange to the beach with my friends still pisses me off. He didn't really *have* to bring a date. He was with friends.

"So last night I was thinking about your invitation and decided you were right. We would have fun at the club. So I get all dressed up and take the train downtown, only to find you drinking champagne in the VIP area with Blend. Can you imagine how I felt?"

"But I tried to tell you, we were discussing my career because I didn't get the deal with Diego." God, this is so frustrating.

"See, that's it. You're right. You have to think about your career." He stops and holds my hand. "And I really am so proud of you." He strokes my cheek with the back of his fingers like he always does. "I'm your biggest fan."

That's why I love him. He melts my heart with those eyes.

"But I can't sit home alone and wait for you to come back and tell me about all your new adventures. I have a life too." He takes a deep breath. "Mari, what I'm trying to say is I don't think we can make it."

"Julian, no! I'm begging you, think it over," I plead.

"I had all night to think it over. I hate these jealous feelings I've been getting when I'm with you. It's not me. I'm miserable. That's not what love is."

What can I say? He's right. Love is supposed to make you feel good, not make you cry.

I turn and walk away.

CHAPTER 21

Sure, Blame Me

I'm halfway home when I veer off in the direction of Casa de Felix. This is the time Vanessa usually has dinner, so I'll keep her company. Oh, who am I kidding? I need company. I need my old BFF.

I push through the glass door, only to find Vanessa already has a friend keeping her company. Raven. I think about turning around and leaving, but Vanessa looks up and waves, leaving me no choice but to go over and sit down.

Ignoring Vanessa's warning look I say to Raven, "Well, it seems we're hanging out with movie stars now. How cool!"

Raven bursts into tears. My comment was snide, but crying like that? Come on.

Vanessa tries to console her, then turns to me and says, "Freddie just broke up with her."

Now I feel crappy. I know firsthand how that feels.

"Maybe we can form a club," I say. "Julian just broke up with me."

That gets everyone's attention. Now they need details so I give them the whole story, from inviting Julian to the club to him finding me with Blend. I omit the part about security escorting him out. I don't want to humiliate him.

"So I went to the motorcycle shop to apologize to him," I say. "He was super nice and apologized too, but he still broke up with me."

If I'm expecting sympathy from Vanessa, I'm not going to get it. One look at her face tells me that she's pissed about something.

Vanessa sucks her teeth and says to me, "So why didn't you ask me to go to Apple with you? We were sitting here right before you left to get ready. Why didn't you want me to go and hang out?"

What am I supposed to say to that? I can't tell her the truth because it would be hurtful. Apple is a cool club, not a high school dance. Vanessa doesn't fit into that scene. Besides, that's Tatianna's territory and I really don't think she wants her little sister there. And if Cisco, her own cousin, didn't invite her, who am I to bring her along?

So I go with a version of the truth. "I didn't invite you because it wasn't my place to do so. Cisco invited me, so it was kind of like working," I explain. "In fact, I was working when I was talking to Blend."

Vanessa usually has the warmest smile for me, but right now she's wearing a sarcastic smirk. "But you invited Julian, right?"

She had me there. I did invite him.

"Forget her, Vanessa," Raven chimes in. "Marisol always does what's best for Marisol. That's the way she is and we both know it."

I feel like I've just been smacked in the face. I can't believe my two BFFs—well, one BFF and one former BF—badmouth me behind my back. I am so not like that. I always think of my friends. Okay, lately a few things have come up that have gotten in the way, but I used to do *everything* with them. This is really unfair. If anyone dropped out of the group, it's Raven.

"Yeah?" I ask. "What about you and Solange? You're the one who stopped being friends with us." I turn to Vanessa for support—but I'm not getting any.

Raven drops her fork with a clang and says in that rat-tat-tat way of hers, "And why did I start hanging with Solange in the first place? Think about it. I became friends with her when you started hanging out with Cisco and thinking you were too cool to hang out with us because you were singing in clubs."

My jaw hits the floor. I am totally shocked at the venom in her voice. I always suspected my friends were jealous of me, but to hear them say the actual words hurts. What kind of friend is envious of another friend's good luck? A sucky friend, that's who. I am so finished with these two. If they are suddenly into the truth, bring it on.

"What? Are you blaming me for your porn video?" I ask incredulously. "Is it *my* fault that you took off all your clothes and did the wild thing with both Freddie *and* Solange?" I start to laugh. "You have to be kidding me!"

Raven starts pouting, sitting there staring at her plate. It's typical of Raven not to take responsibility for her own actions. Nothing is ever her fault.

She gets some surprising support from Vanessa. "But Raven is right. You have been wrapped up in yourself since you started working with Cisco."

Saved from this argument by my ringing phone!

"I have to take this," I say to them, heading toward the door. There's no reason for them to hear my business—especially with their attitudes. "Hey, Pablo, what's up?" I ask once I'm out on the sidewalk.

"Mari, look, I have some good news," he says to me.

"What? Taylor Fox died?" I'm only half kidding. Actually, that thought does cheer me up a little.

"Now, Mari, that's not nice. You're a better person than that," he says soothingly. "But it's good news on that level."

I'm getting excited. Maybe they want to record me, just me. That would be even better than one duet on a CD.

Pablo continues, "Diego feels just awful about the CD deal. You know he's one of your biggest fans—next to me, that is."

Yeah, yeah, yeah, more show-biz bullshit. I'm getting used to it.

"Anyway, he wants you to be his date tomorrow night for the premiere of *Bastille Day*—you know, that new action movie about the French Revolution?"

Oh, I heard about it. I can't imagine how they can turn a historical event into an action movie, but whatever.

Pablo doesn't wait for my response. "Anyway, the premiere is down in Tribeca, followed by a party at Balthazar. Are you in?"

Am I in? In my mind, I'm already there. "Of course!" I yell into my phone, causing heads to turn on the street. Omigod, I'm going to a real movie premiere. I'll be walking down the red carpet on the arm of Diego Salazar! Oh, damn, what am I going to wear?

As if he heard the question in my mind, Pablo continues, "Lola tells me that Kell E has given you some things to wear. I'm going to give her a call now to get you set up. I'm sending a car to pick you up first thing tomorrow morning. I'll have my assistant set up hair, makeup, the works, and give you a call with the details. Got it?"

"Yes!" I yell into the phone. Once again I make heads turn. "Thank you so much, Pablo. I'm so excited. I'll be ready first thing."

"Make sure you are," he insists. "This day has to be timed perfectly if we're going to get you down the red carpet on time."

Omigod, this is the most exciting thing in the world. I start punching in Tatianna's digits as I walk back to my apartment. I feel like I'm forgetting something. Oh, yeah, Vanessa and Raven. Forget them! This will only piss them off even more.

CHAPTER 22

Metamorphosis

It's nine in the morning and I'm gliding down Fifth Avenue in the back of a Lincoln Town Car. I could get used to this.

Remembering Kell E's remarks to me—and her killer look—about always dressing to represent her, I'm wearing her mango light cashmere tunic with the scoop neck and three-quarter sleeves over my white denim mini. I only have my gold flip-flops, which I figure are all right because I'll be getting a mani/pedi later on today. I keep up with them regularly now, because I never know when Cisco will call and I'll have to go onstage. I'm not getting caught with scraggly chipped nails peeking out of my cool boots.

I've actually been on this part of Fifth Avenue to see the Christmas tree and store windows, but I've never been here on a sunny morning. There's a different vibe—less touristy and more everyday people. The more I get to see of this city, the more I love it.

The limo slips further downtown and the streets get a little grittier here and there. It doesn't matter to me. The air-conditioning is pumping and all I have to do is sit back and relax. If I allow myself to think about the premiere, I might explode from the excitement, so I'm concentrating on staying calm.

Stop-and-go traffic clogs the streets of Soho, but we make it to the front of Kell E's. The driver opens the door for me, and a few people turn to see who's getting out, but most keep right on walking. Tatianna is waiting for me inside and brings me straight to the back room to get started. Kell E gives me the once-over. She seems to approve, until she gets to my feet.

"My God, don't you have anything besides those rubber shoes?" She sighs. "They're like sponges absorbing all the filth from the streets." She turns to Tatianna. "Go over to the Roman Sandal. Get the shoes I looked at yesterday. What size are you?"

I tell her, "Seven."

"Get them in a seven and get an acceptable pair of gold flip-flops and a flat gladiator—brown, I think," she says to Tati. "I'm letting you pick. Let me see what you can do on your own."

Tatianna hurries out of the store and down the street. I didn't think anything could scare Tati until I saw her with Kell E. For a girl who waltzes around with an *I don't care* attitude, she sure jumps to please her boss.

"Now you," she says to me, "go behind that curtain and take everything off except your panties. The dress I have for you is a corset. You won't need a bra."

I do as I'm told but after I take everything off, I'm embarrassed to walk out topless. I don't get a chance to dwell on it.

"Hurry up in there! We don't have all day," calls Kell E.

I walk out with my arms covering my boobs, and step up onto a round carpeted platform in front of a three-way mirror.

Kell E is eyeing my Regine's bargain underwear—five for $9.99.

"My God, is this what you wear under my beautiful designs? I can only imagine what your bra looks like." She shudders with disgust. She turns to her seamstress. "Measure her for a bra. I'll have Tatianna pick up some proper underpinnings and send them up this afternoon. If she trips on the red carpet and these things show I'll die of embarrassment."

Kind of like what I'm doing right now. The seamstress measures my rib cage and chest then pronounces, "32B."

That's news to me. I've been wearing camis and sports bras for so long I don't even know my size. Come to think of it, I don't even know how to buy a real bra. I usually sift through the pile until I find something that looks like it will fit.

Kell E brings over the most beautiful confection of a dress that I've ever seen. The pink is so pale it's almost nude.

Kell E smiles at my intake of breath. "I call it Morning Mist."

The two women hold each side and lay it down gently. "Step into it," orders Kell E.

I do as I'm told and they bring it up my body and zip it into place. The outside of the dress looks like soft silk flower petals with feathery edges, creating a translucent skirt that falls mid-thigh. The inside of the dress is like a second skin that cinches my waist and pushes up my boobs.

"It's magnificent," I whisper like a prayer.

"The outside is deceiving. It's actually made like an old-fashioned corset," explains Kell E. "The boning and spandex give you a wasp waist."

I think it's a perfect fit, but Kell E and her seamstress are grabbing and pinning different areas. As they work, Tatianna runs in breathlessly carrying three shoe boxes. She opens one and takes out a pair of pale pinkish-beige metallic sandals covered in brilliants. The thin straps crisscross over the entire foot and fasten around the ankle. They're beautiful, but I've never worn a heel that high. What if I can't walk in them?

Tati fastens the buckles around my ankles as I lean on her shoulders for balance.

"Did you have to get the highest ones?" I whisper in her ear.

"Just shut up," she hisses. "You're the luckiest girl in the world. I'd kill to go to that premiere."

"Perfect!" exclaims Kell E. She turns to her seamstress. "I knew that when I saw them yesterday." She's smiling into the mirror at me, but I'm not sure if she's admiring me or her creation. "Good! Take it off. We'll send it up this afternoon. Now, Tatianna, what else did you bring?"

She flips the lids off the other two boxes while I step out of the dress and stand there with only my bargain panties to cover me up.

Kell E holds up a gold snakeskin flip-flop attached with a crystal circle. They're a little flashy for me but she pronounces them *stunning,* so who am I to argue? The next pair is more my style—a tobacco-color gladiator sandal with a slight wedge heel and metal grommets. I'll wear them to death.

One of Kell E's assistants escorts a hip-looking woman in her twenties to the back room where I'm standing wearing underpants and gladiator sandals. Embarrassing!

"Hi, I'm Brooke," she says, "Pablo's assistant." She swivels her head to look at me and her sleek black hair swings out and falls right back into place, just above her shoulders. "You must be Marisol. As soon as you're ready, I'll take you for hair and makeup."

Kell E says that we're through here and Tatianna will bring everything uptown this afternoon and help me dress. Thank God! I wasn't sure if I could get into this dress unless Lola was home. But Brooke interrupted her.

"Pablo asked me to remind you about the other outfit," she says cryptically.

I have no idea what they're talking about.

"Oh, thank you, I did forget." Kell E turns to Tatianna. "On the rack in the back. Bring it out here."

I had no idea that I was getting two outfits today. I only knew about the dress for the premiere.

Tatianna emerges with a beige skirt made of crocheted circles from a primitive type of cord, giving the bottom a scalloped edge. The black tank top is made from silky cotton jersey. A tortoise-shell clip secures the tank into a V-neck.

"I love it, but what's this for?" I look to Kell E for an explanation.

"I don't know, but Pablo wanted you to have a day outfit as well," she says. "Don't ask questions. You're getting another beautiful outfit. Be happy. Wear it with the gladiator sandals."

I thank Kell E and everyone in the shop, then Brooke and I hop back into the Town Car. We pull up to Butterfly Studios.

"Pablo wants you to have the works," she pronounces as we go into the salon.

"Then I hope Pablo is paying," I say. I can see Kell E providing the premiere dress because it will be photographed. But I can't see her paying for shoes and the other outfit and certainly not a salon visit. I look at Brooke. "Well, is he?"

"Everything is being charged to the agency. That's all I know," she says, following me to the first station.

Thank goodness Brooke thought to take a digital photo and fabric swatch from the dress so we can match the polish and choose a hairstyle. We decide on a pinkish-beige sheer polish with a hint of shimmer.

"Shimmering Blush. It won't compete with the softness of the dress," states the nail tech as she goes to work buffing and polishing.

The biggest surprise is my hair.

"Fabulous color!" proclaims the stylist, fluffing my auburn hair in his hands. "But the length has to go. When was the last time you had a haircut?"

"Never?" I say more like a question.

This guy intimidates me a little. I love my hair. I don't want it cut, but I'm afraid to tell him.

"Trust me. I can see you're uneasy, but I promise you that when I'm done, you'll have more hair on your head than you do now."

After combing my wet hair straight, he spins the chair sideways so that I can see the back. "See what I mean? It's hanging past the chair. Too long! Way too long and your ends are straggly."

He lops off a foot from the length and begins to razor it into long layers. Then he uses a round brush to shape my hair into long soft curls. It's movie-star glamorous.

My brows are tweezed into deep arches, giving my eyes a more open look. It seems like forever, but when the makeup artist is through, I look fresh-faced and natural—but much prettier than the real natural me.

What a makeover! I thank everyone for this small miracle. Now I know why it's called Butterfly Studios. I'm transformed.

Brooke and I get into the Town Car. "Drop me at Madison and Thirty-Fourth," she says to the driver. "Are you excited about tonight?" she asks and continues without waiting for an answer. "You're so lucky. This premiere is the hottest ticket in town and the after-party is supposed to be fabulous." The car comes to a halt. "This is me. Have a wonderful time tonight," she says, squeezing my hand. With that, she's off.

On the ride uptown, I think about what a tough day this would have been if I had to navigate the subways and buses in this heat. As it is, I feel like another shower, but I don't know how to go about it with my hair and makeup done.

We pull up to my curb and the driver opens my door. People are stopping to look. A limo in the 'hood gets a lot more attention than in Soho.

"Have a wonderful time tonight, Ms. Reyes," he says.

"Aren't you taking me to the premiere?" Please don't tell me that, after all this, I have to get on a subway with my new dress.

"Another limo will be taking you, miss."

Thank God! I get to the apartment and Lola opens the door.

"Oh! Let me look at you," she exclaims. I turn around at her request. "You're magnificent."

Tatianna is already steaming the dress and my new shoes are in my room.

"I wish I could take a shower. I'm not sweaty but I feel a little clammy." I fan the bottom of my tunic to get a little air.

Lola purses her lips. "Get undressed and come into the bathroom."

I put on my oversize nightshirt and meet her there. She begins looping chunks of hair into big soft curls and securing them to my head with duck clips. Then she fills the tub with about four inches of warm water.

"Take a little sponge bath. Don't add hot water or you'll come undone. I'll bring in something for you to fill and rinse off with. That way the shower won't spray you."

I ease into the refreshing water and allow myself to chill.

Lola brings in a plastic pitcher. "Did you eat?"

Other than the bottle of water I gulped at the salon, I haven't eaten all day.

"I'm not hungry," I insist. I'm too excited to eat.

"Half a sandwich," orders Lola. "I bought fresh turkey and a rye bread. You need something in your stomach. Tati, you want a sandwich?"

"No, thanks, just a drink."

She keeps me company while I wolf down my sandwich. I didn't realize how hungry I was.

Afterward, Lola brings a bottle of perfume into my room. "Just a small spritz," she says. It smells soft—like baby powder.

Lola and Tati zip me into the dress and Tati fastens my shoes so I don't mess my nails. I reapply the lip gloss they gave me while Lola unfastens the clips in my hair and fluffs it.

"I wish your father were here to see you now," she says, smiling at my reflection.

I feel myself well up with tears and I turn and give her a big hug.

She pulls away. "Don't cry. You'll smear your makeup." Lola unscrews the diamond studs that my father gave her from her ears. "Here, you can borrow these for tonight. They'll remind you that your father is always with you."

Speech is impossible because there's a huge lump in my throat. I push the posts through my seldom-used holes and catch the diamonds winking at me. I feel like a princess.

"There's a huge stretch limo outside," calls Tati from over by the window. "And a crowd is gathering."

"I wonder if Diego's inside." I better not keep him waiting.

Tati hands me an enameled hard-shell evening bag in the shape of a butterfly. "Here you go, you lucky thing. Kell E added this to Pablo's bill."

I raise my brows and Lola bursts out laughing. "Wait until he gets it. Hey, you better be on your way. Let's walk her down, Tati."

The crowd on the sidewalk parts to let us pass. The driver opens the door and I can see that Diego isn't in there. That's a little disappointing. Maybe it's a little old-school, but I always thought a gentleman picks up his date at her door. So I ask the driver, "Where's Diego?"

"We'll be picking Mr. Salazar up at his townhouse, Miss. It's on the way."

It is what it is. I turn back to Tati and Lola. "Thanks for all your help, you guys. I never could have pulled this off by myself."

"Just enjoy," says Lola.

I kiss Tati and Lola and slide into the backseat.

Tatianna sticks her head in the door and says, "You better remember everything about tonight because I'm going to want details first thing tomorrow morning. Got it?"

I blow her an exaggerated kiss. "You got it."

For the first time all day, I allow myself to get excited about the premiere—and my date with Diego.

CHAPTER 23

Paparazzi

The limo slides up to a townhouse and Diego runs out the front door and gets in. He seems a little frazzled at first, but quickly recovers.

"Marisol, you look so beautiful," he says, giving me a kiss on the cheek.

I can't believe I'm on a real date with Diego Salazar! I've been wishing for this moment almost all my life. I know I'm here as a friend and he only asked me because he feels sorry about the duet on the CD, but I'm here and I'm dressed up and I have a glamorous night ahead of me. If a small part of me wants to pretend this is a fairy tale come true, then I'm going with it.

"You look pretty good yourself."

And he does. Diego is wearing a black tux with a black open-neck shirt and no tie. He looks cool and casual at the same time. His killer smile glows in the dimness of the limo.

The theater is a short ride from Diego's place. Our limo takes its position in a long line of cars; we have to wait while passengers emerge to walk the red carpet. When our turn comes, Diego gets out first, smiles for a few photos, and then reaches his hand for me.

Kell E's instructions keep running through my head. *Exit the limo feet first. Stand erect—shoulders back at all times! Smile! Walk slowly. Pause often. Stop for every photographer. Above all else, keep smiling. Photographers love to catch a pout.* Needless to say, walking the red carpet is a slow process.

"Diego, who's your date?"

"Diego, when does your new CD drop?"

"Diego is there any truth to the TMZ story?"

I stick close to Diego, who has a firm grip on my hand. All the while, I keep smiling for the photographers, who keep flashing away. Finally a female reporter asks, "This dress is simply stunning! Whose design is it?"

"Kell E," I say, still smiling, and turn to give her photographer different angles.

"Fabulous. And your name is?"

"Marisol Reyes," I say, loud and clear. *Mental note to self—check every paper tomorrow morning.*

TV cameras are set up further along the red carpet. The questions continue. I expect Diego to step off and speak to them alone—after all, I'm nobody—but he includes me in each interview, introducing me and keeping an arm around my waist so they have to photograph both of us. It's so sweet. He really doesn't have to do this, but he does. What a classy guy.

Once in the lobby, I feel like I've run into an invisible power shield. Blend is up ahead, but that's not what surprises me. It's his date who catches me off-guard. Solange Solis. I can't believe he's with that skank. Is she going to follow me everywhere? Here I'm thinking I'm the only girl from El Barrio ever to go to a hot movie premiere—and here *she* is wearing ghetto chic. Suddenly I'm not feeling so special.

Luckily we don't have to pass them too closely, but I catch her waving at me like crazy from the corner of my eye. I ignore her, but she's so obvious that I'm sure Blend looked up and saw me too. What in the world is he doing with her? He was always telling me how pure I was and that's why he liked me. Now he's with the least pure girl in New York City.

Chimes are signaling everyone to take their seats, and we follow the herd. It takes some time for all these celebrities to stop socializing and settle down. If anyone asks me the major difference between a premiere and a regular viewing, I'll tell them it's the food. Not one person in here is eating candy or popcorn, even though the aroma of hot butter is teasing our noses. And there's silence throughout the film. No one is chatting on her phone or yelling at the screen. Even movies are different when you leave El Barrio.

It's not a bad film and I get into it, even though the beheadings make it gruesome. Maybe it's because I'm zipped into this corset dress—I can feel the pain of the French women of the day. I get a little restless thinking about the after-party, so I'm happy to see the credits roll. Everyone waits until they're done, instead of jumping out of their seats like we usually do, and there's a lot of cheering and clapping. The director and producers all say a few words about how wonderful the cast and crew were to work with. They introduce the feature actors and insist they stand up and receive an ovation. They then invite everyone to join them at the after-party.

Diego and I stroll out of the theater past a few die-hard paparazzi. He keeps his arm around me the entire time and I snuggle in and wrap my arm around his waist. This is starting to feel like more than a mercy date to me. I think he really likes me. Fine with me; I've been waiting for this my entire life. I always knew that, if he got to know me, he'd feel the connection between us.

We find our limo and zip off to the party. I'm checking out the new sights while Diego is frantically checking his messages and texting like crazy.

Balthazar's is in Soho. I remember seeing the restaurant on my way to Kell E's, but never went inside. Once again, paparazzi line the street, calling everyone's name so they can get a good photo. We linger on the sidewalk because there's a crush of people trying to get inside. Diego keeps me glued to his side, smiling for photographers and whispering silly comments in my ear that make me laugh. I never dreamed he'd take such good care of me.

We finally make it into the restaurant. The bar area in the front is mobbed, though only a few tables are occupied. I excuse myself to go to the ladies' room only to be forced onto a line. Nothing new about that, maybe the wait will settle my giddiness, but my luck is about to run out.

"Mari!" squeals Solange, honing in for a hug. "Isn't it great? We're both here."

I'd walk off this line but I'm not sure when I'll get another chance. Once dinner starts, it will be hard to escape. So I just give her a quick smirk, nod, and face front.

But my dis doesn't stop her. She chatters on. "I'm here with Blend." She pauses for a response, but I don't give her one. "I'm his date."

Yeah, like I didn't get that point when I saw them together. She's obviously not going to stop until I acknowledge her and, even though I don't know anyone else here, I don't want them thinking that I'm friends with this tacky chick in the black-and-bubble-gum-pink flamenco dress. I can't believe I ever thought she was hot-looking. My taste has changed.

I turn around and whisper to her, "I doubt that you would be his date tonight if he saw that video you made with Freddie and Raven."

Instead of being shamed into silence, she exclaims, "But he did see it! That's why he called me. He remembered me from the video."

So much for Blend liking pure girls—he likes bimbos, just like the rest of them. I turn back around, determined not to speak to her, but she continues to babble on.

"He invited me to his beach house this weekend," she says, running her bubble-gum pink talons through her hair.

Great, just great! This chick is following everything I do. Now she'll be the one spending a hot July weekend at the beach while I roast in East Harlem. A stall opens up and I march in and lock the door. She's exiting her stall while I'm drying my hands and I dash back to the party.

Diego sees me coming and grabs a flute of pink champagne off a passing tray and hands it to me. Together we go in search of our table. We're seated at a horseshoe-shaped booth with two other couples. Diego and I are lodged in the middle. Blake Madison and Penn Bourne are on Diego's right and Adrian Rainier and his date are on my left. A photographer stops by and takes a group photo. I feel Diego's face press close to mine.

I am so glad that I listened to Lola and ate that sandwich because, even though the waiter places the mussel appetizers in front of us, no one is eating. Finally Blake picks at a mussel and I do the same.

"They're delicious, aren't they?" she says to me.

I wish I could sop up the wine sauce with that crusty bread but I know that would be cheesy, so I let the waiter take my plate. It's replaced with a sizzling steak and a metal spiral filled with a paper cone of French fries. I pick one off with my fingers and nibble it. Blake giggles and does the same. At least there's a real person at the table. Everyone else just has a few bites of their steaks.

Diego keeps checking his messages under the table, as does almost everyone else in the room.

I can't contain my curiosity. "Who keeps texting you?"

"Oh, just Pablo checking up," he says distractedly. "He wants to make sure we're having a good time."

Seems like a lot of texting going back and forth for just that, but I don't say anything. It does make me wonder if this really is a mercy date. Maybe he has a jealous girlfriend waiting at home. Then again, Diego's been super nice to me all night. He can't have a girlfriend because he insisted on including me in all his publicity. No girl would put up with that.

Dinner is over and all of us are heading to the door.

I catch Blend's eye in the crush of people and he nods a greeting. His coolness to me is obvious. It's hard to believe he's making such a big deal about Julian coming over to me at the club. I'm not going to dwell on it and ruin this magical night.

I turn to Adrian and his date. "It was lovely meeting you."

He treats me to a glimpse of his dimples. "Yeah, it was nice meeting you too," he says and gives me a kiss on the cheek.

"This has been fun," Blake says, air-kissing me. "Say, a bunch of us are going over to Apple. Come with us."

I look up at Diego expectantly, but he's already making his apologies. "Sorry, but I'm beat. Some other time." He kisses Blake's cheek and shakes Penn's hand. "Nice meeting you, man."

I'm bummed as we walk out to the sidewalk. Dancing would have been the cherry on the sundae, but I can't go without Diego.

He interrupts my thoughts. "Hey, why don't you take the limo home? I can walk it from here."

I'm crushed. I can't believe he's ditching me. Before I can say a word, a group of paparazzi come running up, taking our pictures. Our limo pulls up to the curb and Diego gives me a long sultry kiss before getting into the car with me.

We ride in silence to his townhouse but, just before he gets out of the limo, he turns to me and says, "I had a great time tonight. How would you like to go out tomorrow—nothing fancy—just a walk around the Village? You said that you never saw this part of the city. I could show it to you. Maybe we'll get a late lunch."

Here I'm thinking that the mercy date is coming to a bad end, and he asks me out for the next day. He must like me!

"I don't know what to say."

"Say yes." He's smiling his sexy grin.

I think about it for two seconds. "Yes!"

"Good. I'll send a car for you about one."

He kisses me on the cheek and slips out the door.

My head is spinning with crazy thoughts. Maybe it's just my wild imagination, but I think I have a real date tomorrow with Diego Salazar!

CHAPTER 24

Total Eclipse of the Heart

Tatianna bangs on my door at ten. I'm awake but still in bed, replaying last night like it was a Disney movie. I let her in.

She rushes past me with several newspapers. "You have to see the photos!"

We spread them out on the dinette table, flipping to the gossip pages. "Page Six" in *The Post* has the biggest coverage.

"Omigod, that's me!" I scream. I'm glued to Diego's side and we're laughing at something—I can't remember what. "The dress looks fantastic."

"There's Blend," says Tatianna, pointing to a sliver of a man near the edge of the page. "Who's he with? They cut her off."

"Oh, you know who that hand belongs to," I tell her tauntingly. "Solange Solis."

"Get out of here!" Tati looks confused. "What in the world was she doing there with Blend?"

"According to Solange, he saw her video with Raven and remembered her. So he gave her a call."

"Sounds strange. You can't believe that girl. I'll ask Reggie." Tati is shaking her head. "Let's see what they have to say about the party."

We scan "Page Six," then "Gate Crasher" in *The Daily News*— they have a small photo of Diego and me kissing—but there's no mention of Diego in either story.

"I didn't think there would be," I say. "After all, he wasn't in the movie."

"But the photos are still great. We'll have to get all the tabloids this week to see if they took pictures of your dress." Tati is scanning the article in *The Daily News*. "Ooh, a blind item. I love these."

What hot singer obviously feels a good offense is the best defense?

"I never get those," I say, closing the papers. "Hey, I'm glad you're here. Diego invited me to the Village today for sightseeing and lunch." I get up and fill the coffeemaker.

"Ooh, look at you. A second date with Diego Salazar." She rummages through the fridge and comes out with fruit salad and yogurt and places it on the table. "Lola buys such healthy things. Everything in our fridge is loaded with fat."

"But is it really a date? See, that's what I'm not sure of. I thought last night was a mercy date, but he threw me off between giving me a lot of attention and texting constantly."

"So? That's what everybody does." She gets plates and silverware.

I put the half-and-half and sweetener on the table. "I know, but something felt off."

"Look, even if last night was a mercy date, he didn't have to ask you out for today." She pulls the lid off her yogurt and digs in. "Just enjoy it."

"I guess." I spoon fruit salad into a dish. "What should I wear? It's probably going to be hot today."

"How about the other outfit Pablo ordered for you? You looked good in that."

The Town Car picks me up exactly at one and, a little while later, we're gliding up to Diego's place. This time he's waiting outside. I get out of the car and he kisses me on the cheek.

"Hey, Mari!" he says with a big smile. "I thought we'd walk. You can't really see anything from the backseat of a limo." He tells the driver a time and place to meet us, and we're off.

Diego's street is nestled between two main roads but has the quiet charm of another time in history. It's a row of well-maintained brownstones decorated with pretty shrubs or objects and window boxes spilling colorful flowers over the sides. And it's clean! That's one of the big differences between nice neighborhoods and mine. People don't throw their junk and garbage on the sidewalk.

I'm glad I took a little time with my appearance, even though Diego is wearing tan cargo shorts with a plain white button-down shirt and flip-flops. My hair still looks good from last night and Tatianna helped me with my makeup. The gladiator sandals feel good, but I hope they don't give me a blister after a day of walking.

"So what would you like to see first?" he asks as we approach the main avenue.

"I'm going to let you be my tour guide," I say to him. "I don't know anything about this neighborhood except that you live on a very pretty street."

"That's the old part of the neighborhood. It dates back to the early nineteenth century when the wealthy people escaped the overcrowded seaport area on the tip of the island." Wow, his knowledge of the city is impressive. Now I'm wishing that I knew more about it. "The real Village, what we think of as the Village, is gritty and raw. It's always been a place for freethinkers and poets."

"And musicians?" I ask. "You always hear about little clubs down here where people got their start."

"Especially musicians," he adds as we approach a park with a huge arch. "This is Washington Square Park."

We walk toward the fountain in the middle. The spray hits me and I turn my face to smile at him. Diego leans in and gives me a gentle kiss on the lips. A prickle of excitement runs through me. Once again I wonder if this is a real date. It must be or else he wouldn't have kissed me. A paparazzo is taking our picture. What do they do, hang out waiting for celebrities or just stalk them? I can't believe they'd intrude on a private moment but I put on my happy face for the camera.

Diego smiles and puts his arm around my shoulders and I feel protected. He points to the buildings surrounding the park, many decorated with purple banners.

"NYU bought up most of these buildings," he explains.

NYU. New York University. I'm too distracted to concentrate on the rest of his story. Just hearing *NYU* reminds me of Julian. It's his dream school and he'll be going there this fall. The image of Julian makes me a tiny bit sad. I wish he were here, giving me a tour of his school.

What am I thinking of? Here I am on my fantasy date with Diego Salazar, the man I've obsessed about all my life, and I'm missing Julian. *Stay in the moment, Marisol!*

"What's the matter?" asks Diego. "You look about a million miles away."

I try to laugh it off. "No, I'm just taking it all in," I say. "It's so old I was just wondering what it was like a few hundred years ago."

We leave the park and walk down Bleecker Street. This is grittier. Actually, so was the park. I never saw so many strange people in one place—men with their dreadlocks piled up in huge knit caps and the smell of weed hanging in the air from so many people smoking right out in the open.

And there are more homeless people than I would have thought after seeing how pretty Diego's block is. A ragged-looking man is mumbling to himself while walking down the sidewalk. He keeps looking people up and down and shouting at them for no reason.

"Getting hungry?" Diego asks.

"Actually, I am," I say, surprising myself. "I didn't realize it until you asked, but there are so many wonderful smells here they're making me hungry."

"I know a great place." We walk hand-in-hand down Sixth Avenue, and a few paparazzi take our picture. Diego is super casual about it. I guess he's used to the attention.

We get to a restaurant with a huge yellow awning shading the outdoor tables. Just the other night I was wishing that I could eat in a restaurant like this, and now I am. How cool is that? A big man with long silver hair envelops Diego in a bear hug.

"Silvano! Marisol, this is Silvano. Do you have a nice table for us?" asks Diego.

"For you? No! For this beautiful girl? Of course." He leads us to a table right in front for everyone to see. "How about a nice chilled prosecco and a bottle of San Pellegrino?"

"Sounds great. Thanks, Silvano."

A waiter brings menus, but Diego sets them aside. Good thing. Aside from pizza, subs, and the chicken parm in the school cafeteria, I haven't eaten much Italian food. The only real Italian restaurant in my neighborhood is Rao's across from my school, and people in limos pull up there for dinner. It's not for the locals.

The waiter pours the prosecco and Diego proposes a toast. "To a beautiful afternoon."

How romantic! We click glasses and a paparazzo takes our picture. I ignore him and keep smiling at Diego. I sip my drink. Mmm. It tastes a lot like champagne. The waiter returns.

"Do you like sausage?" he asks me. I don't know if I do or don't, but I nod. "Bring us the sausage with broccoli di rabe, please." Then to me, "It's my favorite. You're going to love it."

Diego takes my hand as we sip our drinks. I'm confused. Even though he seems to be wooing me, I really don't feel any closer to him. Something's missing. I don't feel like I know anything about him, the real Diego, not the one I read about in magazines. He seems to enjoy showing me the city and taking me to this place for lunch and showing me off, but he hasn't shared anything about himself or asked anything about me.

Diego is busy texting on his phone, leaving me to sit and stew. Maybe it's my fault for not keeping up my end of the conversation. I decide to take the first step.

"So tell me something about yourself that I haven't read," I begin.

"Why? What have you heard?" he snaps. His usual bright smile is gone and there's a challenging darkness in his eyes.

I feel my jaw drop. What kind of response is that? I try to regain my composure, but it's tough. I'm only trying to make polite conversation, but Diego's making me feel like I'm intruding into his personal life. If he isn't interested in me, why did he invite me to spend the day with him and send a driver to get me?

"Sorry," I say, hearing the frost in my voice. The waiter comes over with our lunch so I wait until he leaves. "I was going to ask how you were able to make the transition from El Barrio to this world. I'm only beginning to get a glimpse of life outside of East Harlem and from what I've seen it's very different. I was asking for your advice, not trying to pry into your life."

Sorry if he's offended, but he didn't have to snap at me like that. Between that and my outburst, I'm feeling really uncomfortable. I busy myself with the sausage and the broccoli, which doesn't look like any broccoli I've ever seen. It's a little bitter but really tasty.

Diego begins to say something, but is interrupted by Silvano. "How's everything, okay?" He looks up at the sky. "Is the sun in your eyes?"

We both assure him that we're fine and that everything is delicious, which it is. He refills our glasses and leaves.

"Nah, it's just that I'm really big on protecting my privacy, that's all," he says, grabbing my hand. "I overreacted, sorry." And just like that, he's back to his charming old self.

I look out at the paparazzi. "I guess I can understand that. They haven't left you alone all day."

Diego doesn't respond. He ducks his head and tackles his lunch without making any attempt to have a conversation. I still don't get it. Since when is it a crime to try to get to know someone? I'm not going to sell his story to a newspaper. If he didn't trust me, then he shouldn't have asked me out. This date and last night were his idea, not mine.

I fiddle with my food, but I'm too upset to eat. Silvano comes running over to find out why his celebrity guest is asking for the check without finishing. Diego reassures him that we're tired from the late night and we'll be back soon. I want to leave and am happy to see the Town Car pull up. Now I'm hoping he'll offer to walk home so I can take the car uptown, but no, he slips in next to me as a paparazzo clicks away.

We drop Diego off and he gets out of the car without much of a good-bye. I don't care if he knows that I'm pissed. But as the car glides uptown, I can feel the sting of tears prickle my eyelids. Spending a day with Diego Salazar should have been a dream come true, but this day has turned out to be a nightmare.

I can think of only one reason for his coldness. He asked me out because he thought I was someone he could like but, after getting to know me, he decided he doesn't. That hurts.

CHAPTER 25

Nothing but a Photo Op

I tossed and turned all night. So hearing Lola in the kitchen, I give up and head in. We never had a chance to talk last night because I was already in bed by the time she got home. It was easier to pretend I was sleeping than to go over the day's events with her. Lola is expecting good news and fun details. Well, she won't be getting them from me.

One look at her face tells me something is very wrong. I spot a stack of newspapers next to her at the dinette table and she seems, I don't know, angry.

"I guess I don't have to ask how your afternoon went," she says in a flat tone. She picks up a weekly tabloid and flips through to find a page.

How in the world could a tabloid find out that Diego doesn't like me? The paparazzi only caught one shot of me looking surprised and that was when Diego asked me what I had heard about him. The rest of the shots were all cozy and cuddly. Geez, I hope Lola isn't angry about that.

"Let me see."

She flips to the cover of the tabloid to show the headline to me: *Hot Latino Singer Outed.*

The cover features a huge picture of Diego Salazar, singing. I open the paper to where Lola has her finger and see more photos and a story. There's a photo in a circle of someone who looks very familiar, but I can't place him.

"Maybe that's just a crazy fan," I offer. "What do the other papers say?"

Lola lifts another tabloid.

Life's a Beach!

The cover photo is of Diego and his three friends from the party at Blend's, sitting on the beach. It was probably taken in East Hampton. It's an innocent photo, but the headline makes you think something's up.

"What's the story on that one?" I ask.

I get a sinking feeling in the pit of my stomach as I flip to the cover story. Diego and his friends are dancing at a club. The only thing missing is a female presence. The dance floor is wall-to-wall men.

"Oh, brother," I say, letting out a whoosh of air. "That explains it."

"What does it explain?" asks Lola. "He didn't try . . . I mean, he wasn't *intimate* with you, was he?"

For some reason this makes me laugh. *Intimate!* What kind of word is that? But I don't want to offend Lola, who really looks seriously distressed.

"No," I say, "he didn't try anything. That's kind of the problem." I keep looking at the photos. "I thought it was me. I couldn't figure out why he asked me out two days in a row when he didn't seem to like me." I shake my head. "I spent the whole night tossing and turning trying to figure out what I did wrong, but it wasn't me! He needed a photo op for the press!"

Lola removes the stack of colored national tabloids from the pile and takes out the *Post* and the *Daily News*.

"I'm glad you're taking this so well, because it gets worse." She flips to "Page Six" in the *Post* and "Gate Crasher" in the *Daily News*. Both have several photos of Diego and me taken at the premiere and on yesterday's outing. They even captured my surprised look. The caption underneath: *Is this when she finds out the truth?*

Lola is angry. "I feel Pablo's hand in this. He had absolutely no right to use you like this and I will let him know about it."

She's right. I do feel used—and embarrassed. The whole thing hits home. For years my friends made fun of me because I was madly in love with a big star who didn't even know I existed. Then, by some miracle of miracles, I get, not only a chance to meet Mr. Big Star, but perform with him and date him as well. Now all of New York—including my friends—will be making fun of me because I look like I'm madly in love with that same big star . . . who turns out to be gay. Either way, I come out looking like a starstruck tween who doesn't know what real love is.

I never thought love would be so complicated. Well, be careful what you wish for, because you just might get it.

I say to Lola, "You know, he didn't have to go through this whole charade. If Pablo had just explained the situation to me, I would have gone to the premiere with Diego anyway." I push at the papers. "I wouldn't have kissed him and pretended to be in love, but I would have gone as a friend."

Lola comes up behind me and gives me a hug. "You are a very generous person to say that after all this, but I'm still telling him off." She heads for her phone.

"That's why Pablo insisted on the second outfit. I wondered about that. Do I still get to keep the clothes?" I ask, trying to make a joke. No way I'd give any of it up now. I earned those outfits.

"You better believe it," she snaps. "And he can forget about the beach this weekend."

I run over to her and click off her phone. "Please don't ruin your weekend because of this. That would make me feel worse." It's bad enough that I'll be sitting home feeling pissy. There's no reason Lola has to stay home and watch it.

"I have an idea. Come with us. Some time at the beach away from all this will make you feel better."

"Oh, no! If I have to look at Pablo all weekend, I'll end up telling him off. You go. I need some time." Truthfully, the beach sounds fantastic, but I don't want to be a tagalong on their romantic weekend.

I take another look at the articles. "Wait a sec, I know this guy." The circle photo is small but the guy's expression is the same. "He's one of the waiters from Blend's party. He interrupted me when I was talking to Diego." He certainly moved in fast.

Lola comes over to take another look at the photos, but shakes her head. Then she says to me, "Are you sure you're okay with me going to the beach with Pablo?"

"Of course I'm sure," I tell her. "I'll catch up with Vanessa. Don't worry, I'll be fine."

After Lola leaves, I pour over every detail in every article. It's like a drug I can't get enough of. Part of me is humiliated that I was publically used like that and part of me is relieved that it wasn't my fault Diego rejected me. He'd reject any female. And then I get angry all over again for being so hard on myself. How dare he use me that way!

I do what I always do when I get stressed—I sing. Between my collection of CDs and Lola's, we have just about every song imaginable. Today I pick every angry-woman song and sing it as loud as I can. Lola's collection is better than mine for the scorned-woman type of songs. I flip through to Dusty Springfield singing about a man not having to say he loves her in that smoky, sultry voice of hers.

Then I move on to the get-even songs and let them rip. I need Fergie because I want to be a big girl who doesn't cry. I need to toughen up if I'm going to survive in this business. It's days like today that make me wish I was into country music with all its angst, but that makes me think of Taylor Fox and I get mad all over again.

It's late afternoon when I finally shower and get dressed. Cha-Cha is with Lola but I feel like a walk. I head in the direction of Casa de Felix to see what Vanessa is up to.

I'm wearing my sunglasses, not because I'm famous but I don't want anyone recognizing me from the papers. I don't want to be laughed at. All I want is the company of my real friends instead of the phonies I've been hanging around with. If Raven's there, fine. I'll make the extra effort to be friends.

I get to the restaurant and can see through the glass door that Vanessa already has a friend with her—Julian. Oh, well, we broke up on good terms. He's still a friend, although I wish he were more, but it will be nice to see him again. This is kind of like old times. Vanessa and Julian are laughing at something and I can certainly use a laugh.

I open the door and Vanessa eyeballs me. The smile leaves her face and she looks mad. Instead of waving me in like she usually does, she pretends she doesn't see me and focuses on Julian. She totally dissed me! Then I see it for what it is. Vanessa and Julian are *together* as in *on a date!*

I turn and walk away, letting the door slam. When did this happen? In two days my world has turned upside down. There's nowhere to go but home—alone. I no longer have any friends in this world.

I sit there stewing until shadows start to fall. This is the lowest I've ever been.

There has to be someone. I scroll down the contacts in my phone and a name stops me. Blend. It was useless to ditch him and run after Julian. As it turns out Julian didn't want me anyway. He's looking for a mousy little homebody like Vanessa. Well, now he has her.

A reckless feeling overtakes my reasoning. I hit SEND.

"I was wondering when you'd call," he answers.

"Yeah, well I never had a chance to apologize for the other night."

"Get dressed. I'll be there to pick you up in an hour. I'm going to give you a chance to make it up to me."

I'm not going to let myself get crazy thinking that Blend has an ulterior motive. He probably does. Everyone does. If I learned anything this week, I learned that. Well, I have one too—I want a singing career and Blend is going to be the one to help me get it.

There's nothing left for me here. Diego is over. Julian is over. Vanessa is over. And Raven's been long gone. If my old friends have moved on, then it's time for me to do the same—this time I'll head out into the world wearing an invisible suit of armor.

CHAPTER 26

Caribbean Fantasy

It isn't the Bentley that pulls up to the curb, but a black Lincoln Navigator with heavily tinted windows. No way I'm walking out there; it could be a drive-by shooting. No thanks, I'll remain behind the glass doors of my building. If the window slides down and a gun comes up, I'm out of here.

The window slowly slides down and I have a sudden urge to bolt, but instead of a gun, Blend's face appears on the passenger's side. I walk through the door and head to the curb.

"What in the world were you waiting for?" he demands, hopping out of the SUV.

"I thought this was a drive-by," I admit sheepishly.

He kisses me on the cheek, opens the rear door, and begins rearranging the seating. I'm happily surprised to see Tatianna and Reggie already in the vehicle. Tati is wearing an adorable silk baby doll top in what looks like shades of turquoise or teal. I'll have to wait until we're in the light.

"I love this," I tell her. "You look great." Her white skinny jeans look sprayed on, they're such a perfect fit. I can't wait to see her shoes.

"Reggie, you can ride shotgun next to Lamar." He shoots a meaningful glance my way, making me laugh. "Mari, you can slide in next to Tati and I'll sit next to you."

It turns out that Lamar is not only a friend and driver, but Blend's bodyguard as well. I guess when you're rich and famous, you need to travel with a bodyguard.

"So where are we headed?" In my rush to get out of the apartment, I never thought to ask. I assumed it was Apple, so I put on my leather capris and shimmery bronze tank top. My black booties with the gold zipper are comfortable enough for a night of dancing.

"We're headed to the Apollo," announces Blend.

Omigod, the Apollo. It's a legendary theater in Harlem. So many famous singers have performed there including some of the great women vocalists I've learned about from Lola's CD collection. There are the early singers from the 1930s, like Billie Holiday and Lena Horne, right up to Dionne Warwick and Aretha Franklin. Even Michael Jackson performed there when he sang with his brothers, the Jackson Five. I've always wished that I was around when they held their famous Motown Reviews. They must have been slamming.

"Yeah, a friend of mine is performing tonight," continues Blend. "You know Brooklyn Bobby Biggs?"

"Well, yeah, who doesn't?" Brooklyn Bobby Biggs, or Triple B as he's known, has been heading the charts for over a year now. Every car that passes down the street is blasting one of his tunes.

"I promised Triple B I would make a guest appearance tonight. Laqueesha and I are going to perform 'Caribbean Fantasy' together."

A squeal of pure delight erupts from my mouth. "Yes!" So much for being cool.

Oh wow, "Caribbean Fantasy" is my absolute favorite Blend song. It has a rocking, almost savage base that Blend sings in a low voice. Laqueesha comes in singing the higher melody, kind of like Shakira in "Hips Don't Lie." I've seen the video a million times and it is smoking hot. The two of them perform a dance that should be illegal. Vanessa and I used to practice the Laqueesha part in front of the mirror to see who could dance it best. I know every word to that song. I could sing both parts.

"I take it you like my recording?" asks Blend.

"No," I pause and wait for him to shoot a look at me, "I love it! 'Caribbean Fantasy' is one of my all-time favorite songs. I can't believe I'm going to watch you perform it. And Laqueesha, she's the best." He chuckles appreciatively. "Ooh, I'm so excited."

The SUV rolls north to 125th Street, and over to the west side. I'm not far from my own neighborhood and yet it might be a million miles away. I live in East Harlem, but have never been to Harlem proper. It's an old section of the city. I remember studying the history of Manhattan in grade school. Harlem had originally been settled by the Dutch and was farmland. If they could only see it now, it's a time-capsule from the jazz era.

We enter the theater from the stage door. I can only begin to imagine how many great musicians and singers have walked this way. I'm stepping on hallowed ground. There's nothing more exciting than a theater with its frenzied energy. Musicians are tuning up their instruments. Vocalists are running scales in their dressing rooms. Stage managers are yelling orders. I love this world.

No matter how busy they are, people stop to greet Blend. As part of his entourage, we're also welcomed with great enthusiasm. A man stands off to the side wiping sweat from his brow with a white hand-kerchief. He's looking our way, but seems unsure whether or not to approach. Shrugging his shoulders, he steps up.

"Ah, Blend," he begins.

"Harley, my man!" Blend sweeps the smaller man up into a bear hug. "What's shaking?"

"Yeah, great, great, Blend, how are you?" Without waiting for a reply, Harley continues, "Ah, Blend, we have a bit of a problem with tonight's performance."

"What's the matter, Triple B doesn't need me tonight? That's okay, man, I'll just sit back and enjoy his performance."

"Nah, it's not that, it's Laqueesha." He looks up at Blend sheepishly. "She called in. Can't make it. Said she's sick, mono or strep, something like that."

Whoa! Laqueesha may very well be sick, but it's more likely that she's stoned out of her mind. Her drug escapades regularly make the news. Everyone knows she's a hardcore addict. I've seen pictures of her in the national tabloids smoking crack and shooting heroin. Pictures don't lie. I mean, I've been a victim of tabloid journalism too, so I have some sympathy, but in my case they got the story right. I may not have liked it, but I can't accuse them of making the story up.

"Damn!" Blend smacks himself on the head and begins pacing. "Now what? How am I going to sing both parts of that song myself?" He slams his fist on a wardrobe rack causing hangers and costumes to fly off. "I knew I couldn't trust that woman, but I agreed to do the song with her against my better judgment."

You never saw so many people trying to look away or otherwise engage themselves as those of us around Blend were currently doing. Reggie looks as if he's going to try to calm him down, but turns away before he gets there. Finally, a solution comes from an unlikely source.

"Why don't you sing the song with Marisol?" asks Tatianna.

Everyone turns to stare, and even Blend is looking at me like he's seeing me for the first time. Personally, it never dawned on me to think of myself. I mean, this is the Apollo Theater, for goodness sake, home of legends. My usual venues are frat boy clubs and karaoke for tourists. Even I know I'm out of my league. Or am I?

"Of course, Mari can do it," continues Tati with a lot more enthusiasm than I've ever heard in her voice. "I've watched her and my sister practice it dozens of times in our room." Thanks for sharing that tidbit of embarrassing information, Tati. "Not only can she hit those high notes, she knows all the dance moves too."

Please, God, let the floor open and swallow me whole.

Blend is studying me. "Well, Mari, do you think you can do it?"

I guess I can. I mean, yeah, I know I'm capable of banging this out, maybe even better than Laqueesha, but before I open my mouth to take Blend up on his offer, he says, "Don't say you can, if you can't, Marisol. This is the big time, the real deal. You'll be performing with me. The Apollo may have amateur nights, but tonight isn't one of them."

Now he's pissing me off. Instead of being cowered, I'm empowered.

"Let's do it," I tell him. "And Blend?" He looks my way. "You better keep up with me."

He roars with laughter. "That's my girl. Let's get it going."

There's no time to rehearse. Triple B takes the stage and between the volume of his show and the screaming fans in the theater, you can't hear yourself think, let alone sing. We aren't going to be on until three-quarters of the way through Triple B's performance, so we sit back and enjoy the show from the wings of the stage. Tati, Reggie, and Lamar are with us, as are some other friends of Triple B. He's really doing a terrific job out there. I'm learning a lot about stage presence from his actions. He uses the entire space and keeps everyone's attention focused on him.

"You still sure about this?" Blend whispers in my ear.

"Yeah, 100 percent," I reply. "Embarrassing as it is, Tati was right. I do know every single word and dance move, so you just have to do your part."

"Okay, then."

We're on deck and suddenly I am nervous! What was I thinking? Where did that cocky attitude come from? Now is not the time to rethink my outfit—there's not a thing I can do about it. At least it goes with Blend's black silk shirt and pants. We won't clash, but that's not stopping me from panicking. Too late, Blend is ushering me out to center stage. Deep breaths. Deep breaths. Get the energy redirected to the performance. Yes!

The pounding rhythm for "Caribbean Fantasy" begins with tom-toms thumping and Blend jumps in with his deep base vocals.

Goddess of the sunlight
Goddess of the moonlight
Let me in your orbit
Let me feel your aura
Goddess let me give you some loving tonight.

I'm ignoring him like Laqueesha does on the video, all the while prancing to my own beat. He keeps dancing up to me as if to get my attention, but keeps failing. The crowd goes wild.

Goddess of the fire
Goddess of desire
Let me take your flower
Let me share your power
Goddess let me give you some loving tonight.

Finally it's my turn to sing and I begin wailing in a high soprano, like a siren luring men to their downfall.

Mortal man
If you think you can
Come closer to me
Feel my energy.

Blend continues with his primal rap.

Goddess of the star shine
Goddess of all mankind
I'm reaching out to touch you
To share your world and be true
Goddess let me give you some loving tonight.

Then I drop my voice to a lower range and begin to chant.

Careful, baby, careful
Not to crash and burn.
Careful, baby, careful
Not to crash and burn.

The dance continues with Blend and me simulating an enormous struggle on both a physical and spiritual level.

Never try to steal my powers
'Cause you'll crash and burn.
Never steal my powers
'Cause you'll crash and burn.

I'm getting into it, almost like an opera, where the story is sung as opposed to speaking the words. "Caribbean Fantasy" is a performance piece and the dance is just as important as the song. I begin my banshee wailing in an octave so high only dogs can hear, as Blend chants his mantra in a low range to a tribal beat.

Goddess of the sunlight
Goddess of the moonlight
Let me in your orbit
Let me feel your aura
Goddess let me give you some loving tonight.

We reach the crescendo and our bodies are writhing and inter-twining with each other as if we were making love, yet we never come in contact with each other.

Never steal my powers cause you'll crash and burn.

It's the most sensual dance I've ever seen. I only hope my version does it justice. I'm not a tall, lanky African-American like Laqueesha with a booty so big it could hold a tea tray. I try to compensate with swirling my hair out like tongues of fire.

Blend and I are chanting our own lines at each other.

Goddess let me give you some loving tonight.
Never steal my powers cause you'll crash and burn.

Drums are beating a tattoo, and I know the music is about to end, Blend rolls me into him, bends me back, and gives me a deep soulful kiss. The audience is screaming their approval as he runs his hands up my body and over my boobs. I know that's not part of the original choreography, and neither is the electricity running through me.

"Ladies and gentlemen," Triple B yells into the microphone, "give it up for Blend!" He swirls around and extends his hand. Omigod, does he even remember my name? "And Marisol!"

That's it? Just Marisol? Like Cher or Madonna? Okay, I'll take it.

CHAPTER 27

Chicken and Waffles

We're all at Sylvia's, that landmark soul food restaurant in Harlem, to celebrate the success of the concert. Triple B is there with his posse, which is huge. Compared to his, Blend travels light. The crowd is loud, and even the other customers, most of whom were at the concert, join in the celebration. One big happy family.

I throw my arms around Tatianna, who is sitting to my left. "Thank you, thank you, thank you!"

"For what?" She's laughing and pulling my arms off of her.

"For making this possibly the best night of my life, that's for what."

"Me? I didn't do anything. Blend gave you the shot at performing."

"Yeah, but it was you who put the idea in his head. Even I didn't think of it."

Triple B has his arms around two girls, both of them overly done up, if you ask me. Everything about them is fake, from the extensions in their hair to their eyelashes and nails, and I also suspect that their oversized boobs are fake too. I guess this is the rapper world. I'm not used to it.

Bottles of champagne arrive at the table. Corks are popping and sprays of bubbles decorate the table top and some of our clothes. This isn't the way they serve champagne at Apple. Some of the other girls murmur protests and one openly complains, "This ain't even Cristal!"

No, it's Dom Perignon and even I've heard of that. What an ingrate.

I'm dying of thirst, so I stop a passing waiter and ask for a really large glass of water. Singing is thirsty work.

Blend jumps up and raises his glass of champagne. "To my man, Bobby, great show tonight!"

This brings a rousing chorus of cheers and glasses are drained. I notice the girls have no trouble downing their glasses of champagne, even if it isn't Cristal.

Triple B is wearing a diamond grill in his mouth making him look like a rich kid in bejeweled braces. He gets up and raises his glass. "To my friend, Blend, who is always there to help a brother out."

Another chorus of cheers erupts. Bobby is still standing. "And to this little lady . . ." He's looking right at me. "You've got some set of pipes." He pauses a moment and continues, "I remember you from the party. Fourth of July. Yeah, you were singing with Princess." He raises his glass to me. "I think I like you better than Laqueesha."

Some of the girls roll their eyes and don't bother to raise their glasses, they just drink. Whatever. I'm used to girls with attitudes from my karaoke gigs.

"Hear, hear!" yells one guy. Then someone adds, "And she's sober, too."

Champagne almost snorts through my nose. The guys are laughing at the joke, but I'm not sure it's okay to make fun of someone's addiction.

Without anyone ordering, platters of food begin to arrive—Sylvia's famous ribs, pork chops, and the dish I've always wanted to try, chicken and waffles. I was never sure how those two foods got together, but I guess I'll have a chance to find out tonight.

Everyone begins eating, but I'm too wound up to do anything more than nibble. The cornbread is rich and buttery and the meat on the rib I bite into is fall-off-the-bone tender. Surprisingly, the chicken and waffles is a very tasty combination, even with the maple syrup.

Tati is pushing the food around her plate. "Don't they have salad here?"

"Probably, but no one ordered it." I look around. "Why don't you grab a waiter and ask for one?"

She makes a dismissive gesture with her hand, the same one she learned from Kell E, and begins to pick the heavenly breading off of the chicken.

I nudge Blend. He's said surprising little about my performance since we left the theater. I thought he'd show a little more enthusiasm.

"So, how did we do? Am I your new partner for that number?"

"Baby, you were dynamite." He snakes an arm around my shoulders and whispers in my ear. "What I'd really like to do is practice that number back in my apartment."

Instinctively I know that he's not talking about rehearsing. Blend is interested in the real thing. I could tell that from the way he touched me on stage in front of thousands of people. What I'm surprised about is my reaction. I'm not sure whether it was the thrill of performing on stage at the legendary Apollo Theater, the sexual frenzy of the dance, or Blend himself and the feel of his hands rubbing the length of my body. Whatever is was, it excited me.

Everyone has just about polished off all the food. It's amazing how most people eat when they're wound up. I'm the total opposite. If I'm feeling any extreme, good or bad, my stomach feels jumpy and anxious. Food simply doesn't want to go down.

Triple B pulls a chair up between Blend and me. "Hey, man, you holding out on me? Why haven't you shared this fine young lady with me sooner?"

If there's one thing I hate, it's creepy pick-up lines. I have a very low BS threshold. Anything with the line *fine young lady* in it turns me off. It's condescending. Freddie uses it all the time and it only works on dumb-ass chicks like Raven and Solange.

Triple B continues with the true confidence of a man whose lines have worked in the past. "So, Marisol, that's such a pretty name, where has Blend been hiding you?"

"Bobby," warns Blend in a low menacing voice.

"Oh, come on, man, I never even got a picture of this one. What, are you keeping her all to yourself?"

Blend gets right in his face. "I'm warning you, man, chill."

"*Awright, awright*, I'm going." Then to me, "I hope I'll be seeing more of you."

I've had enough and grab Tati's arm. "Come with me to the ladies' room."

I didn't have to ask her twice. She's out of her seat in a flash.

"Great shoes," I say to her, admiring her bronze snakeskin stiletto sandals.

She does a little samba step to show them off. "God this little party blows," she says on the way.

We get to the hallway where the restrooms are and stand on the line.

"You're telling me. That Triple B character made me feel dirty." I shiver involuntarily. "And to think I was so excited about watching him perform in person."

"I know, right? He's so crude. Every other word out of his mouth is something disgusting," she says with a grimace. "I never want to hear his music again. That guy turns me off."

We are interrupted by a nice elderly lady. "You'll have to excuse me, but I have to tell you how much I enjoyed your performance tonight at the Apollo."

"Why thank you," I reply. It's hard to imagine this nice old lady was part of the screaming audience.

"I was wondering if I could have your autograph for my grandchildren. They will just love your singing. I can't wait to tell them about you when I get back to Detroit. I'm sure you're going to be a very big star." She hands me a little memo pad and a pen. "Make it out to Bertrice." Bertrice is fiddling in her bag while I write my very first autograph. She hands Tati her phone. "Would you be a dear and take my picture with this young lady?"

She shrugs her shoulders and takes the woman's camera.

So there we are, Tatianna taking photos of Bertrice and me in the line to the ladies' room. It doesn't get stranger than this, but it's better than sitting at that table.

The two girls who are with Triple B come out of the ladies' room and have to pass us in the narrow hallway.

"Laqueesha does that song so much better," says one girl loud enough for everyone to overhear.

"You got that right!" the other shouts. She's teetering on her platforms and grabbing her friend's arm for support.

I feel my lips tighten and my face gets hot. How dare they dis me like that? They've been at it all night, but didn't have the nerve to do it in front of Blend. I head after them, but Tati grabs my arm. She rolls her eyes and shakes her head, which brings me back to reality.

"They're just jealous," she says softly.

By the time we get back, the party is breaking up. Lamar brings the Navigator around and we take our places. The magic spell of the night is broken and we ride to East Harlem in relative silence. We pull up to my building and I give Tati a kiss on the cheek.

"Talk to you tomorrow," I say to her. "Night, guys."

Blend walks me to the front door. "So, I promised you a night out and ended up making you work. How about I make it up to you tomorrow night? Feel like Apple?"

I'm feeling better towards him, since we left Triple B behind. "Don't apologize. I had the time of my life. Never in my wildest dreams did I ever imagine performing at the Apollo. You made it happen. Thank you, Blend."

He kisses me on the lips, gently, not like he did onstage. "See you tomorrow night, then."

All in all, this was an exciting night. And the chicken and waffles were delicious.

CHAPTER 28

The Truth Will Set You Free

My phone wakes me from a dead sleep. I can barely pry my crusty eyes open a crack, but the name on the ID looks like Diego. Diego? Nah, can't be.

"Hullo?" I mumble, but it comes out more like a question.

"Are you still asleep?" Who is this person demanding to know my schedule? "It's after one o'clock."

"In the morning?" Man, I know I got home late last night, but I thought it was later than that. "Who is this?"

"Oh, sorry, it's Diego, Diego Salazar. I figured you had caller ID."

"Well, if I could open my eyes I would be able to see it." Why in the world is he calling me? He's the very last person I want to talk to. It's funny how anger gets your motor started. Suddenly, I'm wide awake. "And even if I could see it, I wouldn't have believed it."

I toss the covers aside and stumble to the window. A tug on the blinds and I'm attacked by the sun's death rays. It's daytime all right.

"Yeah, that's why I'm calling, to apologize for the other night, and now I apologize for waking you."

He really does sound nervous and contrite, but I just want him off my phone and out of my life.

"It's nice of you to call, Diego, and I'm sure you're sorry, but it's over and I want to put it behind me. Take care."

I pull the phone away from my ear and am about to thumb the *off* button when I hear him plead, "Wait, wait, Mari, don't hang up."

"What?" I need coffee and a shower if I'm ever going to feel human again.

"Let me take you to lunch today, that's really why I called. I want to apologize in person."

A bitter laugh escapes from deep down in my throat. "You've got to be kidding me. Do you really think I'm going to fall for that trick again?"

"Mari, calm down. I understand that you don't trust me and I don't blame you." His voice lowers to almost a whisper. "But I really feel that I owe you an explanation and I'd rather do it in person."

The very last thing I want is to be seen with Diego Salazar. I'm simply not strong enough to go through that paparazzi frenzy again, and shame on me if I allow it.

"Mari, please, I'm begging you. You don't have to come down here where people will see us, I'll come uptown. You name the place."

"Oh, Diego, you're *killing* me here." I'd hang up on him in a heartbeat, but he really sounds sad.

"Look, I know you haven't eaten, because I woke you up. What do you say? Will you give me a chance? Tell me where to meet you and I'll be there."

I'm not exactly the big restaurant expert. The only place I eat regularly is Casa de Felix, and there's no way in hell that I'm bringing him there. That's the last thing I need, all my former friends gawking at me and making fun of me chasing after a newly outed gay guy. How stupid does that make me look? But maybe Diego is right. We do need closure on this.

"Oh, all right, let me think a minute." Pablo took me to that restaurant last week. What was the name of it? I pound my forehead with my palm to jog my sleepy brain. "El Nuevo Caridad," I say, "on Second and 116th. Do you know it?"

"I'll find it."

"Okay, give me an hour or so."

Once again, I'm about to click off when I hear him.

"And Marisol? Thank you."

———— ◆ ————

The cool blast of air conditioning is refreshing after walking over on the sweltering sidewalks. My white T-shirt is already sticking to me and a ring of perspiration is forming underneath the waistband of my denim mini. I'm wearing Regine's finest because I don't want to look like I'm trying too hard, but I did swap my flip-flops for the gladiator sandals before I walked out the door. I'm trying to keep in mind that I have an image to maintain, like Kell E is always telling me.

Diego is already sitting in a booth tucked in the back, away from the enormous plate-glass windows. His unshaven face makes him look both haggard and hot at the same time. He stands up as I approach and comes in for a kiss on the cheek. I accept it wordlessly. To turn away would only make me look silly and childish.

Diego already has a *limonada* in front of him. The frosty glass looks good, so when the waiter approaches I order the same. I busy myself with the menu, but he sets his aside.

"Marisol, I want to thank you for seeing me. I know you didn't have to, but I'm really glad you did."

"Honestly, Diego, I think it might be best if we let this whole mess drop. You know how the news is, they have to make a big deal out of something until everyone is sick of it, then after a few days—nothing. You never hear about it again. It's over, let it go."

After Diego was outted by the press, he held a press conference and came clean. Yes, he admitted to being gay and was sorry that he misled his fans. Personally, I didn't think an apology to his fans was necessary. Why should he apologize for being who he is? Diego also—and this was very nice of him, again, he didn't have to do it—explained to the press that he and I were simply very close friends and that's why we were together.

"Mari, it may be over in the press, but I can't let it go. I'm too ashamed," he admits.

I drop my menu on the table and look at him. "Diego, there is absolutely no reason to be ashamed of being gay. That's crazy."

"No, I'm not ashamed of being gay. In fact, I never was. That was all Pablo's idea. He wanted all the girls to go wild over me, and he figured they wouldn't do that if they knew I was gay." He concentrates on stirring his *limonada* with his straw. "It's what I did to you, used you like that, that's why I'm ashamed."

How can I still be angry after that? This is a genuine apology, straight from the heart. I cover his hand with mine and give it a squeeze.

"Thank you, Diego, I do feel better," I admit. "And on a happy note, look at all the free publicity I got!"

"If it's any consolation to you, you sounded a whole lot better singing 'Soul Spinning' than Taylor Fox. We rehearsed yesterday. That girl can't sing for shit."

The ice is broken and the past is behind us. Suddenly, I'm starving. A waiter passes with a platter of golden nuggets of *chicharron de pollo* and *papas fritas,* chicken nuggets and French fries Latino style.

"That looks delicious," I say, practically salivating.

He smiles in agreement. "Yeah, I could go for that. It's been a long time since I've had Spanish food." He sounds a little like Pablo.

After the waiter brings our lunch, and two more *limonadas,* Diego continues explaining the situation as we dig into our food.

"You know," he begins, "I have to explain my odd behavior the night of the premiere."

This should be enlightening. I spent the night wondering what all that texting was about, and I seriously doubt that it was Pablo.

"You see, I've been in a serious relationship for a long time, about four years." He pauses to savor a bite of chicken. "*Umm*, delicious. Eduardo—you met him at Blend's party—that's my boyfriend."

So, he must have been the one shooting daggers at me that night.

"Eduardo was hurt that we couldn't come out as a couple. Pablo was absolutely against it. When the time for the premiere rolled around, Eduardo felt this would be the perfect opportunity to make our announcement, but after fighting with Pablo about it for weeks, he made a date for me with you, and that was a done deal."

I'm nibbling a fry and feeling suddenly guilty, even though it wasn't my fault.

"Anyway, Eduardo and I were fighting big time, right up until I walked out the door that night."

"Why? It wasn't your fault, it was Pablo's."

"Yeah, but Eduardo said that I was a grown man and should stand up to Pablo. 'Grow a pair,' is what he actually said."

I giggle and cover it with a cough.

"You okay?"

"Yeah, wrong pipe."

"The fight continued all night via texting. That's what I was doing on my phone, fighting with Eduardo."

This lunch is so delicious that almost all my food is gone. My stomach is starting to ache from eating so fast.

"I kind of understand how Eduardo feels," I say to him. "I would feel the same way if I couldn't be seen with the man I loved. It would feel like he's ashamed of me."

"Exactly Eduardo's point and I'm so relieved that this is all out in the open. It's like they say, 'The truth will set you free.' After everything settled, we were in a good place. Eduardo stayed by my side, and when I confessed to him about how bad I felt about you, he urged me to call you. He said it would give us all a new beginning." He peeks up at me, those chocolate-drop eyes half hidden behind a thick fringe of black lashes. "I was afraid."

"You were right to be afraid," I say with a smile.

Diego looks up to call for the check and sees our waiter snap a photo of us with his cell phone. He's out of his seat like a launched rocket and at the waiter's side in a flash. Snatching the phone out of the waiter's hands, he snaps, "Give me that." Diego deletes the photo.

He walks back to our table shaking his head. "It never ends."

"Well, he probably saw the papers and figured he could make some money selling the photo. In a way, you can't blame him. Money is money. Everybody needs it."

The manager, having seen the interaction, insists that lunch is on him, and begs us to please come back again as his guests.

Diego is wearing urban camouflage—gray T-shirt, faded black skinny jeans, and retro Chuck Taylor kicks. He puts on his Yankees baseball cap and sunglasses before exiting the restaurant. We walk unnoticed through the streets of East Harlem while Diego answers my original question from the other day. He begins to explain his transition from El Barrio to the big world.

"Yeah, it was tough at first," he explains. "I mean, I didn't grow up going to fancy restaurants or dealing with rich people. I'm a kid from El Barrio, playing stickball in the streets and eating rice and beans for dinner." He looks over to see if I'm with him on this. "But I was smart enough to know that I had to learn fast if I wanted to fit in. And I *really* wanted to fit in. So I watched and I learned."

We are at ease with each other, like I always knew we would be. Our fingers are even intertwined as we walk. I mean, we're not romantic, but we're friends, and that's what really matters.

We get to my building and he kisses my cheek.

"I'm glad we did this," he says.

"Me too."

Now I've got to get ready for another big night with Blend—a perfect evening to follow a perfect day.

CHAPTER 29

I'm Getting Pretty Good at This

Apple is banging tonight. It is so cool to pull up to the door in a silver Bentley, be greeted like a star, and prance right past the velvet ropes while the badly dressed line-people gawk.

Blend and I are escorted to his usual booth in the VIP area, where he can take in the scene and not be disturbed unless he grants an audience. I'm not sure if the DJ is male or female but whoever it is, he-she is good. The dance floor is full and throbbing with the beat.

I'm looking cool in the midnight-blue spandex dress Kell E gave me for my weekend in East Hampton. I haven't worn it yet so it's new and I feel good in it. I teamed it with my black ankle boots for a funky downtown look. I'm getting pretty good at this.

Blend holds up his flute for a toast. "To our new beginning. We're going to make lots of music together."

Just what I want to hear, after last night at the Apollo I knew he would be excited about working with me. I clink my glass and take a sip. Remembering his words about contracts, I ask, "So, when are we going to start?"

He indicates the crowd with his glass. "We are starting. First thing is we have to get people to recognize your face."

I feel a deep heat rise from my toes to the roots of my hair. "I think they already recognize it," I admit. Having my face smeared all over the tabloids is already coming back to haunt me. Things are cool between Diego and me, but I'm still embarrassed by the photos.

"That's okay. That's okay. All publicity is good. Besides, that story was all about Salazar, not you." He puts his arm over the back of the booth. "You are a beautiful young girl. How old are you, anyway?"

"I'll be eighteen next week," I say.

"That's it. We'll have a big party for you right here. It will be a great way to generate a buzz."

"Are you serious?" I can't remember ever having a birthday party. Now Blend is going to throw one for me at the hottest club in Manhattan. This is unbelievable!

"Of course I'm serious," he says. "What's the date?"

Oh, wow, this is going to happen. "July twenty-second."

He nods. "I'll get my staff on it."

Just like that? I guess big stars like Blend have a whole slew of people to do things for them. Meanwhile, I'm so excited I can't sit still.

People come up to greet Blend and he acknowledges their words with a silent nod, like a don in a mafia movie. This time he introduces me to everyone as a new singer he's working with, instead of letting me sit there like a zombie. Now I'm part of his world, and it feels good.

Tatianna and Reggie swing by and join us on the horseshoe-shaped couch. Tati's been keeping her feelings about this relationship pretty much to herself, but she always looks happy when I see her with him, so it must be going good. Tati is rocking a hot pearl-gray tunic of slashed raw silk with a thin coffee-colored silk lining. Her long tan legs look even longer in her strappy bronze platform sandals.

"This is fabulous," I say to her, fingering the fabric. "Kell E, right?"

She shakes her head, with a sneaky smile on her face. "Tati," she says.

My eyes widen. "Ooh! You designed this?"

"Designed and made it. You like?"

"Love it," I tell her honestly. "This dress is as beautiful as anything in Kell E's shop." I feel the soft creaminess of the fabric and notice the way it skims over her body. "You rock, girl!" This gives me an idea, but first I have to check with Blend. "Can I invite Tati to my party?"

"Invite whoever you like. Just give the names to my assistant tomorrow." He goes back to talking with Reggie.

I turn to Tati. "Blend is giving me a birthday party here next week. Can you design something for me to wear?" This would be great if I could get her to agree on such short notice. "It might get some press," I add.

"Sure, let me work on it." I can see the wheels turning in her brain. "Come on, let's dance," she says, dragging me toward the floor. We start dancing to the throbbing beat of LMFAO, which allows me to work off this adrenaline rush I'm feeling since learning about my party. Tati keeps dancing towards the other side of the floor and I twirl around to keep up with her. When we get far enough from the table, she pulls me into a hallway and says, "Is it official? You're with Blend now?"

I nod. "I guess so. I mean, he seems interested, and things went well last night."

I never made a conscious decision to be with Blend, we kind of fell into it by default, though I have to admit, I did feel something when he touched me at the end of the song last night. Besides, everyone I cared about has someone else. Diego's with Eduardo, there's no way I'm taking his place. And Julian, *my* Julian, seems more interested in Vanessa than me. At least with Blend I'm furthering my career, even if it isn't love.

"Just be careful." Tati looks serious and grasps my arms, like she really wants me to listen to what she has to say.

This isn't the first time I've heard that. "Why? What is it?"

"I don't know. It's probably nothing, but I overheard Reggie on the phone. He was saying something about legal trouble."

"So? He runs a record label and a clothing line. He probably always has legal trouble of some kind." That gives me another idea. "Maybe he'll be interested in your designs. It wouldn't hurt to ask."

"Maybe, but I'm not so sure the legal problems are just business." She shakes her head. "This sounded really serious. I couldn't figure out what they were talking about, but I'll keep my ears open and let you know if I hear anything more."

We head back out onto the floor and dance for a while. Then we go back to the table and join Blend, Reggie, and a few others who come over. It's a fun night—just what I needed.

Toward the end of the evening, Blend leans over and whispers in my ear, "Let's drive out to the beach."

Lola's chat with me resurfaces in my brain. She's right. I am getting in over my head. I can feel it. Even though I think I might be interested in Blend, there's no way I'm ready for a weekend alone with a man I hardly know. But I am so afraid of dissing him. I can't afford to piss him off again if I want him to help me get my career off the ground. What happens if we go to the beach and run into Lola and Pablo? I'll be screwed. She told me in no uncertain terms that she pays for my phone to keep her informed. I have to get out of this.

"You know, that sounds great," I begin, "but I have an early morning doctor's appointment that I can't get out of. Can we make it another time?"

"Sure, baby, sure," he says, "but we need to talk somewhere more private and I'd like to hear your voice again. Why don't you come back to my apartment for an hour or so and then I'll take you home?"

That nagging little bug is scratching at my brain. Something's up, but there's no getting out of this. I have no choice but to say yes.

Blend lives in this futuristic glass-tower complex overlooking the Hudson River with the most magnificent view ever. I head right to the floor-to-ceiling windows.

"Omigod! Is that the Statue of Liberty?" *Duh!* Of course it is, but my excitement seems to please him. He comes up behind me and hands me a balloon-shaped glass half-filled with amber liquid. I sniff it first. "Ooh, this is strong. What is it?"

"Cognac, very, *very* old cognac," he says. "Let it warm in your hand, then sip it slowly."

I try, but it burns my throat. Blend starts nuzzling the back of my neck through my hair. I'm feeling super sexy and sophisticated all dressed up and looking at this million-dollar view in what has to be a multimillion-dollar apartment. It's like being in a movie and I'm the glamorous woman that every man wants. But I'm not. I'm still seventeen and I'm afraid to hop in bed with a guy I hardly know.

Besides, I always thought the first time would be with . . . I swallow to get rid of the lump in my throat. Why do I have to think about Julian now?

I walk over to the couch and sit down, placing my drink on the huge stone coffee table.

I smile up at Blend. "So, you wanted to talk business," I say, breaking the mood. I would offer to sing but I'm afraid my voice will crack. "When will you sign me to a contract?"

The spell is broken. Blend takes a seat in the chair across from me.

"I'm going to have my people get on that first thing in the morning, right along with your party." He's staring at me strangely. "You know, you're different from other girls."

"What do you mean?"

He shakes his head. "Any other girl would be trying to please me any way she could if I offered her a music contract. You know what I'm talking about?"

"I think I do," I say softly. I remember Cisco's stories about the video girls and how Solange will do anything and anybody to get ahead. "But I guess I'm a little old-fashioned. Does that bother you?"

"I like a challenge," he says to me. "Now let's get you home."

I didn't realize I was holding my breath until I exhaled.

CHAPTER 30

My List of Friends Is Shrinking

Blend's assistant Skye phones me first thing in the morning to talk about the party. I'm kind of surprised. Part of me wondered if Blend was just talking to talk. Promising to throw a party for a girl he hardly knows sounds more like a maneuver to get her into bed. Maybe it was, but now it seems like it's in the works.

"Just compile a list of the names and e-mail addresses of everyone you want to ask and e-mail it to me. Blend will be inviting the bulk of the guests, but he wants you to have your own friends there as well," says Skye in a melodic voice.

I always wonder if people who talk like that are good singers too. That's probably why she works in the music industry. She's probably hoping to catch a break.

It didn't take me long to come up with the names of the people I want to invite, as my list of friends is shrinking. There's Tati, of course, and Vanessa should come even if she did dis me the other day. I'm asking Raven. If she refuses, that's up to her, but she's been a friend all my life and I want her there. And Cisco . . .

I call Skye and ask, "Is it all right if I pick the DJ?"

"Sure, I don't see why not."

That's great. Cisco always has my back and now I have his. I'm asking Randy, Freddie, and, of course, Julian. I want him there more than anyone else. I'm not asking Solange. If Freddie brings her as his plus-one, fine, but otherwise, I really don't want her there. I almost forgot Angel. He's always been part of our group. I'm not sure what's up with him and Vanessa but, just in case it's over, I want him to feel included.

So I guess that's it, I say to myself and hit SEND. Suddenly it hit me. I phone Skye again. "Omigod, I almost forgot Lola—she's my stepmother—and her friend Pablo Cruz." There is still one more person on my mind. "Skye, I have a question for you. Do you know the designer Kell E? She's been super nice to me. Should I invite her or would that be too pushy?"

"Not at all! This is going to be a big event, not a traditional coming-out party." I didn't want to point out that in the Latino community a girl celebrates her fifteenth birthday—*la quinceañera*. We don't have coming-out parties like rich girls. But I got her drift. "In fact, Blend is using this event to introduce you to the music world as his new discovery. You're scheduled to do a new song."

Wow! He's serious about the music thing too. I was hoping he was, but you never know if guys are just shoveling it to get what they want.

Speaking of songs, that reminds me of Diego. Things went so well at lunch that I would love for him to come to the party. Now it's my turn to extend a sign of friendship. "Skye, Diego Salazar is a friend of mine. I'd like to invite him and his partner, Eduardo. Sorry, but I don't have his last name, or Diego's e-mail address. I can give you his cell number, though."

"Not a problem. I'll get in touch with him through his publicist." Before clicking off, Skye gives me her personal cell number and says, "Now if there's anything else you think of or want—food, colors, music—give me a call and I'll make it happen."

I can really get used to this world. I thank her for everything and let her do her thing.

Too antsy to stay in and make myself breakfast, I decide to pick up a coffee and drink it in the park. I'm halfway there when my phone pings. It's Tati.

cant talk hav designs cn u meet me?

Things are looking up. I text back: time/place?

She can meet me in Soho in an hour, so I head to the nearest subway stop. Then I realize that I'm wearing my El Barrio best—cut-offs, T-shirt, and flip-flops—and race back to the apartment to change into something more Kell E worthy. I'm not sure if I'll be recognized, but I can't chance my photo winding up in a fashion column with *Trash Your Stylist* splashed across the top.

I'm running late when I get to the café Tati mentioned. She's not at an outdoor table so I walk in and see her sitting way in the back. This must be a covert mission.

"You're fast!" I say to her. "I can't wait to see." I point to Tati's cup and signal for the waiter to bring one more cappuccino.

Tati opens her portfolio and spreads out her designs. "I started working on these when I got home last night." Wow, she must be really excited about this to get them done on such short notice. "Let me describe them all before you pick, because we can do different colors or make a few changes."

The first design looks a lot like the dress Tati wore to Apple last night. This one is fuchsia and also has slashes, but no lining, so skin can show through.

"I loved this on you last night, but I'm not sure I can carry it off." I'm trying to be diplomatic, but I'm not sure if her feelings will be hurt.

"I agree, but I wanted to try a different version for my own sake." She studies the sketch. "Maybe I'll wear it to your party."

The second design is sketched in a-black-and-white variation of the cut-out dress she wore to Blend's party on Long Island. It's a combination of asymmetrical bands of spandex held together with sheer mesh. It's different, but it doesn't thrill me.

"I'm not sure, I don't think I want to wear black to my party and we just wore white for Blend's. We still have those dresses. What do you think?"

She wags her head to each side noncommittally. "I guess. Anyway, I have one more."

I take a look at sketch three. "Omigod, Tati you're a genius!" I say with awe. "This is a masterpiece." I tear my eyes away from the drawing. "You have to make this for me. I'm begging you."

I never saw Tati smile so wide. She has every reason to be proud. The dress is a confection in shades of persimmon and coral silk gathered like crepe paper to form an hourglass-shaped dress that falls loosely in a micro miniskirt. The sides and shoulder straps are sheer nude silk.

"I love it! It looks like it was made for me," I tell her.

"Well, it was, silly. I focused on you when I sketched it."

I lean over and give her a hug. This is the nicest thing anyone has ever said to me. Tati and I were never close friends. I always thought she tolerated me as Vanessa's tagalong friend. But we're bonding this summer. That's probably because we're two tourists in a foreign land hanging together for support.

"I've got to go," she says. "I took your measurements from the shop. After I get this in form, we'll start fittings."

She dashes back to work. I take my time sipping my cappuccino. I'm in no rush to go back to the real world.

CHAPTER 31

It's Getting Hot in Here!

Blend isn't in the mood for the club scene tonight, which is why we're sitting on the floor in his living room eating Chinese take-out. This doesn't thrill me. One, Blend is kind of weird to be with sometimes, especially when he's zoned out like this. There's something odd about him that I can't quite pinpoint. I like Blend's lifestyle. Hanging out with him at the beach or a club is a lot of fun, but alone I find him a little unsettling. Two, I'm not sure if I'm into a physical relationship with Blend and agreeing to be alone with him is like extending an invitation. I don't want things moving too fast.

But I couldn't say no to hanging out with him tonight. After all, he's throwing a big party for me in a few days and he said he's going to give me a record contract. So here I am, sitting on the floor eating garlic chicken wings and shrimp fried rice, off of a coffee table that's a giant slab of geode, in an apartment that looks like something out of the future.

Blend hardly knows I'm in the same room with him. He's not even eating. He just sits there drinking amber liquid from an over-sized tumbler. When we got here, he mumbled something about legal problems and has been sitting with his eyes closed, rubbing his temples all night. I don't know why he even wanted to be with me tonight. I feel like I'm intruding on his privacy.

I take a sip of my Pellegrino and say to him, "Blend isn't your real name is it?"

Slowly he opens his eyes, but his fingers keep massaging his temples. "Blend is what I go by because Blend is what I am."

"Yeah, I know, but that's not what your mother named you, is it?" Omigod, these famous people are obsessive about their privacy. What are they trying to hide?

He lets out a sigh and begins speaking to me as if he were indulging a small child. "I shed my real name and background to become who I am."

Okay. "Is it true that you're a combination of all races on the planet?"

"True dat," he answers. "My father is black and white. My mother is Peruvian, of Japanese and Inca ancestry. That covers it all. I'm a blend."

I guess he's right. Now that he mentions it, I do see hints of all the races in him. Besides his ruddy tan skin, he has knife-sharp cheekbones and beautiful almond-shaped eyes that do look Asian.

After several minutes of awkward silence, I begin my line of interrogation again.

"I read that you grew up in the Bronx. What was that like?"

"Man, it hurts even thinking about it," he says, slowly shaking his head. "It's hard for a mixed-race kid to grow up on the mean streets of the Bronx." He stares into nothing. "I practically raised myself. My father came and went and my mother worked 'round the clock to support me."

"I'm sorry." That had to be tough. I feel bad that I brought it up, so I drop it.

Blend starts staring at me in a way that makes my skin crawl. "My pure little girl." He gets off the couch and stretches. "Man, I could use a nice Jacuzzi to relax." He looks at me for the first time tonight. "Why don't you join me? Help me unwind. Would you do that for me? Please?"

A bath? He wants me to take a bath with him? That's going to be the first step in our relationship? He's got to be kidding. That is so yucky. Now what do I do?

At my hesitation, he insists, "Come on. Don't be a baby. It's so relaxing."

He grabs my arm, starts pulling me up from where I'm sitting, and begins kissing my neck and rubbing his hands over me in a detached sort of way. It's like I could be anyone. He doesn't even know it's me.

I feel a surge of adrenaline and remember what Tati told me to do when I feel uncomfortable. *Just say no.*

"I'm already relaxed," I say, pulling away from him, but I'm starting to get angry. "Besides, I don't think taking a bath with a guy I don't know very well is relaxing." There, I said it. If he cancels my party, let him. I don't care anymore. He's getting a little freaky.

Blend lets out a sigh. "It's not a bath, it's a Jacuzzi. You know, a hot tub."

Yeah, I know, I've seen it. It's a big whirlpool bathtub in the middle of his bathroom. It does have a spectacular view of the harbor, but then, so does this room.

"I don't have a bathing suit with me."

"You don't need one, it's just the two of us," he says, running his hand up my thigh. "Don't you want to get closer?"

The hand gets too high. I pull away. "No, thanks, I'll pass."

"Well, I'm taking a soak," he continues. "If you're going to be a baby about it, you don't have to get in. Come and keep me company."

He heads to the bathroom, leaving me to sit there uncomfortably. What I really want to do is go home, but I don't even know where the nearest subway stop is. I'm stuck here, at his mercy. Tears well in my eyes and I realize I'm shaking. This doesn't feel like love. It doesn't feel like anything I want to be a part of.

I hear him turn off the water and the bubbles kick in. He yells over the noise, "Hey, Mari, bring my drink in."

So much for my waiting this out. I pick up his glass and walk into the steamy room. He takes it and says, "You don't have to get in. Sit on the edge and keep me company." He stares at the glass wall. "I love this view."

It is magnificent. I always feel such energy from the lights of Manhattan. There's something magical about this city. The melody of "New York Nights" runs through my head.

Suddenly he grabs me and pulls me onto his chest and begins kissing me. I'm struggling to pull away, but he's got a tight grip on me. His hand comes up and tries to grab my boob, soaking my Kell E T-shirt in the process.

"Quit it!" I force myself up and step away from the tub, sliding on the wet marble.

"Somebody's all wet." He begins laughing and splashes me some more, getting water all over the floor. "Now you have to take your shirt off."

I look down. The fine cotton is completely see-through and so is my sheer nude silk bra. There's nothing left to imagine.

The other night at the Apollo a jolt of electricity ran through me when Blend touched me during our onstage kiss. I felt like I was becoming attracted to him and would enjoy getting to know him better. But instead of taking it slow and bringing me along, he ignored me all night and now assaults me like this. Yes, that's what it feels like. He doesn't need *me*. Any girl will do.

"Come on, take it off to dry. You can leave your panties on. I promise I'll be a perfect gentleman." He's laughing at his own joke, but it's not funny to me.

I'm trembling more from nerves than the air conditioning. How did I get myself into this mess? I should have listened to Lola's advice about him wanting more than a professional relationship. I feel so stupid. Everyone told me to be careful of Blend. Now I know what they were talking about. This night is getting more and more bizarre.

"Come on, get in here," he says excitedly.

Without warning he zones out. His eyes are closed and his head leans back. He's alone in the tub moaning all by himself. I've have to get out of here.

Blend's shirt is hanging on a hook. I grab it and throw it on over my T-shirt. Never mind the car; I'm hopping on the first train I find. For all the glamour and glitz of this apartment, I'd rather be home—safe in my little room in East Harlem.

CHAPTER 32

It's Never Really Over Between Us

The night was a rough one for me, tossing and turning, and replaying that horrible night in my head. I'm not sure what I could have done differently. I don't even know why I feel responsible for getting myself into that entire situation with Blend. He's the one who should be ashamed, not me. I want to get back to a simpler life, being the old Marisol, and hanging with my real friends. That's why I'm so excited when I get Julian's text in the morning.

got ur e-vite. want to hang?

Do I ever! Suddenly being with Julian seems like the most normal thing in the world. I text him back: time/place?

I'm going to meet him at the playground—our playground—at eleven. It's hard to remember that when I first met Julian, when I was fourteen, I was a little taken aback by the intensity of his attention. I was so overwhelmed by his energy. He chased me for a long time before I finally started seeing him.

Even then, being with Julian meant being together in our whole big group of friends. We spent our afternoons eating French fries and drinking Cokes at Casa de Felix. Movie "dates" involved a bunch of people, not couples. Kisses were snuck in dark public places like the park. We were never really alone.

Things were beginning to get physical, at least on Julian's part, but then my father died. That really rocked me and the last thing I could imagine was getting into that kind of relationship. It seemed as if I would be dishonoring my father. Julian and I fought about things and broke up.

After a few months, we got back together and were working our way slowly to where we left off. We were older now, and I was finally able to climb out of that black hole that sucked me in when my father died, so getting into things with Julian finally felt right. Then Cisco started calling me to sing for him on his karaoke gigs and that became a big problem for Julian. Again, we fought about things and broke up.

After being out with Diego and Blend, I realize that Julian's love was innocent and genuine. It was the real deal. I blew it by always putting my music career first. He must have felt awful every time I cancelled plans because I had a gig or wanted to hang out in a club with Cisco. Anytime something better came up, I blew him off. That had to be painful.

This morning I take as much care with my appearance as if I were going downtown. I wash my hair and scrub my skin to try to get the creepiness of last night off of me. After blow-drying my hair, I wind the top around big rollers for fullness while I put on a light touch of makeup.

My denim mini and citrus Kell E T-shirt with my gladiator sandals will give me a polished yet casual look for a day in the park. I want Julian to notice me. Who am I kidding? I want Julian back.

He's already sitting on our bench when I get to the playground, even though it's eleven on the dot. Beside him is a Dunkin' Donuts tray with two large coffees and a paper bag.

"Ooh, what do you have?" I ask. It took so long for me to get ready that I completely forgot about eating.

"Blueberry muffins and coffee. Two Splendas and half-and-half."

"Perfect," I say, and take a sip. I pick off a piece of the crunchy muffin top and pop it in my mouth. "Mmm, this is so good."

"Only you could get so excited about a muffin," he says, shaking his head.

The muffin is good, but it's not just that. I'm always overwhelmed by Julian's thoughtfulness. He didn't ask if I was hungry. He knows that I always forget to eat. That's why he brought breakfast. How sweet is that?

Even on our dates, he always took me to Enzo's and made me eat a slice of pizza, or to Casa de Felix, even though I told him I wasn't hungry. And he always holds doors for me when most boys let them slam in my face. Julian has these gentlemanly habits like a boy from a hundred years ago. They're just little nice things, but they always make me feel special.

I notice Julian checking me out and I sit up a little straighter. He's looking good too, in khaki cargo shorts and an olive green graphic T-shirt. He's wearing cool-looking kicks with low socks.

"So I got the e-vite to your party," he begins. "Sounds like a big deal."

My mouth is full of muffin, so I just nod. Then I swallow and say, "It's going to be banging. You coming?"

"Of course I am. I would never miss your birthday."

And that's another thing. Even though I never have birthday parties, Julian always comes over with a gift and takes me out someplace special. Last year we took the train to Coney Island for the day, just the two of us. We swam in the ocean and rode the rides at night. That day is one of my favorite memories.

Why did it take me so long to appreciate what I already had?

"It's going to be off the charts. Cisco is spinning and Tatianna designed a dress for me. I'm really excited."

I don't want to tell him that it's my professional debut with Blend's label and that I'll be singing a new song. My career is what always comes between us and I don't want to blow it again.

"Will you be bringing Vanessa?" I ask innocently.

"Why are you asking?"

"I saw the two of you having dinner together at Casa de Felix this week and you looked, I don't know, like you were on a date or something." I take another sip of my coffee. "Were you?"

"I don't know. Kind of, I guess."

I try to lighten it up but I have to know everything. "That's impossible, Julian. How can you not be sure if it was a date?"

He sits there eating his muffin while staring at the cars racing down the FDR in the distance. I think he's playing for time. Fine, let him think, but I will get to the bottom of this. One thing I do know: Vanessa seemed sure it was a date.

"Vanessa called me the night we—" he kind of chokes up—"the night you and I broke up."

That skunk! I told her about it right after it happened and she wasted no time going after him. Unless she had some major revelation at that moment, Vanessa must have been scoping Julian for a while.

"I don't know. We were both missing you and we started hanging together."

Oh, give me a break! If Vanessa missed me so much, why didn't she wave me into the restaurant like she always does? The look she shot me was poisonous. But I'm not going to badmouth Vanessa. I remember what happened when I talked about Solange.

He looks at me for the first time. "I thought she'd make me happy."

"So does she?"

He shakes his head. "I'm not sure what would make me happy."

I know. I'd make him happy if he could get over his jealousy.

Then he asks me, "Are you happy?"

I let out a bitter laugh. "That's a loaded question. Did you read the papers this week?"

He starts to laugh, which gets me going too. Leave it to Julian to make me see the funny side of the whole mess.

"Well, at least you looked pretty."

"Thanks a lot," I reply. "That's a big help." But it really is.

He looks me over again. "You look really pretty." He picks up a lock of my hair and winds it around his finger like he used to do when we were a couple.

See, I knew he still has feelings for me. But I have to close the lid on this Vanessa thing once and for all.

"You know what I don't get? Poor Angel, how did he feel about all this? He's crazy about Vanessa."

That should make him feel guilty. Julian loves his cousin and Angel worships him.

"He doesn't know about it. At least, I don't think he does." Julian sips his coffee. "It didn't go that far, we were only in public that once." He brings the lock of my hair up to his face and rubs his nose against it. Julian always loved the coconut smell of my shampoo. "I never even kissed her." With that, he leans in and kisses me. It's a long, soulful kiss and this kind of tingling feels just right.

Squealing girls interrupt our kiss. Summer school just let out and kids flock to the playground. This group is led by Raven—who has to pass gym before she can graduate—frantically texting, her eyes wild with excitement. When she's through, she comes running over to us.

"Hi, Julian," she says in a whiny sarcastic voice. She turns to me. "Hi, Marisol, what are the two of you doing here?"

As in—*together*.

I ignore the question and ask, "Are you coming to my party?"

"I guess. Is it really at Apple?" She can't hide her excitement about going to the trendiest club in the city. She'll be there. "What's everybody wearing?"

"I don't know. Tati and I are wearing dresses that she designed," I answer truthfully, but my statement causes her to pout.

"That's not fair. You two are going to have the best dresses there."

Well, it *is* my party and Tati *is* a clothing designer. I know better than to say it aloud.

I could swear I hear the Colon twins, but that's not likely. Suddenly they're climbing all over me.

"Mari, Mari!" They give me hugs.

I hug them back and give them kisses on the tops of their heads. "Hey, guys."

Vanessa comes running up, panting. She takes one look at Julian and me and her face gets pinched. She wasted no time coming down here to see if Raven's text is true. Now she can see for herself that I'm here with Julian. She eyes the Dunkin' Donuts stuff and knows we didn't just meet up. This was planned.

She says to Julian, "I thought you were working today."

He shrugs. "I decided to take the day off. It's too pretty to work."

If I look a little harder, I'm sure that I'll see steam coming out of her ears. Vanessa's eyes are darting back and forth between us, trying to get the whole scoop. Raven has that manic look she gets when she thinks there's going to be some action.

Personally I've had enough drama this week, so I ask Vanessa, "Are you coming to my party? Cisco and Tati are coming." Then I add mischievously, "I asked Angel too. Maybe the two of you can go together."

"Woo-hoo!" roars Raven. "Did you hear that, Vanessa? She doesn't know you're going with—"

"Raven!" Vanessa glares at her. She turns back to me. "Of course I'll be there," she says calmly. "Are you going with Blend? Tati said that he's giving the party for you."

Bitch! It's tough to have a verbal duel with someone who's smart. Vanessa was always a fast thinker but I'm not used to her sharp side. She used to be so sweet.

Her comments wipe the smile off Julian's face and he shifts on the bench. Once again my career barrels through, knocking us down in two different directions. Time for triage.

"Blend is giving the party to announce that he's signing me to his label," I explain sweetly to Vanessa. "It's a professional relationship, not a date." There, hopefully Julian will understand without me having to beg. "I'll be singing my new single at the party."

"Oh, good," she replies smoothly. "We'll get to hear it then."

How did our friendship get this strained? Only a few weeks ago we were so close. I guess I saw little hints of jealousy during these past few months, but I figured if I ignored them they'd go away. I love Vanessa, but now she can't stand the sight of me. It's not my fault she decided to move in on Julian and got hurt. She should have known that it's never really over between us.

Vanessa continues, "Well, I have to take the twins to their playgroups. Julian, will I talk to you later?"

He shrugs noncommittally. "I don't know, maybe."

Somehow, I doubt it and so does Vanessa.

All is not lost. Julian might have been rubbed the wrong way with the news about Blend, but he's not writing off our relationship. Maybe he's toughening up a little.

As for Vanessa, now I know I won the duel. Take that. *Touché!*

CHAPTER 33

No One Has a Soul

"Stand still while I'm pinning this," orders Tati. She managed to cram a sewing machine into the bedroom she shares with Vanessa. "Or else you're going to get jabbed."

That seems like the least of my worries. I haven't heard from Blend since that night and I'm not really sure I want to talk to him either. He really grossed me out with that whole hot tub thing. If it were anybody else, I would have told him where to go, but it's Blend, a powerhouse in the music business. I can't afford to offend him, but I'm not going do anything that makes me uncomfortable. I decided not to see him alone. I'd rather keep our relationship strictly professional.

I have to be smart about this. So instead of calling him directly, I'm communicating with his assistant, Skye. She keeps telling me that the party is still on, but she knows nothing about a song for me. How in the world am I supposed to learn a song well enough to perform as a pro?

"You framed some of your old sketches," I say to Tati, looking around the room. She has been creating outfits since forever. Now some of her old designs are pressed in distressed white frames over her bed.

She looks up. "Yeah, I was going through an old box of sketches and picked out a few that still would work." I try to sneak a peek at what she's doing, but she grabs my leg. "Stand still. You can look when I'm through."

I'm getting anxious. I have all these people coming and I don't have a song to sing. I'm going to end up looking like a fool two times in one week—first as Diego's fake girlfriend and now as a clueless singer. At least I'll be looking good. This is one amazing dress. Tati's a genius.

"This dress is even more spectacular than the sketch you showed me. Say, have you heard from Reggie?"

She shoots me an impatient look. "When have I had time? Between your dress, my dress, and work, I haven't had a minute to myself."

"I know, I know, I was wondering if he said anything about Blend. I haven't heard from him since our last date and that didn't go well."

"Why? What happened?" she mumbles with pins in her mouth.

I'm embarrassed to admit the details, but I need someone to talk to, and Tati is the only person who knows all the players.

"He groped me and tried to get me into the Jacuzzi." Even thinking about it turns my stomach.

"What?" she screams, shooting pins at me. "How did you get yourself into that mess?"

So I explain the whole story to her and tell her that my T-shirt was clinging and see-through and so was my bra. "I was so scared. But the weird thing was, by the time I turned around, he was . . ." I've had a long time to think about this, but I'm afraid to admit it to myself.

"What?"

"I'm not positive but he was kind of in his own world." I can tell she's confused, so I say, "You know, his hands were under the water, his eyes were half-closed and he kept saying, 'That's right. That's right.' And then he zonked out. You don't think he was—"

"*Eww!*" she screams. "Yeah, I'll bet he was. That's so disgusting."

I cover my face with my hands. We can't both be wrong.

"Tell me about it. I was there. Anyway, I stole his shirt off the hook and tossed it over my wet T-shirt and ran up to Christopher Street to catch the subway." Just repeating this makes me queasy. "I haven't heard from him since. That's why I wanted to know if you've talked to Reggie."

"We'll call him later and see what he knows." Tati continues pinning. "God, Blend's such a perv. Just forget him."

"Believe me, I want to, but I don't want to piss him off. He's powerful in this business."

The bedroom door opens and Vanessa walks in.

"Hey, *déjà vu*," I say to her, trying to be upbeat. "It seems like we've been here before, trying on party dresses." That's always been our ritual for any party we ever went to.

She plops down on the bed and flips through a magazine.

"Yeah, but it's always been you and me, and now it's you and Tati."

I look at Tati and she rolls her eyes. Vanessa *is* jealous but I can't get into this with her. Part of me wants to apologize—for what, I don't know—and part of me wants to smack her and tell her to snap out of it.

"Well, it's Tati's design. Beautiful, isn't it?" I ask.

She looks up from the magazine. "It would be nice if she made something for her *sister* to wear to the party."

"Give me a break!" shouts Tati. "How many dresses can I make in a week? Between the two of us, we have a closet full of clothes. Pick something and wear it. It's not like you're going to be photographed."

Vanessa jumps off the bed and leaves the room, slamming the door behind her. She just got on my last nerve—and Tati's too.

"You know," I begin softly, because I'm not sure if she's listening outside the door, "she likes Julian."

Tati wrinkles her nose. "I don't see that happening. Besides, he likes you. That's obvious."

That's good to hear, but I'm not so sure about it. After the showdown in the park, we kind of went our separate ways. Suddenly Julian had to work that afternoon, so I told him I had to go home and practice my song—the one I don't have yet.

On the one hand, it's good. I don't want Julian thinking that he's my date for the party. Even if Blend doesn't pick me up, he will send a car. He wouldn't want to see Julian getting out of it with me. Plus, this is a business party. If Julian is there, I'll keep worrying about his feeling left out when I have to meet different people. I don't want him to throw another fit and storm out.

Tati's phone rings and she checks to see whose calling. "It's Reggie," she says. "Hey, what's up?" Instead of making myself scarce, I'm hanging on her every word. "Uh-huh, uh-huh." Oh, that's helpful.

"Ask about Blend," I hiss.

She holds up a finger. "Okay, that's great, I'll see you then." She flips the phone shut.

"Well?"

"Reggie's been with Blend," she explains. "It seems that he's having this huge legal thing going on, and when he's not in meetings with his legal team, he shuts himself off in his apartment."

"What kind of trouble?" I ask.

At least he's not pissed at me. I need the professional exposure this party will give me even if it means I have to face Blend again. Something else is bothering him. Still, shutting yourself off in your apartment seems a bit extreme even for a big legal issue.

"I don't know, but Reggie said he's picking me up for the party tomorrow night, so we know that's still on."

The party may be on but the party girl doesn't have a new song to sing. "No mention of a song for me, I suppose?"

"*Nada.*"

The other thing that's bothering me is that I don't have a contract with Blend. When we were at the beach, he made such a big thing about if Teddy Bear Barnes or Pablo Cruz really wanted me, they would have signed me to a contract. He swore that's what he would do. It's been over a week since we got together and there's no song and no contract.

I always dreamed of a career in music, but I had no idea about how the business end of it was run. Now that I'm getting a taste of it, I'm not sure I like it. No one has a soul in this business. They don't care about anyone because they have no hearts.

A melody drifts through my mind while I'm standing here thinking about Blend. Without thinking I begin singing along with it. *"You have no soul. You have no heart. You're a beautiful shell, but you tore me apart."*

"Cool song," says Tati. "Is it new? I haven't heard it yet."

"That's because I just made it up."

"Just now? Just like that?" She shakes her head. "You know, you should write your own song. Forget about Blend. Write your own and sing it at the party."

I laugh. "Yeah, and how am I going to do that? I can't write music and I don't play an instrument."

"No, but Cisco can."

That's right. Cisco always used to play the piano at family gatherings and everyone would sing along.

"Yeah, but doesn't Cisco play by ear?" I remember that people would call out tunes and he would play. "He can't read or write music."

"No, but I remember him telling me about some computer program he has on his laptop. He plays a tune on his keyboard, and the notes appear on the screen, something like that. He was going on and on about it, but I zoned out."

"Wow, that's really cool." This might work. "So if I sing a melody, he can play it on the keyboard and it will record on the computer. Then he can mix it." Now my mind is racing with possibilities.

"Yep, all you have to do is write the song." She unfastens the million little buttons running down the back of the dress. "You're done for now."

All I have to do is write the song. How hard can that be? But where in the world do I begin?

CHAPTER 34

I Want to Growl

I grab a long white legal pad from the supply in Lola's desk, along with a new gel pen from the box. Ever since Lola began doing freelance paralegal work from our apartment, she keeps a full stock of office supplies. I have no idea where to begin, so I jot down the lines I was singing for Tati.

You have no soul.
You have no heart.
You're a beautiful shell, but
You tore me apart.

That sounds more like a chorus to me. I've got to think of a way to begin the song. I have to tell a little story. This gets me thinking. It must be great not to have a soul. Nothing makes you feel bad. You certainly have no regrets. And the best thing about it is you have absolutely no trouble sleeping at night.

That's it!

Do you ever lie awake
All alone in your bed
Just trying to shake
Thoughts running through your head?

I keep working along these lines, scribbling my thoughts as fast as I can. I'm scratching out and trying to rhyme. It's not as easy as I thought, but not really that hard either. When I think I have it down the way I want it, I give Cisco a call.

"Hey, Mari, what's up?"

"Hey, Cisco, good buddy, good friend."

"Uh-oh, now you have me worried."

"No, no, nothing like that. I wrote a song and I need to put it to music. Tati said you have a program on your computer that writes music."

"Yeah, it's great." He starts to give me a detailed version of the technology involved, but not only don't I need to hear it, I'd never understand it.

"Whoa, whoa, Cisco, TMI." I shake my head to get the technical thoughts out. "Do you think if I come over and sing it you could play it on your keyboard?"

"I don't see why not." I detect a hint of enthusiasm in his voice. "What are you doing now? Want to come over and give it a try?"

"I'll be right there." I grab my trusty pen and notepad and head out the door.

———— ◆ ————

Randy is at Cisco's place when I get there, drinking beer and hanging out. Good, the more minds on this, the better. Besides, Randy has been surprising me lately with his raps and ideas. He's not just the roadie I had him pegged for when we started.

The equipment is already set up. I maneuver my way around the speakers and amps crowding the sparse living room. Cisco has his keyboard and laptop set up on the kitchen table and wires are running everywhere, like snakes making a mad escape from the reptile house.

"Hey, guys, thanks for this," I tell them, putting my stuff down and pulling out my pad.

"Nah, it's a good idea. It's going to work." Cisco motions for me to join him at the keyboard. "Grab a drink from the fridge."

I see dozens of beers, a few cans of soda, and way in the back, a lone bottle of water. I stretch my arm in and snag it.

"So I hear somebody was singing her little heart out at the Apollo the other night?"

"Yeah, how'd you hear about that?"

"Tati." He takes a long pull of his beer.

Of course.

Cisco puts his beer down and says, "Sing the song through for me once and then I'll come in on the second try. I have to hear the melody through once before I can play it."

Taking a deep breath, I begin to sing.

"Do you ever lie awake, all alone in your bed, just trying to shake, thoughts running through your head?"

It's kind of weird singing a song I wrote. It's like baring my innermost thoughts to the world. My nerves start to settle and I'm able to continue calmly, concentrating on getting the melody from my lips and into Cisco's head.

"Do you ever regret, all the things that you said, or did you simply forget, that you messed with my head?"

I break into the chorus, the same words I sang for Tati. Cisco's eyes are closed as if meditating on the tune. Randy is smiling and nodding his head to the rhythm. They like it, I can tell.

Now comes the rest of the song. This is the part that I plan to wail, but for now I simply sing it softly, making sure to get every note in.

God gave you a beautiful face
And a body to die for
But in your chest there's an empty space
To be a person you need so much more.

Now I can tell that Randy is really getting into this. That encourages me to really sing the rest.

So stay away from me.
I need to set myself free.
I can't live this way anymore.
I thought it out and I'm sure.

I finish by repeating the chorus, repeating the signature line, and sing the last word up one octave.

Randy starts hooting and clapping and Cisco comes out of his trance.

"Whoa, Mari, that is banging!" Randy keeps clapping those ham-like paws of his, the sound echoing through the apartment. The best thing about having no rugs, no curtains, and almost no furniture is that the acoustics are great. It's like singing in the shower.

"You really wrote that Mari?" asks Cisco. "It's really, really beautiful."

I preen a little. "Thanks, you guys." Then I ask Cisco, "Do you think you can play it?"

We practice it several times, recording each take. Cisco then sets it up with other instruments, playing background on the keyboard. You don't need friends with this gadget, he's a one-man band.

"Okay, Mari, this time we're going to give it a real try, so sing your little heart out."

I take a long sip of water and wait for the opening bars of my song. My song!

Do you ever lie awake
All alone in your bed
Just trying to shake
Thoughts running through your head?

Do you ever regret
All the things that you said
Or did you simply forget
That you messed with my head?

You have no soul.
You have no heart.
You're a beautiful shell, but
You tore me apart.
You have no soul.
You feel no pain.
You walked away from me
Without the need to explain.

God gave you a beautiful face
And a body to die for
But in your chest there's an empty space
To be a person you need so much more.

So stay away from me.
I need to set myself free.
I can't live this way anymore.
I thought it out and I'm sure.

You have no soul.
You have no heart.
You're a beautiful shell, but
You tore me apart.
You have no soul.
You feel no pain.
You walked away from me
Without the need to explain.

You have . . . no soul.

We play it back and Cisco and Randy are high-fiving each other. They turn to include me, but to tell you the truth, I wasn't *that* crazy about it. I mean I like the song, but it wasn't quite what I had in my head.

"What's the matter?" asks Cisco. "You don't like it?"

"No, I like it. It's just that . . ." I hesitate, not wanting to offend his arrangement. "Do you think it sounds a little too, I don't know, poppy?" Is that even a musical term?

"You mean like a pop tune?" He raises his eyebrows and wags his head back and forth. "Yeah, kind of, but that's what's in right now. Like Katy Perry, she's really hot right now."

"I like Katy Perry," adds Randy.

"I like her too, and she has a really wide vocal range, but she is who she is. I'm not like her."

If there's one thing I always care about it's not sounding like or imitating another singer. I want the version I sing to be my own.

"What do you mean?"

"Well for one thing, Katy is a performance artist as well as a singer, like Lady Gaga."

"I like Lady Gaga," adds Randy. Oh, brother.

"I like her too." Haven't we been here before? I need to take charge of this—it *is* my song. "It's just that I had something else in my head when I wrote it. I was trying to channel Janis Joplin singing 'Piece of My Heart' or Steven Tyler singing 'Dream On'. Those guys are really gritty and rock a ballad. That's what I was going for."

Cisco folds his arms across his chest. He's obviously not open to another interpretation.

Randy pipes up with, "I think you should do it like Mariah. You know, do some runs with the melody. You've got the vocal chops for it."

"Thanks." He does have a point. Mariah could sing the hell out of this. "But I really wanted to rock it. No one is doing that now except maybe Kelly Clarkson. I want my singing to be unique."

"Mariah is unique." Cisco feels the need to point out another Mariah Carey factoid. "And, may I add, she has a five-octave range."

That's a low blow. My range is still very impressive at four octaves, but now is not the time to be petty and quibble.

"Please, Cisco, can we try it more of a rock beat? Pretty please?" I ask. "I want to growl."

He laughs and rubs the top of my head. "How can I say no to that?" He kisses me on my forehead. "You're so pretty when you beg."

Cisco resets the background instruments and beat, giving it more rock. "How's that?"

"Great." I get ready to run through it again. This time I'm not afraid to let it rip.

God gave you a beautiful face
And a body to die for

I'm rocking it. Sneaking a peak at Cisco and Randy, I can see that they're into it too. I finish up the song, and we play it back.

"I like both versions," says Randy. "I'm not just saying that. They're both really good, different, but good."

Cisco is nodding in agreement. No one needs to ask which one I prefer.

Randy continues, "Here's what I think. We film Mari doing both versions and post them on YouTube. We'll see which gets more hits. Let the public decide."

"But I need this song for the party," I protest. "Blend still hasn't come up with a song for me to sing. I wrote this one to have something original to sing. If we put it out now, it won't be new."

Cisco is grinning one of his crazy grins. "So wait until after the party to post it. But there's one thing I know for sure, we're going to make a shitload of money on this song." He looks at me. "You're going to have to share the rights for the melody with me."

"You got it," I tell him. "This baby wouldn't have been born without you."

Randy claps once like a coach getting his team's attention. "Okay, let's record!"

I look down at my cut-offs and T-shirt. My hair is in a ponytail and I'm wearing next to no makeup. Never did I think I would be seen by millions of people today. "No way I'm going on YouTube looking like this, guys."

Cisco looks me up and down. "Yeah, you're right. Run home and change while we get everything set up."

Who needs the record companies when you have YouTube?

CHAPTER 35

It's Rocking, It's Raw

What to wear? What to wear? I'm confused about this. I'm not even sure who my audience will be. I could be getting hits from kids all across American. I might even go global. I have to get my look right without making it seem as if I'm trying too hard.

When in doubt, call Tati. "Hey, I know you're busy, but I need fashion advice."

"Well, you called the right person. What's up?"

"You were right about Cisco. He not only recorded the song, but we did two versions of it. That guy is a musical genius."

Tati lets out a little laugh. "I know. I know. Genius happens to run in our family. Now what kind of fashion advice do you need from this fashion genius?"

I run through how we're going to have a contest on YouTube and let the public decide if they like the pop or rock version better. "I'm going through my closet, but I'm not sure what my look should be. If I wear one of my performing outfits, I'll look like a New York hootchie mama. On the other hand, if I wear a mini and T-shirt, I might look like those people lined up to get in the clubs. You know the ones who don't get in because they're not dressed up enough?"

"Umm, yeah, I see your point." Tati is silent for a moment and I know better than to disturb her thinking process. "Here's what you do. Put on your jeans, good ones, not your hang-out-with-my-sister jeans, and your boots to give yourself a long, lean line." Good, this is all good. "Then take the black top from the daytime outfit you got from Kell E, the one with the tortoise shell clasp, and wear that on top. Wear your gold hoops and that's that. Sexy, but casual."

"Oh, Tati, that's perfect. That's just the look I should have," I tell her. "Hey, I know you're super busy, but why don't you take a break and meet me at Cisco's? You can hear the song, and then maybe we can do something afterward."

She hesitates. "Yeah, you know what? I could really use a break. Besides, I'm almost finished here. I only have to put up a hem and I can do that tomorrow. That sounds good. I'll meet you at Cisco's place."

Yes! Tonight's going to be a great night.

"And Mari," adds Tati, "remember to blow out your hair and take some time with your makeup. You're going viral."

From her lips to God's ears.

————— ✦ —————

By the time I get to Cisco's Tati is already there. She's wearing a version of my outfit, jeans, a halter top made from a tan chamois material, and her bronze heels. Tati, being Tati, added a jaunty little raffia-cropped fedora for a statement. She looks fantastic as always, and inspects her creation, me.

"Perfect." That's all I need to hear, but I get a "Whoa" from Randy and Cisco encourages me with "You look hot!"

Remembering what he said to me the other night when he picked me up for work, I ask him, "Not like a hooker?"

He laughs his braying laugh. "No, but you looked hot then too."

They've already cleared a space in front of the one wall in Cisco's apartment that's painted an industrial gray. I never knew why, but never cared enough to ask.

Randy explains, "I thought this would work with your hair." *Aww.* "And I was afraid the white walls would be to stark and reflect too much light."

Who knew Randy had such an artistic eye? I take my place in front of the wall and Randy gives me the microphone.

"You want to practice again or should we just go for it?" asks Cisco.

"Nah, we practiced enough today. Let's do it." I tell him. "We'll record the pop version first." This way I won't have to worry about straining my voice during the rock version.

I begin the opening verse, "*Do you ever lie awake all alone in your bed . . .*"

Tati is sitting in a space that she cleared for herself on the sofa. I can tell from her face that she's impressed. I finish the pop version, and she says, "Mari, I can't believe you wrote that. It's as good, maybe even better, than anything on the radio."

High praise, especially from Tatianna, who doesn't get excited about much.

Cisco starts up the music for the rock version. I give it everything I've got, singing with a passion that I didn't know was in me. By the time I get to, "*So stay away from me. I have to set myself free . . .*" Tati is sitting up on the arm of the sofa, rocking to the beat, and I know I nailed it.

I sing the closing line softly, and bring the last note up one octave. I did the same in the pop version, but I think it has so much more impact in this one.

"And we're clear," announces Randy.

Tati jumps up off the sofa, applauding wildly. "That's the one. That's my favorite."

"Really?" asks Cisco, like he can't believe it. He's sticking with his version.

"Absolutely. The first version is great—I loved it—but it sounds like the other songs out there. This version is unique. It's rocking. It's raw. Best of all, no one but Mari could possibly sing it."

That's my girl! I'm glad I thought to invite her. Now it's not two against one. Cisco always listens to his cousin.

———— ◆ ————

Being at Casa de Felix tonight feels like old times. Julian, Angel, and Vanessa are already at our usual table waiting for their dinner. I'm thrilled to see that Vanessa is sitting next to Angel and not Julian. Randy and Cisco pull up another table and put it next to theirs, while Julian and Angel arrange the chairs. Vanessa is busy glaring at everyone while trying to ignore both Tati and me.

"Sit over hear, Mari," says Julian, pulling out the chair next to him. I take him up on his offer. Let Vanessa see once and for all that she doesn't stand a chance with him.

"Man, I'm starving," says Randy. "I feel like I put in a full day's work."

"You did," I say to him. "And you did a great job." I lift my Coke. "To Cisco and Randy!"

We toast with our sodas and Julian asks, "What are we drinking to?"

Randy bursts in to explain. "Mari wrote a song and Cisco helped her set it to music. You have to hear it, it's banging."

"You wrote a song?" asks Julian. Now even Vanessa is paying attention. "Wow, I didn't know you knew how to do that."

"Neither did I," I admit. "I just gave it a shot. Cisco is the one who brought it to life. He set it to music and Randy filmed me singing it."

"It's going out on YouTube right after the party," adds Tati, studying her menu. "I want the chicken, but I can't eat the whole half, I only want the white meat."

Felix makes the best rotisserie chicken in the world. It's really moist and tasty, but he won't tell anyone what kind of rub he uses to season it.

"I'll split it with you," I tell her. "I like dark meat better, anyway."

We order the chicken and two mixed salads with avocado and lime.

"Girl food," announces Randy. "Give me a big platter of *ropa vieja* with rice and beans." The shredded flank steak is another specialty of the house.

"Sounds good," says Cisco. "Make that two."

It feels so warm and toasty to be back together like this. It reminds me of all of those times after school, sitting around, eating French fries and drinking Cokes. The group falls into its old patter, except for Angel who never really says much anyway. Even Vanessa gets over her mad and starts chatting with Tati and Cisco. We talk about everything and nothing, like good friends are supposed to do.

The food comes and we're about to dig in when Freddie walks through the door. I haven't seen him since the viral video he made with Raven and Solange. Apparently, neither has anyone else by their response.

"My man," shouts Randy, standing up to pull him in for a hug and clap him on the back.

Vanessa and I eyeball each other. At last, something we agree upon.

Cisco stands to give Freddie a hug. "Hey, great video, I put it up on the flat screen. You know, give the ladies something to consider."

Ugh, even Cisco liked it.

Tati rolls her eyes. At least Julian has the decency to just say hey to Freddie, and leave it alone. What is it with these guys and that kind of stuff? I'd be mortified if it was me.

"Hey, Mari, I got your e-vite." He pauses to order a Coke. "Can I bring a date?"

"Sure, why not?" I wonder if he can hear the sarcasm dripping from my voice. Tati does and smothers a laugh. Now I feel that it really doesn't matter who he brings. My life is finally on the right track. I'm the one having a big, glamorous birthday party at Apple. In a few days, a song that I actually wrote is going to be viewed by millions on YouTube.

Who cares if he brings Solange? It was a waste of my time and energy to worry about her in the first place. It's amazing how freeing it is to put old negative feelings behind you.

I turn to Julian and smile as I watch him eat his burger.

"What?" he asks through a mouthful of food.

"Nothing, I just love being with you." And with that I steal one of his fries.

CHAPTER 36

Surprised by Love

Around midmorning a messenger arrives at my door and hands me a package. It's a small box from a jewelry store. I open the gift card first.

Happy Birthday. Wear these tonight.

Blend

At least I know he's alive and my party is a go. Maybe he didn't write a song for me, but that's okay, I wrote one for myself. I open the blue velvet box. Omigod! Diamond earrings are winking at me. They're not those huge ghetto studs, but they're much bigger than Lola's. Of course I'll wear these tonight.

I run to my mirror and slip them in. Thank goodness they're screw-backs or else I'd be afraid to lose them. Fluffing my hair back to show my ears, I turn my head from side to side. They're gorgeous.

The apartment door opens and Lola comes in. I haven't seen her in a week and I run to give her a hug.

"I missed you," I tell her, as Cha-Cha jumps at my legs to get in on the action.

She squeezes me back. "Me too. Happy birthday, baby."

We pull away and she notices my earrings. "Where did you get those?" she asks with a frown.

I kneel on the floor to play with Cha-Cha. He missed me as much as I missed him.

"A messenger just delivered them. They're from Blend."

She looks a little angry. "Well, you're not going to keep them." It sounds more like a statement than a question.

"Why not?"

"Mari," she says, like she's explaining something to a small child, "Those are very expensive earrings. It's not a proper gift for a grown man to give an eighteen-year-old girl that he barely knows. You're going to have to return them."

Oh, no, I'm not! I love these earrings and I'm keeping them. There's no way Lola can force me to give them back.

"He wants me to wear them tonight for my performance," I say to her. "I need to shine."

"And trust me, there's something he wants in return," she says bitterly.

If only she knew. I sit on the floor and stew while Cha-Cha jumps in and out of my lap.

"Oh, Mari, you have to have faith in my judgment on things like this," she says more gently. "I know you're a strong young woman from the way you've been handling your singing career, but when it comes to men, you're very naïve. If you're father was here with us, I'm sure he'd agree with me."

That's a low blow. Every time Lola wants to prove her point, she reminds me that it's exactly what my father would want—and I cave.

"Can I at least wear them to the party?" I feel my voice choking. "I promise I'll return them at the end of the night."

Lola starts to chuckle. "I suppose so."

I clap my hands. "Good! Because they're perfect with my dress. Ooh, you have to see it. Tati is a genius! The cleaners are giving it a professional pressing."

"I can't wait," she says, more like her old self. "Cha-Cha, go get Mari her gift."

He runs to Lola's tote bag and retrieves a slender box wrapped in pink paper with a big gold bow on top, and drops it in my lap.

"Happy birthday from Cha-Cha and me," she says. "Open it up."

Too late, I'm already tearing off the wrapping. I lift the lid on the jewelry box.

"Omigod, it's beautiful."

It's a gold link bracelet with a little heart charm dangling off. On one side of the heart are my initials: MR. On the reverse is the inscription: Love, Lola & Cha-Cha 7/22.

I say to her, "No one ever gave me anything so lovely."

I jump up and give her another hug, which triggers a demanding yip from Cha-Cha. I pick him up and smother him with kisses. Tears flood my eyes and I can feel myself getting choked up.

"Why are you crying?"

Taking a long sniff, I tell her, "It's been such a hard year for both of us." I keep fingering the gold heart. "And, I don't know, this heart, it just means . . ." I'm sobbing full-out now and feel like such a jerk.

"I know. I know," Lola says softly, giving me another hug.

But I feel I have to get this out now because we've never said it before. I don't think I fully realized it until now.

"The heart means we love each other. We're really a family, you and me." Crazy barking interrupts me. "And Cha-Cha."

Papi and Lola had only been married a little over two years when he was killed. He was the glue that held us together. After the accident, Lola and I kind of stuck together by default and because I have no other family, she became responsible for me. But now I realize that our feelings grew into real love. I'm not all alone. I have Lola.

"Lola, I never thanked you for taking care of me after Papi died."

"Mari, we took care of each other," she insists. "I'm not sure how I would have survived if I didn't have you to come home to each day."

So I guess that's how love grows, without thinking about it or forcing it, just two people who like and respect each other. I wonder if that will happen with Julian.

"Come on," she says, "I'll make some tea. I'll bet you didn't have breakfast."

She's right, of course. Once again I forgot to eat. I follow her into the kitchen along with Cha-Cha.

"So how was the beach?" I ask.

"I absolutely love it out there. We might return later tonight instead of waiting for morning."

"You drove all the way back just to go to my party?"

"We drove back so that I could spend your birthday with you."

Omigod, I'm getting welled up again. See, that's what family is. That's real love.

CHAPTER 37

Nothing Can Bring Me Down

My errands for the day are done. I got a fresh mani/pedi and picked up my dress from the cleaners. I wish I could have gone back to Butterfly Studios for my hair, makeup, and nails, but Blend didn't offer and I didn't want to ask. It doesn't matter. I can do it myself and probably better than one of the tacky salons in the neighborhood. As it is, I had to fight with the nail tech to use the bottle of Shimmering Blush nail polish that I got at Butterfly Studios. They wanted to use hot pink!

Blend hasn't called me since that awful night at his apartment, but his assistant did and told me that a car would be sent to pick me up. Once again, I asked her if he had a song for me, even though it's too late to learn it in time for the party, but she didn't have any info about that. I'm not going to worry about it. In fact, it will actually be better if I sing my own tune. That way it will get noticed by a lot of people in the industry. Maybe someone will offer me a record deal. Right now I need to practice my vocals because I didn't get a chance to do it this morning.

Even on a super busy day, I always make time to exercise my voice. I've got to; that's the only way to keep my instrument tuned. I can't afford to get lazy, and besides, I'm happiest when I'm singing. Whatever problems I'm having become more manageable after a good vocal workout.

I run my scales while flipping through the stack of CDs to see what will catch my mood. Something upbeat, I think, loading the Black Eyed Peas. Tonight is going to be a good night; it's my party, after all. I sing through all the party songs—Cee Lo, Ne-Yo, Gaga—even though they're not vocally challenging, they suit my feelings. Nothing can bring me down.

The shrill sound of the phone interrupts my practice. Normally I'd let it go, but because tonight is the party, it might be important.

"*Hel-loo* . . ." I sing into the phone as I lower the volume on the system.

"Hey, Mari, what's up?"

Julian! I get a little adrenaline rush. Lately I never know if I should be excited or fear the worst when I hear his voice. I hope he's not mad about the upcoming YouTube video. With Julian you can never tell.

"Nothing, just practicing," I answer, trying to sound cool.

"Look, I know tonight's your party—"

Omigod, is he calling to cancel?

"—and you're probably really busy, but I was wondering if you could get away for a few minutes?"

That's it. He's cancelling. I know it. The new song pissed him off.

"Sure, Julian, where do you want to meet?" I try to keep my tone light and upbeat.

"I'm almost at your block. Come down and I'll meet you in front of your building."

A hundred different reasons for why Julian needs to talk to me in person go through my mind as I wait out front, anxiously looking for him. What if he heard about my singing at the Apollo with Blend? Whatever it is has to be too important to say over the phone. But when Julian rounds the corner, I can see that he's carrying a small gift bag. Aww! Of all the thoughts I've been thinking, giving me a present didn't come into play.

"Is that for me?" I ask, grabbing for the bag.

He snatches it away. "Maybe. Let's go to the park."

Once we're settled on our favorite bench, the very same one where we first kissed, Julian hands me the bag. "Happy birthday, Mari."

"Ooh!" I grab the bag and take out a little box wrapped in silver paper with a pink bow. "This is a surprise. I love surprises," I say, looking up into those puppy-dog eyes.

"I know. I didn't want to bring it tonight. I figured either we wouldn't have time alone so I could give it to you or it would get lost on some gift table. Go ahead, open it."

He's as excited as I am as I rip off the wrappings. I look at him before opening the lid. "Want me to guess?"

"Just open it already." He's laughing because he knows me. I don't have the patience to guess.

"Oh, Julian, it's beautiful!" Inside the box is a creamy white pearl, attached to a fine gold chain, nestled on peach velvet. I'm fascinated by the pinks and greens reflecting in the sunlight. To think that such a beautiful pearl grew inside a shell at the bottom of the ocean. Maybe this is what I really wished for when I threw that shell back into the sea.

Julian is smiling down at me. "Do you like it?"

"Oh, Julian, this is magnificent. Thank you so much. I love it."

"I wanted you to have something special for your eighteenth birthday." He brushes my cheek with the back of his fingers. I love when he does that. "Something to symbolize the two of us."

Tears run down my face. I refuse to cry because I can't have swollen eyes for tonight.

"Here," he says, removing the necklace from the box, "let me help you put it on." He fastens the chain around my neck.

I touch the pearl with my fingertips. "I can't believe you did this for me."

"Of course I did. I love you, Mari." Those words make my heart melt.

"Oh, Julian, I love you too." I throw my arms around his neck.

We hold each other for what seems like forever, just feeling the comfort of our hug. This is real love.

CHAPTER 38

Some Party!

The Town Car drops me off at the club well before the party starts so Blend and I can greet our guests at the door. There's a big sign out front:

Private Party

Invited Guests Only

But it doesn't stop a group of gawkers from hanging out to catch sight of a celebrity. My friends from the 'hood will have a good time posing for the paparazzi and feeling like celebrities, so that's kind of cool.

I walk into the club. To the left of the front entrance, a huge wall is set up with repeating ads for Cristal champagne and Tag Heuer watches. Spotlights are set up to focus on it.

A small group of photographers are hanging out. One says to me, "You're Marisol, right? Pose in front of the wall."

It feels really weird to know absolutely nothing about what's going on with my own party, but I do as I'm told without question. Kell E's advice about posing for photographers rings through my head, as I turn sideways and twist forward, always keeping a smile on my face for the camera as the photographer snaps away.

I ask the photographer, "What's with all the ads?" I've seen backdrops like this behind pictures of celebrities in the tabloids, but this is only my birthday party.

"Pretty standard. Cristal and Tag Heuer are underwriting the party," he answers.

"As in, paying for it?" No, that can't be. Why would two big companies pay for my birthday party?

He nods. "Yeah, you got it."

I think to myself, *Blend put no effort into this.* His assistant put the whole thing together and Cristal and Tag Heuer are paying for it. The only thing Blend had to do was come up with a song for me and he didn't even bother to do that.

At that moment, Blend walks in, dressed to kill in a buff-colored suit with a peach shirt and tie. Following him is his usual entourage of Lamar and Reggie, along with a few other guys I recognize from the beach house and Sylvia's.

But wait a minute. Reggie is here, but where's Tati? Don't tell me she's not coming, or even worse, he forgot to pick her up. I better give her a call and find out what's happening, but Blend approaches and leads me to the wall of advertising.

Blend poses with me for the photos, but doesn't greet me with a kiss on the cheek or anything other than businesslike professionalism. I feel like he doesn't want to be seen with me, which is strange. He's announcing me as a new singer on his label. It's only natural that we have a cordial working relationship. Besides, this is a happy occasion. Well, who knows, maybe there's a new girlfriend in his life and she's jealous. Fine with me; I only want to sing, not romp in his Jacuzzi.

When the photographer is through, I say to Blend, "I thought I'd hear from you this week. What's up with the song I'm supposed to sing tonight?"

He looks away and swipes his hand over his chin. "Ah, there was no time for that this week. Maybe you can do one of your numbers with that guy you work with."

That guy I work with! This is the night I'm supposed to be launching my new career and he wants me to sing a song with Randy? Well isn't he going to be surprised? I'll be up there with Cisco, but I'll be performing a song of my own. This is my chance to shine.

I stomp my foot and spin around. Let him think that I'm upset about the song. He'll be even more surprised when he hears me sing. I know I keep saying to myself that things don't matter, but they do, even though I have a Plan B. Blend was supposed to supply a professional song and sign me to his label. Deep down inside, I envisioned myself up on that stage performing my new future hit for the music community. Now I feel like I was hired to sing karaoke at one of Blend's parties. I mean, what if my song isn't as good as my friends are saying? Then I'm really going to look like amateur night at the Apollo.

Cisco and Randy are setting up, so I go over to hang with them.

"Hey, Singer Girl," Cisco calls out. "Are you ready for your big number tonight?" He takes a good look at my face. "What's up, did Blend come through with another song?"

I shake my head. "Blend didn't arrange anything for me."

"You've got nothing to worry about," Randy says. "This party is all about you singing your new song. You've got this one covered."

"Are you sure it's good enough?" Now that the time is near, I'm beginning to doubt myself. That super shot of confidence I was riding high on yesterday is beginning to fade away.

Both Cisco and Randy protest, but I'm scared. I can't fall on my face in front of all these people.

"Cisco, hand me the catalog, the big one with all the songs." I thumb through in search of an old tune. That's what I'm focused on right now. I'm going to sing a number that really shows my range and wow these people. Big deal, so it's not my song. But from now on, every time these people hear it, they'll think of me.

"Load up 'Piece of My Heart' for me, Cisco." It's an old Janis Joplin tune that I love to wail. The lows are gritty and dirty, and the high notes hit the stars. I can rock the heart and soul out of this song. Lola introduced me to Joplin and when I sing this at home, I really let it rip. Besides, with all I've been through lately—with Diego, Blend, Julian, and even my friends—I feel like I really did lose a little piece of my heart. Move over Janis, I'm making this song my own. Tonight is going to be my night after all.

But before I get a chance to check the arrangement that's on the loop, I get called away.

Guests are arriving and I have to be there to greet them. I stand next to Blend and shake the hand of everyone he introduces to me.

Tati walks in and I immediately jump on her, "Omigod, I'm so glad to see you. When Reggie walked in with Blend and you weren't with him, I worried."

"He called earlier and asked if I could get to the party on my own." She looks a little peeved. "So I hitched a ride with the gang from the ghetto, Julian, Nessa, that whole bunch."

"Well, I'm so happy you made it." I kiss her cheek.

"Let me see how you look."

I twirl around slowly to model my outfit.

Tati takes in the total look. "You are rocking that dress!"

"It's from a talented new designer—Tatianna. Have you heard of her?" We burst out laughing. "You look fabulous too." She's wearing the super-distressed version of the dress she wore the other night. It has the same slashes as the other one, only in bronze sueded silk this time. And instead of a contrasting silk lining, Tati is wearing a flesh-toned body stocking that makes her look like she's naked underneath. Her silky black hair is flowing straight down her back. Only Tati could carry it off.

People keep pushing in so there's no time to chat. Finally all my friends from the neighborhood walk in together.

"We rented a limo," gushes Raven, "and the paparazzi were taking our pictures when we got out of it." So that explains the lag time between Tatianna's arrival and the rest of the crew. The ghetto gang, as Tati branded them, was posing for the paparazzi as if they were celebrities. Good for them.

"This is so great." Vanessa gives me a hug and a kiss. "Happy birthday, Mari."

"I'm so glad you're here," I say to her and I mean it. It feels like the old Vanessa is back and I'm thrilled.

Angel follows her, awkwardly nodding and mumbling, "Happy birthday." That's Angel. I'm surprised he got that many words out of his mouth.

Then in come the glamour couple. Freddy and Solange walk in with more swagger than Beyoncé and Jay-Z. I can't believe she's got those stupid knock-off sunglasses on top of her head. I mean it's dark out.

"Happy birthday, Mari," says Freddie, giving me a kiss. Solange just shows her Chiclets teeth and waltzes past. Some attitude—she wasn't even invited.

"Happy birthday, Mari, you look beautiful," Julian whispers in my ear. "You're wearing my pearl." This makes him smile and he looks as happy as I feel.

My hand automatically goes to my neck. "Of course I am. I love it." And I love him. "I haven't taken it off since you put it around my neck."

"Have fun," he says. "I'm going over to hang with Cisco for a while. I'll catch up with you later."

He walks into the party and I admire his cool retreating image. Maybe, just maybe, he's going to be okay with me working this party. It *is* business, but that never stopped us from fighting about it before.

He's followed by Kell E, who gives me the once-over. "Who designed your dress?" she demands.

It would have been impossible for her not to notice. This dress is amazing; I've never seen anything else like it. These large crinkles of silk in soft shades of coral and bold persimmon look like flowers. The way Tati arranged them on the sheer silk netting tricks the eye. Of course the dress would make Kell E curious—she thinks that she's the only designer dressing me.

I'm not sure if Tati wants me to say anything but, if she didn't, she should have said something earlier. "It's a gift from Tatianna. She made it for me for my birthday."

There, no one can find fault with a birthday present. Kell E storms away, in search of someone—most likely Tati.

My throat is dry, and I would kill for a bottle of water. But Lola and Pablo arrive and he pulls me off the line. "We have to talk."

While he's perp-walking me to a dark corner, I'm wondering if I messed up by letting Blend give me this party. After all, Pablo was kind of representing me and he did tell me to stay away from Blend.

When we're far enough away from the other guests, he says, "Taylor Fox can't do Diego's CD. She checked into rehab this afternoon." Yeah, so what? That's her problem. This has nothing to do with me.

"The cut is yours if you want it. Can you be at Teddy Bear's studio tomorrow morning?"

"I guess so," I murmur. I'm not sure how this conflicts with Blend's signing me to his label.

"No guessing, Marisol, this is business. Yes or no? Do you want to do it and will you be there?"

What am I thinking? Blend never offered me a contract. He doesn't even have a song for me to perform tonight. Forget him!

This time I don't hesitate. "Yes!"

Pablo smiles and pats me on the shoulder. "That's my girl. I'm taking Lola back to the beach later tonight. Will you be okay at the studio by yourself? If not, tell me and I'll be there for you. We can always head out there tomorrow night."

"Of course," I tell him. "I'll be fine." And I will be. I feel like I can do anything. "And Pablo, thank you, this is the best birthday present ever."

"My pleasure, just knock them dead the way you did during the demo."

We head into the main room just as Blend gets onstage to welcome everyone and make his big announcement.

"Ladies and gentlemen, thank you all for coming to this evening for a double celebration. Tonight you're going to meet the newest star in Blend's constellation. I signed her today."

Oh, no, he didn't! I never signed anything. Blend ought to know better—he's the one who taught me that if a label really wanted me, they would make me sign a contract right then and there. I walk up onto the makeshift stage to a polite round of applause and wait for Cisco to cue up "Piece of My Heart." But as the opening bars begin, it's a different song. Cisco is going with the rock version of "No Soul."

I look back to find Cisco and Randy grinning at me. This makes me smile. Hey, when they're right, they're right. I have no choice but to go with my tune.

Did you ever lie awake
All alone in your bed

Just trying to shake
Thoughts running through your head?

I sneak a peek out into the audience. The talking died down and they're listening. At least I have everyone's attention.

Do you ever regret
All the things that you said
Or did you simply forget
That you messed with my head?

I look at Julian, not that those words are meant for him, but I want to see if he likes the song. He is positively beaming. He's proud of me!

You have no soul.
You have no heart.
You're a beautiful shell, but
You tore me apart.

Now I'm looking directly at Blend who has the decency to flinch a little. Good.

God gave you a beautiful face
And a body to die for
But in your chest there's an empty space
To be a person you need so much more.

I'm growling this song right at him and he knows it. He can't even hold my eye. If he still thinks there will be a business relationship between us, I will leave him in no doubt.

So stay away from me.
I need to set myself free.
I can't live this way anymore.
I thought it out and I'm sure.

I bring the chorus home for the last time and hit that high note on the word *soul*. The cheering begins before I can complete that note and take a bow. I'm looking at all these music people cheering for me—omigod, even Diego and Eduardo are out there smiling. But it's the sight of my friends and Lola smiling and clapping that fill me with so much joy, I feel like I'm going to burst.

Blend walks up on stage as the ovation is dying down. "Tonight is a very special night for this young lady as she's celebrating—"

He's cut off by a commotion near the door and then a loud crash. Police officers and people in FBI jackets burst into the room. "FBI!" shouts one man. Then he looks right at Blend. "We have an arrest warrant for Norman Katzenbaum."

Norman Katzenbaum, who's that? Police rush the stage and hand-cuff Blend. Why are they handcuffing Blend when they should be going after Norman Katzenbaum?

The FBI agent says to Blend, "Norman Katzenbaum, you are being charged with molesting minors, possession of child pornography, trafficking in interstate pornography . . ."

Stunned, I tune the rest out. I can't believe this is the same man I know. What am I saying? I don't know him. I didn't even know his real name. No wonder he's been preoccupied this week. He must have had a clue this was coming. But I'll bet he didn't think it was going down here.

I cover my mouth with my hand as they trot Blend past me. He stops and looks me in the eye but doesn't say a word. I search for some sign of remorse but there's none. His eyes are cold and unrepentant.

Suddenly the room is filled with paparazzi who snuck in through the kitchen door. More of them storm in through the front after the police escort Blend out. Cameras are flashing and microphones are being stuck in everyone's faces. Once again I'm smack in the middle of a scandal. Only last week I made the papers as Diego Salazar's scorned lover. This week I'll be the minor Blend molested.

Molested! Yeah, that's what it was. When he grabbed me, wet my shirt, and stuck his hands up my skirt he molested me. I wasn't a willing participant in that. Being physical with him was the last thing I wanted. Not that I'll ever tell. I don't want any more bad publicity. His ugly secret is safe with me, even though he doesn't deserve it.

I can't believe the cast of characters giving interviews. Kell E is holding court with a news crew, posing in her own design. Raven is gushing to a reporter and smiling for pictures. Solange is telling reporters that she starred in Blend's last video as the entire crew hangs on her every word.

Cisco turns the music up, adding to the circuslike atmosphere.

I'm almost blinded by a bright light in my eyes. "You're the girl who used to date Diego Salazar." A reporter shoves a microphone in my face.

"No, no, Diego and I are good friends."

"I remember you from the red carpet," he insists. "What was your name again?"

"Marisol Reyes," I stammer. I don't want to dredge up that nightmare again.

A strong arm circles my shoulders. I can smell the soft citrus scent of Pablo's cologne.

"Remember her name. Marisol Reyes will be recording 'Soul Spinning' tomorrow morning with Diego Salazar for his *Duets* album."

"Wait!" shouts another reporter. "Wasn't Taylor Fox scheduled to do the 'Soul Spinning' duet with Diego?"

"Thought you people knew your news," says Pablo, with a chuckle. "Taylor Fox entered rehab a few hours ago."

This sends the reporters off in a frenzy. They'd rather cover a big star like Taylor Fox than a little nobody like me. I'm not sure if that makes me happy or not.

"One thing that jerk Blend did right, he wrote a terrific song for you."

I laugh. "Blend didn't write that song. I did."

Pablo is stunned.

"Cisco set it to the tune in my head and Randy filmed it," I say proudly. "It'll probably be up on YouTube tonight, if I know them."

Pablo is nodding with approval. "We'll talk when I get back from the beach."

Maybe I'll finally get my contract after all.

Someone tugs on my arm.

"Julian! I have to get out of here."

"Come on, let's go."

"Good idea, Julian," says Pablo. "Get Marisol home. She needs to rest up for tomorrow." He looks at me. "I'll handle this. Are you going to be okay?"

I nod. I mean I'm shaken and upset, but I'll be fine once I get away from this craziness.

"That a girl. Call me if you need anything, promise?"

I nod again, but I don't care. I only want to get as far away from this madness as soon as possible. Julian leads me through the kitchen and out the back door.

Before I know it, Julian is pulling me up the side street to Eighth Avenue in search of the nearest subway station.

Once we're seated on an uptown train, he says, "Some party."

That's my Julian—the master of the understatement.

CHAPTER 39

Think I'm in Love

We slam the apartment door behind us and lock it as if to keep the crazies out. We're laughing from the absurdity of everything that happened.

"Omigod, what a night!" I turn and stare Julian right in the eye. "The entire day has been so crazy. I feel like I'm on a roller coaster that's out of control."

"What are you talking about? I gave you that nice necklace. What's crazy about that?"

I finger the pearl and enjoy the warmth on my fingertips.

"Nah, that was a good thing, it's beautiful. Thank you again." I kiss him gently on the lips. "But even that was crazy. When you called, I was positive that you were going to tell me you weren't coming tonight, and my heart was breaking."

"Why would you even think that? That's insane."

"Is it?" I ask, forcing him to meet my gaze.

He closes his eyes and kisses me deeply until we feel the need to come up for air.

I cling to him. "Oh, Julian, we've been through so much drama. I just want to be a normal couple."

"We will be," he says. "We'll make it work." We stand there holding each other like two people on a life raft. Then he says, "Hey, let's see if we made the news."

He picks up the remote and begins surfing as we snuggle on the couch.

"Trouble tonight, at the hottest club in New York City. Apple, home to many celebrities, was the scene of a joint FBI and New York City

Police sting. Norman Katzenbaum, the rapper who goes by the name of Blend, was arrested for trafficking in interstate child pornography."

Julian looks at me. "He didn't take any pictures of you, did he?"

I shake my head. "No, no, never."

But it gets me thinking. What if he had hidden cameras that I didn't know about? There could even be photos of Tati and me changing and showering in his East Hampton house. Who knows what that sicko was up to? He may have even had cameras in the bathroom of his own apartment. That whole nightmare in the Jacuzzi might be on film.

"No," I continue. "It's like I told you, we had a professional relationship." But I better call Pablo first thing in the morning and tell him everything. He'll know what to do.

Julian is content with that explanation and continues to flip through the channels. Cable has a more in-depth report on Blend with footage from the party rolling in the background.

"Blend, whose real name is Norman Katzenbaum, is a well-known rapper who makes a point of claiming that he is a combination of all races on the planet. While that *may* be true, fans will be disappointed to find that his claims of growing up on the mean streets of the city are quite a stretch." A photo of a luxury high-rise appears on the screen. "Riverdale, though technically the Bronx, is a far cry from the inner city. Blend enjoyed a comfortable life while growing up, which included a summer home in Sag Harbor. His father, a pilot for United Airlines, and his mother, a corporate lawyer for a Wall Street firm, sent their son to Fordham Prep and then on to Boston College."

"Well, at least he didn't lie to me," I tell Julian. "He said his father came and went and that his mother worked around the clock."

This amuses Julian, but not as much as the huge picture of me that pops up on the screen.

"Tonight was to be the night that Katzenbaum announced the signing of his protégé, YouTube phenomenon Marisol Reyes, to his record label. Reyes has been romantically linked to the rapper, as well as the Latino singer Diego Salazar."

"Ugh!" I groan. "Will I ever live that down?" I bury my face in my hands. "They make me sound like a skank."

"Relax. It's all good publicity for you."

I hit Julian with a throw pillow.

"Kidding! Kidding!" He yells, laughing like crazy. Then he looks around. "Hey, when's Lola getting home?"

"She and Pablo went back to the beach. They only came out for my birthday party." He's staring at me. "What?"

"So that means we have the place to ourselves?"

It does, but I'm still not sure I'm ready for *the works*. One thing's for sure, I'm not going to chase him away like I always do. He pulls me closer and begins kissing me softly. His kisses feel so right.

My beautiful dress is making me feel claustrophobic and my feet are throbbing from standing for hours. Strappy sandals are made for limos, not subways and running through the streets of Manhattan. I unfasten my sandals and slip them off.

"Help me get out of this dress and we can get comfy."

He turns the TV off and we walk hand in hand into my room. I realize there's no way I can get out of this dress without help. Tati must have sewn a hundred little buttons with loops down the back.

"Can you unfasten these little buttons for me?"

When they're undone, I grab my cami and shorts and run into the bathroom while holding up the front of my dress. It takes me a while to scrub the makeup off my face, rub in a little moisturizer, and comb out my hair. By the time I return, Julian is lying on my bed in his boxers with the covers down, and snoring!

Ever so gently, I pull the comforter up over him. He mumbles something incoherent, but basically he's dead to the world. So much for my big romantic night.

I guess it wasn't meant to be. Maybe Tati was right; Vanessa and I should have a bet to see who will be the last remaining virgin in El Barrio. I might make a few bucks out of this. Then again, you never know what the morning will bring.

A cup of tea would be perfect right now, so I put the kettle on and wait by the window for the water to boil. They say New York is a city that never sleeps and that's especially true in El Barrio. There's traffic in the streets, people laughing and singing on the sidewalks, and a general party atmosphere as if every night were New Year's Eve. I always believed that it was the rhythm of this neighborhood that gave me my love of music.

What I didn't know when I started on my musical path was the kind of crazy nonmusical things that would happen to me along the way. I mean, the whole Diego thing was so weird. I kind of became famous for being a gay man's date. And then there's Blend, or Norman, or whoever he really is. Never in my wildest imagination did I ever think I would somehow get involved with a child predator. This reminds me, I really have to call Pablo first thing in the morning and find out if there are any photos of me out there. I could be in for another media nightmare.

The tea is ready and I add a little honey to soothe my throat. I have a long day of singing ahead of me. This time I'll take Diego's advice and make sure they take care of me the way they do him.

Probably the most important lesson I learned this summer—as if all that wasn't enough—is about friends. And frenemies. You'd think you'd know about friends with eighteen years of experience, but I guess it's an ongoing evolvement. Never again will I waste time or energy on people who don't like me. If they decide to turn their attitudes around, fine, if not, good luck to them. But more importantly, I know I have to make more time for those friends I love, like Julian and Vanessa. They deserve it.

And I'm always going to keep my eyes open for new friends. Tati, Cisco, even Randy, and I became so close this summer even though I've known them forever. I owe so much of my newfound success to them and we're only headed up from here. They're as focused on their goals as I am on mine. Together we're a great team.

I think I learned more this summer than I have in my eighteen years on the planet. As long as I'm growing, it's all good, even the bad and the ugly.

Exhausted, I slip gingerly into bed next to Julian, careful not to wake him. He looks so sweet lying there lost in slumber. Wonderful times are ahead of us too. I just know it. We're young and have the rest of our lives to work it all out. What I'm sure of is that Julian is made of the right stuff and he's going to grow into one heck of a man—a man that I'll be proud to share my life with.

My last thoughts before drifting into dreamland are: I finally found the man I love *and* tomorrow afternoon I'm recording my first record! Tomorrow. The past is far behind me. It's what's ahead of me that counts. Life is what we make it, and each day is a new beginning. I'm going to make sure to live each and every day on my terms. All of the tomorrows are mine to conquer.

Happy birthday to me! Let the dreams unroll. Tomorrow, and all of the tomorrows are mine.